Prologue

As the sun sank below the horizon, dust layers ... atmosphere turned it from yellow to blood-red. A fitting sentiment for what they about to do, Alex thought grimly.

Elaine tugged at his arm. 'You okay?'

Alex shook his head.

She held his hand and gave it a squeeze. Alex knew she was only trying to console him, ease the pain by showing that she understood. But she didn't. Cliff had always been there, almost from the very start of this nightmare. He had counselled him through his own personal darkness, the work camp, Tina's death, the grim struggle of the Welsh community. And stood side by side as they fought their way into Genesis – the subterranean city they now lived in. There would be no measure of words or gestures that could console him.

They were standing in the middle of a small group of survivors next to a makeshift scaffold. On top of the scaffold was a corpse wrapped neatly in a white sheet – standard issue for funerals. In front of them was a deep pit filled with glowing coals. Each time the wind swirled into the pit a column of sparks fled into the night air. The heat from this pit itself was so intense that no-one could stand at the edge for more than a few seconds.

'We are gathered here to pay our last respects to Cliff Steward,' a man dressed in a black robe with a grey beard began. 'I did not know Cliff personally, but I understand he was one of the first surface people to liberate Genesis from military rule. Alex has told me how Cliff fought alongside him in in those terrible days after the holocaust and his important role in the Welsh community. Throughout this time, he proved to be a loyal and devoted friend. Like so many others from the surface, he leaves no next of kin and died from the all-too-common disease of cancer. His companionship and wisdom will be sorely missed.' He paused and looked around the small gathering. 'I will now let Alex Carhill, his closest friend, say a few words.'

Alex drew a breath, stealing himself against his own emotions. He had not prepared a speech. Words could not describe what he felt, and no-one, except maybe Elaine, would ever understand. Only the people who had survived those days would have an inkling of the bond they had formed. 'If it wasn't for Cliff I would not be here today,' he began then paused, not so much to collect his thoughts but to gather the strength to continue. 'He was the only constant in my life through those dark times. He counselled me through my suicidal thoughts, reasoned with my insanity and dragged me forward when no-one else could. I will miss him every day for the rest of my life.' He paused again as the emotion welled in his throat. 'Rest in peace my friend,' he finished quietly, as Elaine squeezed his hand.

The priest walked over to the scaffold and made the sign of the cross, then prayed over the body. Alex had remembered that Cliff had once told him that he was a Catholic before the holocaust. Like most survivors, his religious beliefs went quickly up in flames with the bombs. But as the sickness took hold, Cliff seemed to soften his distaste for God. Maybe he saw some resemblance of hope for the future or saw his own end and he wanted to make his peace; Alex wasn't sure which. Either way, a religious send-off seemed appropriate.

'I now commit his body to the fire.' The priest made the sign of the cross again. 'May his soul find peace.'

He nodded and another man in a black robe pulled a lever. The metal tray Cliff's body was lying on tilted upward, and his body smoothly slid off the end and into the pit. When the body hit the coals it immediately flared into a ball of flame, filling the air with the scent of burning flesh. Alex turned away from the scene, not wishing his last memory of Cliff to be a charred and crumpled corpse.

The Rise of Alpha
The Sequel of Nuclear Midnight

ROBERT COLE

Copyright 2021

Contents

Post-Holocaust Britain

Chapter 1

Alex woke early, as he always did, and climbed out of bed. Elaine, still sound asleep, was curled up in the corner of the bed with her hands over her head, as though trying to block her ears from some hideous noise. She had been very restless during the night and had cried out several times. Bad dreams – everyone had them. Often when her sleep had been disturbed, he would wake to find her in a foetal position, curled up into a tight ball.

Alex had not slept well himself. Visions of Cliff's body sliding into the coal fire pit hadn't helped. When sleep finally arrived, it was fitful and filled with images he would sooner forget. The work camp, desperate struggles at the shore of Cardiff, the death of Tina and the hand-to-hand fighting on the surface only a month ago. These nightmares had subsided in the last few weeks, now with Cliff's death, they were back. Apart from Elaine, Cliff was the only person who had survived the recent battle against the military. He was the last link with those times.

They were housed in an apartment in the science sector of Genesis. Apparently, its occupants called the city Genesis because it would be the seed of a new beginning for the world once they had eradicated all the surface people. Clearly, things hadn't gone to plan. Now everything was different. This city's future and the survivors' future were now intricately entwined.

Alex padded over to the bathroom and opened the wall cabinet. Inside was his electric razor, toothpaste and toothbrush. Three things he deeply treasured. He took out the electric razor and quickly ran it over a three-day growth. He still couldn't get used to shaving on a regular basis. Elaine liked him clean shaven; still the sight of a clean-shaven chin after so many years of having a beard seemed odd. He squeezed out some toothpaste onto his toothbrush. After years of cleaning his teeth with his fingers and what soap he could find, his teeth had taken on a decidedly yellow appearance; but at least he still had some. Many survivors had lost teeth. With no real dentists' facilities on the surface, painful or rotten teeth were just pulled out. Down here it was a different story. Like before the war, teeth were cherished and quickly nursed back to full health if something went wrong.

He brushed his teeth carefully, taking time to savour the taste of the toothpaste. It was heaven. Sometimes he would even swallow some just to savour the taste. When he finished, he peered into the mirror. He had barely looked into a mirror for nearly three years before he came here, and his image still shocked him. He was only 25, but his face told a different story. His grey eyes were surrounded by a face worn and beaten from extreme cold then blistering sun. There were permanent crow lines around his eyes and creases hanging from each eye that should not belong to one so young. His hair, once thick and bushy, now thinly framed his face.

In many ways, he realised, he was still in a state of disbelief about what had happened. Still alive when so many others were not. His only goal for so long had been survival, then he had become consumed by hatred for what the military had done to the survivors. Their destruction was all that mattered – justice in a world without justice. It had driven him to kill, to slaughter. Everything that he endured he used to focus on that one final act of revenge which he fully expected to take his life. But it hadn't. The battle had swept everyone away but Elaine and himself. Now he had to reset and find a new goal. The world had suddenly changed again. He knew he had to adjust; his greatest fear was that he couldn't.

Elaine stirred and rolled over in bed.

Alex watched her for a moment, taking in the lines of her body. The food at Genesis had put flesh on her bones again. Her tall frame was quickly filling out into more womanly proportions. Her hair had also regained some of its lustre, due largely to the use of hair conditioners and shampoo. Like him, her skin bore the ravages of the sun, but as she regained her health some of the softness had returned to her features.

'How did you sleep?' he asked when her eyes opened.

'Hmm...' She paused thoughtfully. 'Strange dreams...'

'You called out a few times in the night.'

'Uh...what did I say?'

Alex shrugged. 'The usual stuff. Mainly just groans and cries.'

'The usual,' she agreed, brushing away some hair from her eyes.

Most of Elaine's nightmares seemed to revolve around her mother's death from a rat plague and her own torture at the hands of the military. And his...well, they were many and varied because he had such a rich tapestry of horrors to choose from. His worst dreams revolved around the deaths of people he loved – his brother Jason, Ron and Tina... But the most vivid were about Tina's death. Watching the life seep out of her with no-one there to help and nothing he could do. Sometimes, in his dreams, she would even survive the flu. Her temperature would break, and she would wake up weak and pale but alive with a big beaming smile. He would always wake up then. Those were the hardest nightmares. Ones that offered hope when there was none.

'Peter McCaffrey has called a committee meeting which will start in about half an hour,' Alex said, climbing into his clothes.

Elaine rolled onto her side. 'What's it about?'

'Hmm...not sure, but the full committee is meeting so it must be important. I'll get some breakfast on the way.'

5

'I'll probably be at work when you get back,' Elaine replied, watching Alex dress.

Elaine had just started work in the hospital as a nursing assistant. Her dream job. Although she had worked in a pathology lab before the holocaust, she was also enrolled in a part-time nursing degree. The opportunity to continue her nursing had been too good to pass up. Although the first day had been traumatic, there was a light in her eyes that night that Alex hadn't seen before. She chatted continuously about the things she had learned and the people she had met. After all the cruelty, slaughter and terrible things she had experienced, she only wanted to heal the sick. He admired her for that. To survive in this world, most people built a wall between themselves and the atrocities they witnessed. They became numb to it all, focussing only on their own survival. Not Elaine. When she saw pain or suffering, she wanted to heal it; she had seen the worst of human behaviour and chose not to build a shell of indifference against it. Something that Alex found impossible; the horrors he had witnessed had eaten deep into his soul and dissolved much of his humanity. His anger at the world always simmered just below the surface.

But nothing seemed to affect Elaine. She understood and accepted the things people did to each other and still loved them. She was his compass that reorientated him when his world became too terrible to bear. And he loved her for it.

'I'll drop down and visit you when the meeting is over,' he said with a smile.

'That will be nice. I can give you a tour. They have some amazing equipment down there. Then we can catch a movie.'

Alex laughed at this. There were two things above all else the survivors loved about this city. Flushing toilets and movies. Every second night in a large auditorium in the shopping precinct they showed classic movies on the big screen. This venue had quickly been packed out. So much so that the city people had stopped coming, preferring their computer screens and TVs to associating with the surface people and their rough and ready ways. 'What's on tonight?' he asked.

'The last of the Star War movies.' Elaine replied with a grin.

'Ah...definitely worth seeing.'

Alex gave her a quick kiss then headed off to the canteen for breakfast. Their quarters were not far from Dr Crean's place. He took the lift down three floors and exited to the delightful smell of food wafting along the corridor. He followed the smell until he came to a large hall filled with tables and chairs. Along one side was a glass-encased serving area filled with steaming trays of food. Alex took a plastic tray from a rack and surveyed the assortment of food. There were fresh eggs, chips, fried tomatoes, mushrooms and hamburgers. The hamburgers were made from cultured meat but tasted exactly like the real thing. The place was indistinguishable from any canteen in any city before the war. He still felt that he was living in a dream and that he would soon wake up where he belonged; in a waste land under a blazing blood-red sun.

He filled his plate with a sample of everything and moved down the line to a woman serving hot tea and coffee.

'Good morning,' she said brightly when he approached. 'What would you like?'

Alex took a moment to observe her. He judged she was in her late twenties with a plump fleshy face and glossy sandy-coloured hair, neatly pinned back in a short ponytail. Although her lips curled up in a smile the rest of her face remained frozen, like a porcelain doll. He wondered what she was really thinking behind that frozen smile. 'Dirty mutant', maybe, or was there a hint of pity in those grey eyes?...

'What sort of teas do you have?' he asked.

'Well, there's various mixtures of herbs, usually infused with lemon.'

'In the Welsh community, we had our own tea that was very popular. Unfortunately, I don't think the recipe made it down here.'

At the mention of the Welsh community a flicker of sadness crossed her features and she turned her face away.

Alex waited, feeling increasingly awkward as it was becoming obvious that she was on the verge of tears.

'It's alright, Jess, I'll take over.' A large woman with greying hair, again pinned back behind her head, moved across to take her place. 'You must forgive my colleague,' she said in a formal tone. 'She recently lost both her parents.'

Alex studied her for a moment. She was not angry; he detected no trace of resentment in her eyes, just sadness.

'I understand,' he said. 'We also lost many good people.'

His words hung in the air between them like an invisible wall. She clearly did not want to talk about an event which had taken thousands of the city's lives. Alex wondered what she would have said if she had known that he was the cause of most of the deaths. 'I'll just have some lemon and ginger tea.'

She poured the tea in silence without making eye contact and put the cup and saucer on his tray. Alex wanted to say something reassuring, like 'the future will be much better' or 'with time the wounds will heal,' but realised reciting clichés would only make matters worse. There was a terrible, impassable gulf between the city and the surface people that only time would heal.

He muttered a 'thank you', then moved off to eat his breakfast.

***

The meeting was to be held in a small conference room adjacent to the central dome of the city. Fortunately, this area had been left virtually untouched by the invading surface people. On one side of the room there was a large glass panel that overlooked a beautiful subterranean forest and parkland that was infused by natural light from the diamond-shaped roof. The sight of such lush growth, and the smell of the trees and plants never failed to lift his spirits. Still clutching a carton of orange juice, Alex stood in front of the panel admiring the view while he waited for the rest of the committee members to arrive.

As it turned out, the underground city had had a similar governing structure to the Welsh community. There were ten board members – six were military, and the other four represented the scientists and food production, although these positions had little voting power and served only in an advisory capacity. The newly formed committee had adopted a similar structure; five members were from the surface and five from the city. In the case of a voting deadlock the chairman, who was from the surface, had the casting vote. The committee had been meeting every second day since it had been formed two weeks earlier. Alex, who had found the city and been instrumental in planning and carrying out the attack, had been one of its first members. This was a position he was still uncomfortable with as he hated politics; and politics among two groups of people who hated each other was almost unbearable.

'Hello, Alex.'

Alex turned to see a short, balding man in his mid-forties smiling broadly at him as he walked over. Alex returned his smile, noting that his face had filled out in the last few weeks, and the shadows under his eyes had retreated. Dr Martin Crean and his wife Debbie had tried to help Elaine and himself over two months ago when they were hiding from the military. They had both been thrown in prison for their troubles and were facing a death sentence when they were found in a cell in the military sector of Genesis after the attack. Alex had been delighted to find they were both alive. Given the ruthless nature of the military, he suspected that they would have already disappeared – like so many other civilians – if they asked too many questions. The editor of the Chronicle paper and his assistant, who were also trying to help, had not been so lucky.

'How are you settling in?' Martin asked, reaching out to shake his hand.

'Good, but the place certainly takes some adjustment. Still hard to believe I'm here.'

Martin nodded with genuine warmth in his eyes. 'And Elaine?'

'She's really happy, loves working at the hospital.'

'Glad to hear that. We need all the help we can get.' He paused, making eye contact. 'I was very sorry to hear about your friend Cliff.'

At the mention of Cliff, Alex felt a wave of sorrow. 'He was a good friend' was all he could come up with.

Martin seemed to sense Alex's emotions and put his hand on his shoulder. 'You must come for dinner soon. There's a lot we need to discuss.'

Alex smiled at this invitation. It was hard to believe that only two months earlier he had seriously contemplated killing him. But circumstances were vastly different then. 'Yes, we would be delighted,' he said warmly.

'Good, I will arrange it with Debbie, and you can fill us in on everything that's happened.'

The other committee members began drifting in, nodding politely to each other as they took their places around a polished cedar table. Over the last few weeks Alex had come to know them all. A mixed bunch, he thought grimly. Representing the surface there was himself, and Arthur Fennel and James Rawling, who had served on the Welsh community committee; and Peter McCaffrey and Alison Weaver, who were from the Scottish community. Three men and two women represented the city. Neither side trusted each other. That was obvious from the many tirades he had witnessed since the committee had formed. The resentment and hatred ran deep. Four of the five city members were scientists, representing the disciplines of computing, medicine, science and agriculture. The fifth member was one of the few military commanders who had survived the attack and not been thrown in jail, or worse. His name was Garrett

Minster, a thick-set man with a square face and short cropped hair. Alex had yet to see him wear anything more than a grimace. Apparently smiles or pleasantries were beyond his social range. His men called him Bulldog. An apt name, as it turned out, as once an idea lodged in his head it was impossible to remove. As a section commander, he had refused to fight the invading surface people and surrendered a small arms stockpile. He was also instrumental in convincing many soldiers to lay down their arms rather than continue a bloody fight in the tunnels, saving many lives on both sides in the process. For that, he was automatically promoted to the committee, and his knowledge of the city and the military had proven invaluable.

Peter McCaffrey, the only survivor of the three-man junta that ruled the Scottish community, arrived with Alison and smiled warmly at Alex. Peter had been the first of the Scottish leaders Alex had met when he made contact with the Scottish community; he was the most likeable and optimistic of the three. A trait, Alex thought grimly, would be put to the test in the coming months as he had been elected chairman and faced the unenviable task of negotiating a peace between the surface and city people.

Alex and Martin sat down in the middle of the oval-shaped table with the Scottish and Welsh community members on their right and the city members on their left – their usual battle positions.

'Good morning, everyone,' Peter said with a quick smile, remaining standing once everyone was seated. 'Sorry to drag you all in here for an unscheduled meeting. I know you are all very busy men and women, but something urgent has come up that needs our immediate attention.'

There was a sombre note to Peter's words that immediately caught Alex's attention and he found himself glancing around the room to see who else shared his mood.

'There have been some very disturbing developments over the past few weeks that we have been monitoring,' Peter continued solemnly. 'I had been hoping that the

11

situation would resolve itself but clearly it will not. If anything, matters will only deteriorate unless we take immediate action. As I'm not in charge of surface matters I will hand over to Garrett.'

Alex followed Peter's gaze as it fell on Garrett, who immediately straightened in his chair.

'As you all know,' Garrett started, after clearing his throat. 'The military have been monitoring conditions on the surface since the holocaust, largely by listening in on radio broadcasts. We were particularly interested in what was happening in Europe. We even sent drones on short trips over there. France, The Netherlands and Germany were decimated, and only small communities survived. However, there were larger pockets of survivors in southern Spain and Portugal. About a year ago, radio broadcasts from this region started talking about a plague that was sweeping north from southern Spain. At first, we thought it was flu, but the symptoms didn't match, and the mortality rates were extremely high.'

'How high?' Alex asked.

Adriana, Genesis's chief medical officer, wiggled her large frame into a more comfortable position in her seat and pushed her glasses further up her rather generous nose. 'We don't know for sure. As this plague swept north, radio stations were abandoned. Their last messages spoke of people dying of respiratory failure. Severe coughs, high fevers, and many coughing up huge volumes of sputum and blood, even urinating blood.'

'And you don't know what it is?' Arthur asked.

'No,' Adriana said, 'we can only speculate. We have sent drones across to south-east England and watched these people fleeing across the channel from France. They appear to have an atypical form of tuberculosis.'

'Consumption,' Alison volunteered, quoting an ancient name for the disease. 'My grandfather died of consumption.'

'Aye,' Peter said. 'Tuberculosis killed some of my relatives too. But atypical? What type of TB is that?'

'The usual form of tuberculosis is caused by Mycobacterium tuberculosis, a bacterium that infects a third of the world's population,' Adriana said dryly. 'And before the holocaust, it was re-surging, killing 1.5 million each year. But there are many other Mycobacterium species which don't usually infect people unless they are immune supressed in some way like...say...because of malnutrition or radiation poisoning.'

'And you think that this atypical species of Mycobacterium has somehow managed to infect healthy humans,' Arthur surmised.

'Healthy may not be the right word, since all surface people have been exposed to high levels of radiation,' Adriana replied, 'and most are malnourished.'

'But I still don't understand,' Alex interjected. 'I studied tuberculosis in one of my courses at university. From what I remember, it is very infectious, but it grows slowly. It takes a long time to kill someone.'

'Mycobacteria tuberculosis does. But not all strains of Mycobacteria grow slowly. Mycobacterium smegmatis, for example, grows quickly and has been known to infect humans, but it mainly causes skin infections, so it's unlikely to be the cause. What we appear to be dealing with is a Mycobacterium that causes very similar symptoms to Mycobacterium tuberculosis but kills more rapidly and is highly infectious.'

'So, we think it's a new form of tuberculosis,' Peter surmised. 'Something that no-one has ever seen before.'

'That's right,' Adriana agreed. 'Probably there has been some gene exchange between Mycobacterium tuberculosis and an atypical mycobacterium. The resulting organism is a new species that we have no resistance to. This explains why it is spreading and killing people so rapidly. Look at the Spanish flu of 1918, HIV, Ebola...the trend is always the same. In other words, no matter who is exposed to this disease, city of surface people, this disease is likely to kill them both.'

'We are facing a plague that is spreading rapidly across England,' Garrett concluded. 'The survivors carrying this plague could reach here in a matter of weeks if we don't stop them.'

This time, both surface and city people alike looked surprised. Only Garrett and Adriana showed no emotion.

'So, what do you mean by 'don't stop them?' Arthur asked.

Garrett didn't respond to the question straight away; instead he shot a glance across at Adriana, as though he was hoping for her input. When she said nothing, he continued. 'You all know the strategy we had adopted before we were attacked by you.' He waved a hand at Alex and the other surface people on the committee. 'We picked that particular time because our drones were detecting a large number of people crossing the channel. We needed to stop them before they spread the disease across England.'

'You were going to kill them too,' Alex blurted out, verbalising the look of horror on many of the surface people's faces.

'We were protecting our people, exactly like the Welsh and Scottish communities did,' Garrett said defensively, his features folding into a snarl that reminded Alex of an angry British bulldog.

'There is a big difference between what we were forced to do to survive and you deciding to kill survivors because it was the easiest option,' Alex replied, feeling the blood rise in his own face.

Garrett stood his ground. 'We needed to stop this disease from reaching England,' he stated.

'A bit like eradicating a rat infestation,' Arthur said angrily.

'There were other ways,' Alex weighed in. 'You had the technology to isolate the sick. Instead, you decided to kill us all.'

Garrett's features hardened and for a moment the two men glared at each other across the table. 'I'm not defending what we planned,' Garrett said, deciding to take a softer tone after a quick scan of the furious faces around the table. 'I'm just stating the reasons for it.'

'Doesn't sound like it,' Arthur growled. 'Sounds like you approved.'

'I did not approve, but I understood. There is a big difference. And I cannot be blamed for the actions of my superiors.'

'Same defence used in World War II,' Arthur scoffed.

Alex glanced around the faces of the survivors. They all had that murderous look he had seen so often before the attack on Genesis. In contrast, the city people looked more pale than usual. Except Garrett, who was flushed and looked like he wanted to exterminate every surface person in the room.

'That's enough,' Peter raised his voice. 'I thought we all agreed to work together.'

'There is another solution to this threat,' Adriana said quickly, 'one that may offer an alternative to killing survivors. Firstly, it's clear that we barely have enough antibiotics for our own needs let alone trying to treat the waves of plague-infected foreigners that are crossing to our shores. So, our scientists went back through the records to see if there was anything that worked before the advent of antibiotics. It turned out there was. Bacteriophage therapy. Using viruses called bacteriophages to attack and kill bacteria.'

'I've heard of this,' Martin said. 'There were companies around before the holocaust that were promoting bacteriophage therapy as a way of fighting multi-drug resistance bacteria.'

'That's right. The Food and Drug Administration in America had also approved their use on compassionate grounds for treating people with multi-drug resistant infections,' Adriana said. 'We checked the scientific literature. It worked. In fact, before the advent of antibiotics in the early 1940s, it was the main way to treat bacterial infections and it was being used routinely in parts of Russia right up to the holocaust.'

'And these bacteriophages,' Alex said, 'they killed all bacteria?'

'Yes, everything in nature preys on everything else,' Adriana replied. 'The microbial world is no exception. For every bacterium, there are 10 viruses. It's the oldest war on the planet. If it wasn't for viruses, we would be overrun with bacteria in 24 hours.'

'And these viruses never attack the human host?' Arthur asked.

'No, they are extremely specific. They will only attack the species of bacteria that they prey on and once they are gone, the viruses also disappear as they are cleared by the immune system.'

'Neat little system,' Peter commented. 'One wonders why we ever stopped using it.'

'Because antibiotics could be produced in bulk and a lot cheaper than live viruses. And you can't patent viruses,' Adriana commented dully. 'But none of that matters anymore. The fact is we have a natural biological system we can use to destroy bacteria, including whatever type of tuberculosis that's killing the survivors.'

'So, what do you need to find these bacteriophage viruses?' Alex asked.

'We need samples from the infected people,' Adriana replied. 'The bacteriophages should be there. We need to find these bacteriophages and grow them up in large quantities, then inject them back into all TB patients.'

'If I understand correctly, you have to first grow the bacteria on culture plates and look for plaques,' Martin said.

'And what are plaques?' Arthur asked.

'They're clear spots on a bacteria lawn that indicate that the bacteria have been destroyed by a bacteriophage. We just need to grow the bacteriophage from these spots in large volumes, filter away the bacteria, and we have pure bacteriophage we can use to treat tuberculosis patients.'

'Sounds simple,' Martin commented.

'It's a little more involved than that, but basically that's what we need to do,' Adriana explained. 'The problem will be finding the bacteriophage in the first place. We don't know how common they are in a new strain of tuberculosis.'

'So, you want to capture some of these sick people and bring them back here?' Arthur asked.

'No, that would be too risky,' Adriana replied. 'We have a number of mobile medical buses that can be refurnished with the necessary equipment within a few days. We can then send medical teams with these buses to the shores of Kent to intercept these people and take samples.'

'And who would be in charge?' Arthur asked.

'We would co-ordinate the operation,' Garrett said. 'And Adriana's medical teams would conduct the medical examinations.'

'No way,' Arthur growled. 'We're in charge here, not you.'

'We have the medical skills and can provide a military escort,' Garrett replied, looking to Peter for support.

'You think we're idiots,' Arthur shot back, 'Once you have the cure, you could do anything. Even turn this epidemic against us. Just like you did with the typhus plague.'

'What...?' Garrett face began to change colour again. 'Are you suggesting that we would use this epidemic against you?'

'You've done it before.'

'The people behind that plan are all dead. Aren't we trying to build trust?'

'Trust has to be earned,' Alison cut in. 'I agree with Arthur; the military can't be put in charge of this operation. We need to be in charge.'

Another uncomfortable silence settled on the committee as neither side was willing to offer a compromise.

Alex felt Peter's eyes on him. 'What's your opinion, Alex?' he asked.

Alex studied Peter's face for a moment, feeling this was not a simple question. 'I think,' he said carefully, 'that Arthur's right; a surface person should be placed in charge of the operation. We know surface conditions and how to survive. We should be the ones in charge.'

'Agreed,' Peter said immediately. 'And you are by far the best qualified person to lead. No-one else has your experience.'

Alex looked around the committee. The surface people in unison were all nodding agreement. Martin was also nodding. Only Garrett looked upset – he folded his arms and stared blankly ahead.

'We would also be happy with this arrangement,' Adriana nodded. 'As long as our medical staff are left alone to do their work.'

All eyes were now fixed on Alex. If he refused, how would they solve this? Garrett would be the next choice and he was watching Alex with a measure of distaste akin to finding something disgusting stuck to his shoe. This mission couldn't fall into his hands. With this realisation, he found himself nodding acceptance. The relief on Peter's and Arthur's faces was palpable. But all Alex could think of was what he was going to say to Elaine.

Chapter 2

'So, what do you want me to say?' Elaine stood, hands on hips, glaring at him. 'Hope you have a nice trip? Hope you don't die?'

Alex and Elaine were facing each other in their apartment. When he had told her about the committee meeting and his decision to lead the expedition to Kent she had said nothing. It was her typical response to disturbing news. She mulled it over, digesting the information carefully and brooding up a storm. Not until they had returned to their apartment had she erupted.

'After everything that has happened, you still want to risk your life...our future?'

'Well, you weren't there. Everyone was at each other's throats. Someone from the surface had to take the mission. I was the best choice,' Alex said simply.

'You were the most expendable you mean. The dumbest person in the room.'

'I was the best choice,' Alex repeated, deciding not to rise to the barb. 'Both sides trust my judgement. I have been doing these missions for three years and I have more experience than anyone else.'

'You have just volunteered yourself for a mission hunting down what sounds like the deadliest disease anyone has ever faced. It may be so infectious that you all die just collecting the samples.'

'It's dangerous, I admit, but we have full protective gear, and I won't be collecting the samples myself. Anyway, I would prefer to be directing the operation than watching from the sidelines,' he added as an afterthought.

She flung her hands in the air. 'I thought we had an understanding after the last time you ran off by yourself and nearly died.'

'We did...we do,' Alex stammered, seeing the pleading in Elaine's eyes. 'But this is different. I'm not going off to fight a war. I don't have any intention of killing anyone. This is just a quick trip. I'll be back in a couple of weeks.'

'What rubbish,' Elaine spat. 'You have no idea how long it will take. You don't know what's out there or how infectious this disease is. Or if there even is a cure. Don't make it sound like you are just going down the road to pick up some milk from the local shop.'

Alex tried to put his arm around her, but she pushed it away. 'You weren't there,' Alex repeated lamely. 'There was no other choice.'

'You always have a choice,' Elaine shot back. 'Don't try telling me that Peter ordered you to go. I know he wouldn't do that. You chose to go because you can't stop yourself. Even now after all that has happened, you are still hunting death.'

Alex saw her watching him carefully for his reaction. This was an old argument. She knew his history. The almost suicidal missions he had continually volunteered for while he was at the Welsh community.

'It's not true,' he said in his most convincing voice. 'I'm doing it for the people of the city and the survivors. I don't have a death wish.'

'So, you think that it will be a short trip and perfectly safe?'

'Yes.'

'Then I'm coming too.'

'What...no.'

'Why not, you said it was perfectly safe.'

'Not that safe.'

'So, it's not safe?'

'No trip on the surface is completely safe. You know that.'

'But it's not about travelling on the surface, is it? It's about exposing yourself to a disease that appears to have wiped out most of the remaining survivors in Europe. That's the real danger.'

Alex glared at her but couldn't fault her logic. 'Well, I don't want you to go,' he said stubbornly.

'Well, I don't want you to go, but you're going anyway. You don't have the final say on what I do either.'

'You're not qualified to go.'

'I do have medical training and I've worked in a pathology lab in the microbiology department for three years before the holocaust and I know how to culture bacteria and viruses; that's exactly the type of training they need. You are not in charge of selecting the medical staff to go. I'll ask Adriana if I can go.'

'I thought you were happy working in the hospital here.'

'I am, but I think I would also like a trip on the surface,' she said with a quick smile. 'It will be nice to fill a breeze on my face and breathe the fresh air.' She walked over and collected her cardigan. 'Well, are you coming to see Star Wars?'

***

It took four days to outfit three buses with the necessary medical equipment to perform the microbiology tests. Alex used this time to plan the route to the Kent coast. Six armoured vehicles would also accompany the buses. Overall, 12 medical staff and 18 soldiers would be going. Alex had insisted that half the soldiers should be from the surface and the drivers of the buses would also be surface people – two per van. He would be one of the drivers.

The best route was to head north and link up with the M4. Travel along this motorway should be relatively quick since it had previously been cleared by the military as the major route to the east. At Newbury, they would turn off and head south to Basingstoke, then pass through the South

Downs National Park to the coast at Brighton. From there the convoy would head out along the coast of Kent. The medical buses would travel in the middle of the convoy with the armoured vehicles front and back.

Hopefully many of the survivors would be found along the coastline of Kent as it provided a ready source of seafood. Aerial photos taken by drones showed that along this route much of the area was deserted but small walled communities still persisted, each with accompanying farmland and crops. These communities would be avoided – armoured vehicles could easily be misinterpreted as hostile.

Elaine's assertion that Adriana needed her skills had proven correct. Her experience working as a pathology technician in microbiology was exactly what Adriana wanted. As there were few volunteers from the city who were willing to risk their lives on such a venture, Elaine was accepted immediately. Alex had contemplated trying to change Adriana's mind, but decided that if Elaine ever found out she probably would never forgive him. That, he couldn't live with. At first, he thought he would assign her to another bus, but then he would only be worried about her, and she about him. So, in the end, Elaine had her way. She would ride with him in the front of the bus, which was where she wanted to be from the beginning anyway. After that had been settled, Elaine set about trying to organise him. Something he was definitely not used to, but he didn't mind. He knew, as always, she had his best interests at heart. He even began to look forward to the trip, telling himself that with the military escort and medical personnel there was minimal risk. With Elaine by his side, it might even be fun – an adventure they could share.

***

On the morning of the fifth day after the committee meeting, the convoy assembled at the main tunnel entrance. Alex flicked through an inventory list and carefully ticked off each item. He had estimated that the round trip would be over 1000 kilometres, so he had brought twice the fuel and food.

This was the standard formulae he used whenever he embarked on one of these trips. He had also ordered extra supplies that might be useful to barter with. This included medical supplies, dehydrated food packages, blankets, clothes and even seed packs for growing vegetables. Elaine was busy checking the supplies of culture plates and nutrient blood agar for culturing TB bacteria. Alex ticked the last item off his list, then headed over to Peter and Adriana who were talking quietly together a short distance away.

'How's it looking?' Peter asked when Alex approached.

'We're ready. Just waiting on the medical staff to finish checking their supplies.'

'Good. We will do our best to monitor your progress every few days with drones,' Peter said. 'We may even be able to point you towards possible targets.'

'I've instructed the staff to collect samples from at least 20 different patients,' Adriana said. 'This should give us a good selection of bacteriophages. When you reach this number, you can turn for home.'

Alex nodded. 'Sounds easy.'

'Let's hope it is,' Adriana said.

'And make sure you take good care of Elaine,' Peter added.

Alex knew full well what Peter was referring to. During their last mission, the military had captured Elaine and himself and savagely beaten Elaine. 'I'll take extra care of her this time.'

'And don't take any unnecessary risks.' Peter came forward and gave Alex a warm embrace. 'We need you back here on the committee as soon as possible.'

'I'll see what I can do.'

Adriana gave him a brief smile and offered her hand. 'Hope all goes well.'

Her smile was genuine, Alex thought, but there was an air of superiority about her. A lack of empathy perhaps, he mused. In any case, he didn't warm to her.

When they had disappeared back into the tunnel, he turned his attention back to the shimming red orb of the sun as it slowly climbed above the dust layers on the horizon. For the first few hours of every day the earth was bathed in rich colours of magentas and reds. It was beautiful. And it never failed to take his breath away. He realised that he had really missed the surface. The changing colours of the land as the sun rose through the dust clouds. The heat of the midday sun, the freezing cold of the nights. Even the brutal landscape had a certain appeal: the twisted dead trees, the parched land, the packs of wild dogs. After the ordered technological advances of Genesis, it was like walking onto a different world; an open wound – only slowly healing itself.

'We're almost ready.' Elaine appeared beside him and put her arm around his waist. She was dressed in a grey tracksuit and top with a hood attached, and a leather utility belt pulled tight around her waist. Standard issue for travelling on the surface. The tracksuit offered protection against the UV laden sun while the utility belt contained all types of medicines and supplements, a knife, torch, compass and handgun. Everything that could be useful on such a mission.

'Are all the buses ready?' Alex asked.

'Yeah.'

Alex looked back at his bus. Two fresh-faced city people – a man and a woman – were watching him with a mixture of anticipation and trepidation on their faces. They looked younger than himself and Elaine, but he knew from their files that they were around the same age. Casey was the infectious diseases expert; a tall, ungainly looking man with grey eyes and a nervous smile who was always willing to drop some scientific fact or usually irrelevant statistic into the conversation whenever he felt nervous. In contrast, Susan, a medical doctor, was a short, stocky blonde with a plump face and infectious laugh. 'What do you think of your fellow medical staff?' he asked.

She glanced over her shoulder. 'They're excited to be on the surface.

'And scared,' Alex added.

Elaine nodded. 'Yes, that too.'

Alex turned his attention back to watching the sunrise. There was low cloud on the horizon which had turned a deep crimson, which only added to the spectacle. One thing he had learned since being on the committee was the state of the rest of the world, particularly America. In the first committee meeting, Garrett had graphically described the situation when he briefed the surface people on the intelligence the military had gathered on the holocaust. Before all communications had been cut off from the outside world there had been some desperate broadcasts, largely from ham radio operators throughout America. Apparently, there had been several nuclear explosions directly on top of the caldera of the super volcano in Yellowstone National Park. These detonations had opened fissures to the magma chamber. The resulting eruption was horrendous. Volcanic ash, magma and pyroclastic clouds spread over most of northern America in a matter of days. This was why the nuclear winter had been so severe and why the blood-red sunrises and sunsets would persist for tens maybe even hundreds of years.

The San Andreas Fault had shifted too, sending large parts of California into the Pacific Ocean. Atmospheric bursts had also destroyed all electronic equipment and it was assumed that as a consequence all the nuclear reactors had melted down. America was a basket case. No wonder there had been no communication with them since the holocaust. One thing was certain, Alex thought. The surface was still a frightening place. In the next few days, these city people would see and hear things that would quickly test their mettle.

Chapter 3

As Alex had anticipated, progress along the M4 was rapid by surface standards. He and Elaine shared the driving as they made steady progress eastwards. They had reached the turn-off to Newbury by mid-afternoon. On the way, they had passed one large settlement on the outskirts of Swindon. This settlement had a 5-metre brick wall around it with guard towers spaced every 100 metres. The wall appeared to stretch for kilometres right around the southern part of Swindon. Alex figured a large part of the town must had been demolished just to build the wall. Drone surveillance had put a population inside the wall of upward of 1000 individuals. They knew all about Genesis and kept their distance. A wise decision considering the military had a policy of shooting anyone who came within a ten kilometre radius of the city.

As the convoy passed, there was an initial panic and more people poured onto the walls, largely armed with longbows and the occasional rifle. But when it was obvious they were not the target of the convoy they just stood and watched. Alex could only guess what they were thinking. They had probably seen or heard the war just over a month earlier. Maybe they thought the city had won, so they were even more afraid than before. Who knows? But they made no attempt to signal them; they just trained their guns on the convoy as they passed in complete silence. Most were ragged, dirty-looking men and women with no sign of children. If it was anything like the Welsh community, they would be having trouble conceiving and giving birth to live babies. He knew from his previous trips that the southern part of England was much more contaminated than the north. This town could well be dying. The thought sent a shudder through him. Alex made a mental note that when they had found a cure for this disease, this walled town would be one of the first places they would contact.

By late afternoon they had passed through the centre of Newbury. The place felt completely desolate. Alex remembered the map Garrett had shown them during the first meeting of the committee. Reading to the east, and Southampton to the south, had both been bombed. Blast waves would have hit from both directions shattering all windows and stripping the trees within minutes. But this damage seemed worse. Whole houses had been reduced to piles of rubble; cars had been overturned and their metal shells physically battered into twisted metal. It was as if the local population had taken to smashing cars and demolishing buildings in some kind of prolonged rampage. Several times they had to stop to cut their way through fallen trees and the armoured vehicles had to push lines of upturned vehicles from their path. It was clear that the road at one time had been deliberately blocked.

Bullet holes and signs of explosions were also evident among these roadblocks. There were bodies too. Skeletons covered in clothes, some piled on top of each other, others fragmented, their bones scattered by scavengers. Several piles of bodies had also been burnt. Charred bone and ash now the only remains of people's lives. But now, as they passed through the town centre, there was nothing; no people, no packs of wild dogs, just the sound of the wind and the occasional stray cat scurrying between the buildings. Once a fox looked up at the passing convoy, then went back to sniffing out its next meal. He had seen this sight once before, up in the north of England, after the typhus plague several years earlier. The population had tried to outrun the plague by heading north. Whole towns had been abandoned to disease and rotting corpses. Down in the south, so close to the bombs, with a higher population, he could only imagine what type of nightmare had unfolded.

By late afternoon, they had passed out of Newbury and were heading south to Basingstoke. The sun was changing from a yellow to a shimmering blood-red orb and the temperature had dropped. Alex radioed to the leading vehicle and told them to pull into a field off to the left of the road. He had already discussed with Luke, the leader of the armoured vehicle convoy, how to set up camp. The armoured vehicles would form a ring around the three medical buses, which would in turn form an internal triangle. The inner triangle would be their camp where they could light a fire and cook. In this way, they could maintain a 360-degree surveillance of the surrounding houses and fields.

When the vehicles were all in their correct positions, Alex stopped the bus and turned back to his passengers. 'How are you all going?'

'Okay,' they mumbled back.

They didn't look okay, Alex thought. Two pairs of frightened eyes stared back at him. He couldn't blame them. Four years in the sheltered, controlled environment of the city, quietly working on whatever project they had been assigned to. Meanwhile the world they had known burned and decayed. The harsh reality of what was left must have been like being suddenly smacked around the face with a cricket bat. 'Don't wander to far from the camp without a guard,' he warned. 'No telling what's out there. Especially at night.'

Both nodded obedience.

'We will light a fire as soon as we've gathered some wood,' Elaine added more gently. 'We can then discuss what we have seen today in more detail.'

'Those bodies...I mean skeletons,' Casey queried. 'What do you think happened?'

'The same thing that always happens,' Alex replied. 'The strong killed the weak, then disease killed everyone.'

Elaine glared at him. 'We don't know,' she said. 'Probably some local struggle. The population probably moved away because of the typhus plague.'

'Started by the military,' Alex added.

'We were not involved,' Casey said quickly.

'I'm not blaming anyone,' Alex replied. 'Just stating what happened.' He picked up his automatic weapon, ignoring the scalding look from Elaine, and headed out off the bus. He knew Elaine was annoyed with him for opening old wounds, but he wasn't about to let anyone forget what had happened.

It took around half an hour to set the fire and sort through the supplies. Most of the food was in cans or dried and didn't require cooking, but a blazing fire, especially when the chill of the night set in, always eased people's worries and created a more congenial atmosphere. Once Alex had checked that guards were in place around the camp, he wandered a short distance away to watch the sunset. Winter was only a few months away, so many of the trees were losing their leaves. Before the holocaust, the autumn leaves would have been a beautiful sight. But the trees that survived the holocaust were stunted now. The fallen leaves revealed a forest of twisted limbs stretching toward the sky like many knotted arthritic fingers.

When he finally headed back to the camp, the smell of cooking was wafting through the air. A man was standing over the fire ladling out soup to a growing queue of people. Elaine was over the other side of the fire in deep conversation with the medical staff. Feeling a little guilty over his earlier words, he decided to join the conversation.

'I was just saying to Susan,' Elaine said, as Alex approached, 'that the surface is showing definite signs of recovery. I've noticed an improvement, even in the short month that I've been away.'

Alex hadn't noticed any improvement. Elaine was trying to calm the horror evident in Susan's eyes. 'Yes, the trees seem to be healthier,' Alex lied.

29

Susan was looking across at Alex. A slight crease forming across her forehead. He knew she was wondering if he was telling the truth. 'It's like being on another planet,' she said finally, shaking her head. 'I knew it was bad, I expected it...we all did. But seeing it.'

'Seeing it,' Alex agreed. 'And knowing what it once was like. That is the difficult part.'

'But it's what we have to work with,' Elaine added, 'and with the technology Genesis has to offer...'

'Yes. We should be able to make a difference,' Susan agreed.

Alex watched their fresh-faced enthusiasm and hopeful looks return. Elaine's soothing words were having their effect.

'Excuse me, sir.'

Alex turned towards an approaching guard.

'We have spotted someone.' He pointed toward a cluster of trees by the road.

Alex glanced across at Elaine then grabbed his rifle and headed in the direction of the voice. A small man dressed in tattered clothes with a thick ginger beard that stretched down to the middle of his chest was walking towards them with his hands on his head.

'DON'T SHOOT, I JUST WANT TO TALK!'

'STOP WHERE YOU ARE!' the guard ordered.

The man stood perfectly still, blinking in the harsh beam of the searchlight. 'I JUST WANT TO TALK!' he yelled.

'What do you want to do?' Luke asked Alex.

Alex took out his binoculars and studied the man carefully. His face was scarred, possibly from typhus, and he had the familiar sunspots of someone who had been exposed to the harsh sun for long periods of time. He wore tattered jeans, dirty runners and a thick woollen jumper which had a muddy stain down one side.

'WHAT DO YOU WANT?' Alex yelled.

'HELP!'

'WHAT KIND OF HELP?'

'WE HAVE MANY SICK PEOPLE. WE WERE HOPING YOU COULD GIVE US SOME MEDICINES!'

'We should help.' Elaine had appeared beside him. 'They may have tuberculosis.'

Alex nodded. 'Check he has no weapons then we can talk to him.'

'YOU CAN COME!' the guard called.

When he arrived, he was quickly patted down. The man had a long narrow nose and dark eyes that darted back and forth nervously.

'Would you like some soup?' Elaine asked.

The man's eyes widened instantly, and he nodded enthusiastically. His brief smile revealed a row of yellow teeth with two missing. 'Yes, please.'

Elaine returned his smile then disappeared to fetch some soup.

'What's your name?' Alex asked.

'Thomas Levy.'

'Are you from Newbury?'

He shook his head. 'Basingstoke.'

'Ah...we're heading that way. Is there a sizeable community there?'

'There used to be, but not anymore. Most have left or died from the sickness over a year ago.'

Alex watched him carefully. The man still looked nervous and had taken to stroking his beard as he talked. 'How many are in your group?'

'About sixty, but many have died recently. That's why I'm here. We are camped about a mile away in that direction.' He pointed across to the tree line that he had emerged from earlier. 'We desperately need antibiotics and medicines. I've come to ask for your help.'

'What do your friends have?'

'Fevers, festering wounds, coughs, vomiting. You name it and someone's got it.'

'How many are sick?'

31

The man thought for a moment. 'Eight seriously; like, they can't walk. Then maybe another 10 are sick but can still walk.'

'So nearly a third of you are sick?'

'Like I said. We really need your help.'

Alex thought for moment. 'Are you near a road?'

'No, you will have to go by foot.'

Elaine arrived back with a steaming mug filled with soup. 'It's beef broth.'

Thomas accepted the mug eagerly, warming his hands on it and sniffing the vapours before venturing a sip. 'Hmm...haven't had something like this since before the war.' He grinned.

'How long have your friends been sick?' Elaine asked.

'Some awhile. But others have recently come down with something we've never seen before. Foreigners from the east brought it.'

Elaine glanced across at Alex. 'What are the symptoms?'

'High fevers, they cough a lot and spit too. Bloody spit mostly.'

'Anyone died?' Alex asked.

Thomas shook his head. 'Not yet, but some of the foreigners have. I tell you it's scary. Not seen anything like this before.'

'When you say foreigners,' Alex asked, 'where exactly have they come from?'

Thomas pulled a face. 'They sound French...I think, but I'm no expert, maybe also Spanish.'

'We better go,' Elaine said.

'First thing tomorrow, we'll see if we can help,' Alex said.

'No, no tomorrow's too late. Why not tonight? We're only a short distance through the trees. My wife's also sick. Can't even sit up. She could be dead by tomorrow. She needs a doctor and medicine now.'

Alex looked into the pleading eyes of Thomas, then back at Elaine, nodding her agreement with Thomas. 'Alright,' he said, 'come with me. I have a map in the bus. You can point out exactly where your camp is.'

'Thank you, thank you,' Thomas said, gripping Alex's hand and shaking it rigorously. 'You're a Godsend. A champion.'

Alex couldn't help but smile at the obvious gratitude he saw in Thomas's eyes. When they reached the bus, Alex pulled out the map he had in the glove compartment.

'We're here.' Thomas pointed to a clearing through a cluster of trees about a mile away. 'It's only about a 15-minute walk.'

'Susan is a medical doctor and Casey specialises in infectious diseases. I can ask them to come along,' Elaine offered. 'We also have some antibiotics and anti-virals. I can put a kit together.'

'Okay,' Alex agreed. 'I'll talk to Luke and see if I can arrange an escort.'

Thomas sat by the fire, wolfing down a meaty stew and chatting to the medical staff as the necessary arrangements were made. After a discussion with Luke, it was agreed that they would have four soldiers as escorts. All would be heavily armed. Alex also decided as a goodwill gesture to include some food supplies, which he would carry himself.

Fifteen minutes later the party assembled in front of the fire. Except for the armed escort, everyone had backpacks strapped to their backs. It was agreed that if Casey confirmed that some of the sick had TB they would not try to treat them but would come back the next day with the buses to take samples, using strict safety protocols.

With Thomas in the lead, they reached the thicket of trees and followed him down a narrow twisting path and through several farm gates. Behind Thomas were two soldiers followed by Alex, Elaine, the three medical staff and the two remaining soldiers in the rear. As was typical these days, when the sun set, a mist crept into the valleys, reducing the visibility to less than 20 metres.

They had not gone far when Thomas called a halt. 'Sorry, I think that the soup has gone straight through me. I'll just be a minute.' Rather surprisingly, he ran off into the bushes to relieve himself while the company waited.

Alex saw the flashes before he heard the shots. Both soldiers in front of him went down with barely a sound. By the time he realised they had been shot, the two soldiers behind had also fallen. Susan screamed as more shots rang out. Alex swore; he had opted to take a full pack of supplies instead of a rifle. He felt Elaine's arm on his shoulder pulling him to the ground. Searchlights were everywhere, blinding them. He heard more gunfire and hurried footsteps crashing through the undergrowth. A strong beam of light found him. 'Don't move,' a harsh voice called. Alex shielded his eyes and tried to look up. All he could see were army boots, a green khaki uniform and the muzzle of an automatic weapon pointed at his head.

Susan's screams stopped abruptly.

'Don't hurt them,' a voice called.

Alex recognised Thomas's voice.

'Hands on heads,' the voice growled. Elaine, beside him, put her hands on her head and Alex followed. The two soldiers in front of them were rolled onto their back and kicked a few times. 'Both dead,' another voice called.

'Same here,' a further voice called from behind.

Alex noticed that although they were wearing military uniforms these soldiers were unshaven and their clothes were dirty and tattered. They also wore night vision goggles – his soldiers never stood a chance.

At that moment, explosions and rapid gunfire filled the air. Alex looked back in the direction they had come and saw the sky light up.

'That will be the rest of our unit,' the soldier closest to Alex said. 'We'll soon have plenty of new supplies and weapons.'

Alex realised then who these people were. They were the remnants of the military that had escaped through the tunnels when the survivors had invaded Genesis. They had been preying on the communities on the surface ever since and were the only force capable of attacking and destroying the convoy successfully.

'On your feet.' The soldier waved his weapon in Alex's and Elaine's direction. Alex noticed Susan and Casey slowly climbing to their feet. Susan had a trickle of blood running down the side of her face from above her hairline.

'I told you not to hurt any of them.'

Alex turned his attention to Thomas, who had reappeared and was examining Susan's face with his torch.

'She was hysterical,' the soldier replied.

'So what? I'm sure if you had just told her to shut up, rather than using the butt of your rifle, it would have been just as effective.'

Thomas turned his attention to Alex and Elaine, shining his torch in their faces and up and down their bodies, like he was inspecting prize pieces of merchandise. 'Well, at least you both look undamaged,' he said, coldly. Gone was the nervous, pleading manner that had been so convincing half an hour earlier. In its place was a sly, self-satisfied grin. 'Fooled you good, didn't I?' he said brightly, like he had just played an amusing joke. 'Bet you never suspected a thing. Just thought you were helping some poor sick locals.'

'Who are you?' Alex asked.

In response to this question, Thomas rolled up his shirt sleeve. On his forearm was a crudely tattooed image of a Viking helmet. 'We're the Vikings. We rule. No-one moves through our territory without paying us a fee.'

Alex knew full well what Thomas was. The Welsh community had built elaborate defences against these parasites; groups of armed men and woman who roamed the land preying on smaller communities that couldn't defend themselves. They raped and killed at will and demanded food and supplies from whoever they came across.

Alex turned his attention to the soldier who was still guarding them. Despite his beard, his skin was clear and unblemished and his hair, like the other soldiers, was cropped close to his skull. 'You're ex-military from Genesis aren't you?'

The soldier stared coldly back at him. 'And you're a mutant from the surface that attacked my city.'

The hostility behind the soldier's words seemed to amuse Thomas. 'Looks like you two have a lot to talk about.' He grinned at Alex. 'Should be entertaining.'

The sounds of gunfire and explosions had died down.

'Thomas there?' A voice came through a walkie-talkie clipped to the belt of a nearby soldier. Thomas unclipped the walkie-talkie. 'Here.'

'Site secured. Are the medics safe?'

'All safe. What are the causalities?'

'Six dead. Four injured. All military killed.'

'Damage?'

'Two armoured cars destroyed and one bus.'

'Okay. We'll be there soon.'

Thomas gave the walkie-talkie back to the soldier. 'Shame about the armoured cars and bus,' he muttered under his breath.

The soldier came forward and nudged Alex with his rifle. 'Move.'

In the torchlight, Alex glimpsed Casey and Susan's faces. Casey's face was the colour of a newly ironed white bedsheet, and Susan was sobbing as she wiped away some of the blood from her face. Welcome to the surface, he thought grimly.

Chapter 4

When they reached the clearing, there were gasps of horror from Susan and Casey, and accompanying laughter from Thomas. The two closest armoured vehicles had been totally destroyed and were still burning fiercely, and the bus immediately behind had also received a direct hit from some type of explosive, as the front cabin had been ripped apart. Bodies were scattered around each of the vehicles – most already stripped down to their underwear by men dressed in army fatigues. The initial assault must have come from the trees they had just emerged from, as both armoured vehicles and the bus on this side of the convoy had been destroyed. The other two vehicles on the opposite side hadn't moved from their positions, suggesting they had been overrun swiftly. Alex estimated that around 50 soldiers were picking through the smoking wreckage.

They were led through this wreckage to the bonfire they had left only half an hour earlier. The fire had been stoked higher with several large logs and the flames now reached head height. Around the fire, groups of men were sifting through the supplies that had been taken from the buses. Some were laughing and joking, while others appeared to be cataloguing what they had found. On the far side and under guard, Alex counted five people who were sitting quietly on the ground with their heads bowed. Three of them were from one of the other medical teams. The other two were drivers – surface people, like himself. They looked up when they saw Alex's group, but their faces only registered misery.

Thomas led them to a grey-haired man sitting at a foldout table in front of the fire.

'Just as I promised, Major Harrow,' Thomas said proudly, stopping in front of him. 'Here they are, safe and sound.'

The man didn't look up immediately but continued studying a map spread across the table. When he raised his head, he looked straight past Thomas at the four captives. Unlike most of the other soldiers, he was clean shaven, with a broad fleshy face and grey watery eyes. Alex noted with some satisfaction that his face also was bright pink and peeling from severe sunburn.

'Two people from the surface and two from Genesis,' he said, studying each person in turn.

'Who are you?' Elaine asked.

'They're the remains of the military that escaped from Genesis a month ago,' Alex said.

Harrow's eyes settled on Alex. 'That's right,' he said coldly.

'This man is the leader,' Thomas said, placing a hand on Alex's shoulder, which Alex instantly shrugged off.

The major studied Alex for a moment. 'Is that right?' he queried. 'You seem a bit young to be in charge.'

'I'm not,' Alex lied. 'You shot the men who were in charge.'

'Hmm...' The major nodded, then frowned. 'I can't place your accent.'

'I was born in London, but we moved to Australia when I was seven. I was on holiday when the bombs dropped.'

'Bad timing,' Harrow said, amused, 'although who knows what's happened in Australia.' His eyes narrowed on Alex. 'So, if you're not in charge, what do you do?'

'I just co-ordinate things. I have had a lot of experience running missions for the Welsh community.'

At the mention of the Welsh community a flash of disgust crossed his face. 'And you are?' he asked, switching his attention to Elaine.

'Elaine.'

'And what do you do?'

'I'm a microbiologist.'

'And Thomas says you two are doctors.'

Susan and Casey nodded.

The major switched his attention back to Alex. 'This brings me to the question of what you are doing out here.'

Alex stared back coldly at the man but said nothing.

The major gave a half-smile then turned his attention to Elaine. 'Your mission?'

Elaine, like Alex, remained tight-lipped.

'I've already looked inside your buses and spoken to the other medical staff we captured,' he said, a trace of amusement in his voice. 'I know a lot more about you than you think. You have been sent to the surface to collect samples from TB patients to develop a cure.'

'We are trying to find a cure to stop a plague that could kill all of us,' Elaine added.

'You are trying to find a cure for Genesis,' Harrow corrected. 'You are now working for us. When you find a cure to this disease, I want control of it.'

Alex and Elaine looked at each other.

'You're using this disease as a weapon?' Alex asked.

He shrugged. 'Of sorts... At the very least a powerful bargaining chip. I think Genesis will be keen to negotiate with anyone who has a cure. And if they don't... Well, then...we will then have a weapon more powerful than any bomb or army that Genesis could throw at us. I will leave that up to your imagination what we could use it for.'

'So...' Harrow shifted his attention back to Alex. 'If you are co-ordinating this mission, you must be in contact with Genesis.'

Alex shrugged. 'I talk to them.'

'How often?'

'Twice a day, morning and night-time.'

'Have you contacted them tonight?'

'No.'

'Good. I want you to call them now and report that everything is fine and that you have been talking to some locals who say that there are some sick foreigners to the south in Wash Common. Tomorrow you plan to take a detour to try and find them.'

'What if they don't like that idea?' Alex asked.

'I doubt they would say that. If they trusted you enough to lead such an important mission I hardly think they would question your judgement. Don't take me as a fool.'

'And where will we be really heading?' Elaine asked.

'Where you were heading in the first place; towards the TB-infected people spreading across England. We will be your personal escort. Your team will be able to collect as many samples as they need and develop a cure. We will act as your protectors. The only change will be that when you develop a cure you will give it to us, not Genesis.'

'We still don't know if a cure is possible,' Susan replied.

A lopsided grin appeared on Harrow's face. 'Well, for all your sakes, you better pray that it is.'

No-one asked for further clarification. It was clear from the menace in his voice what Harrow meant.

While Elaine, Susan and Casey were led away to join the other captives, the major, and two soldiers, escorted Alex to one of the buses and told him to contact Genesis. With the major threatening to shoot the captives if he deviated in any way from what they had discussed, Alex contacted Peter and relayed the major's message. Peter sounded excited by the news and wished him well, ending the message with a warning to be careful because a scavenger group called the Vikings was active in the area. The major smiled broadly when he heard this.

'Good,' Harrow said when Alex had signed off. 'By tomorrow morning the whole site will be cleared. There will be no sign that we were ever here. We will travel eastwards until we find some infected people. Then,' he said with a smile, 'you can find a cure.'

Alex was escorted back to the medical staff who were sitting in a small group by the side of one of the buses. Apart from Alex's group, there were three other staff who had survived the attack. A grey-haired man in his fifties called Simon, who was a trauma doctor, and Parker and Nolan, both microbiologists in their thirties.

'What's happening?' Simon asked when Alex sat down.

Alex explained what the major had ordered him to say.

'I thought as much,' Simon said. 'They were very interested in our buses and our medical experience.'

'Were the staff all killed in the third bus?' Alex asked.

'They were at the front of it when a rocket hit them. Three were killed instantly and the fourth died from blood loss a few minutes later. The major was really annoyed when he found out.'

Now Alex had had a chance to look around he noticed that two trucks and several Land Rovers had joined them. The soldiers were busy transferring all the supplies out of the buses, and what they could salvage out of the remains of the third bus.

'I count around 50 soldiers,' Elaine said, moving across to sit next to Alex.

'There's more,' Simon said. 'There's a base around here. Apparently, it's the remains of the Vikings' camp. The major's soldiers all but wiped them out and took it over. I was talking to one of the soldiers. Apparently, about 300 soldiers escaped from Genesis under the major's command. When they passed through Newbury they encountered the Vikings, who demanded payment for passing through the town. Instead, the major attacked them and wiped them out.'

'So how does Thomas fit into all this?' Alex asked.

'He switched sides,' Simon said, 'and helped the major attack the Vikings. I don't think he's very popular with the soldiers, but he seems to have some authority over them.'

'How are Parker and Nolan coping?' Alex asked.

'In shock, but they don't appear to be hurt,' Simon said.

41

Alex looked over. Nolan was visibly shaking. It might have been the cold, but he doubted it. Parker looked in better shape; at least he was alert and looking around. They reminded him of how he felt the first few days after the holocaust. He just hoped they would recover their wits quickly because there was one thing he did know; they would need all their physical and mental strength to survive what was to come.

Chapter 5

'Come on, pick one,' Thomas said eagerly.

Thomas was standing over a foldout table watching Susan. On the table, was a row of three walnut shells with a dried pea under one of them. The object of the game was to shuffle the walnut shells then guess which one had the pea. Today it was Susan's turn to guess and she looked terrified. As always, she had watched him carefully when he showed her which walnut had the pea under it. He had then rapidly switched them around then asked her which walnut the pea was under. She had already guessed right on both previous occasions. This time they were playing for her rations. A pile of sanitary pads, toilet paper, soap, headache pills and several packets of sweets were at stake.

'This one.' She pointed to the left walnut shell.

Thomas lifted up the walnut shell and the pea was under it.

'Great pick,' Thomas announced with a grin. 'But you know the rules, if you win, I am entitled to a second game which is double or nothing.'

Susan expression of misery only deepened.

Thomas laughed cruelly then placed the walnut over the pea again and began swiftly moving the walnuts around. Alex followed the walnut with the pea in it to the right walnut. One thing was for sure. The pea wouldn't be under this walnut. Susan also knew this and picked the middle walnut. When she pointed to it, Thomas laughed cruelly and quickly lifted up the shell. It was empty. He lifted up the left walnut, revealing the pea. 'Let's see.' He grabbed the packet of sweets and the sanitary pads. 'Maybe next time you will watch more closely.' He chuckled.

Alex looked across at the major who was sitting by the log fire reading a book. He had been watching the show out of the corner of his eye and now had that familiar lopsided grin on his face which everyone had grown to know and hate. Thomas's little magic tricks had occurred routinely every night since they had begun their journey eastwards in search of TB patients.

Thomas looked through Casey's pile of rations. 'How about some three-card monte?'

Casey's expression hardened but he said nothing. Alex knew what he was thinking. When Thomas first started playing these tricks and it became obvious that he was very skilled at sleight of hand, everyone had protested to the major. He had just smiled, saying it was just harmless fun and he saw no reason to interfere. When everyone had refused to play, however, he had made participation compulsory. Refusal would result in all rations being withheld. There was no choice. The best Casey could hope for was that Thomas wouldn't take away all of his rations.

Thomas pulled out three playing cards, two were red jacks and the third was a black ace. Each card was slightly bent up length ways, so he could grip the card and quickly shuffle them. Thomas laid the cards on the table, face-up to show Casey where the ace was. The object of the game was to quickly shuffle the cards like the shell game. When finished, the observer had to guess where the ace was. Thomas swiftly shuffled the cards then turned to Casey. 'Where is the ace?'

Casey pointed to the left card.

Thomas flipped it over. 'Very good; want to try again?'

Casey didn't respond, triggering a ripple of laughter from Thomas as he quickly shuffled the cards again. 'Where is the ace?'

Casey pointed to the middle card.

Thomas turned it over, revealing the ace. 'You're hot tonight,' he said, grinning. 'Now we will play for your rations.'

He turned the cards over and began shuffling. When he stopped, Thomas turned to Casey with a big smile. 'Third time lucky?'

If looks could kill, Thomas would be dead, Alex thought. This scenario had been played out before. He didn't know how Thomas did it, but the ace was never where it should be. Casey paused, scratching at his stubble on his chin as he contemplated what to do next. The ace should have been the middle card, but it wouldn't be. Casey would have to decide whether to believe his own eyes or assume that the ace was either the left or right card, therefore he would have a fifty–fifty chance of picking it. After glaring at Thomas briefly, he picked the middle card.

Thomas laughed with delight and turned it over. It was the Jack of Hearts. Thomas laughed again, while Casey turned over the other two cards and showed the ace was the left-hand card. Casey swore and swept the cards off the table. 'You're a cheat and liar!' he yelled before storming off.

'Remember the rules,' Thomas called after him. 'If you don't play the game you forfeit all of your rations.'

'You're just a pig,' Susan spat before she also ran off after Casey.

Alex watched them disappear into the darkness beyond the camp. Twice before, in the past two days, Casey had lost his temper. He looked over at the major who had a big smirk on his face. Casey couldn't afford to show his emotions. In the few days they had been travelling together, Thomas had proven to be a master tormentor. Always needling, always probing to find a weakness that he could exploit for his own entertainment. Casey had to be stronger, play the game and bide his time. A quick temper could lead to a world of pain.

'Well, that's it for tonight,' Thomas said cheerfully. 'Tomorrow we can play again.' When he walked over to collect Casey's supplies, Elaine intercepted him.

'Can I trade?' she asked.

Thomas looked up from bundling Casey's supplies into a sack. 'Trade what?'

'A packet of lollies for the sanitary pads.'

Thomas thought for a moment, while stroking his beard. 'Two packets.'

'Okay.'

Alex watched Thomas hand the pads over with a big grin. He then leant closer to Elaine and whispered in her ear.

A look of disgust momentarily crossed her face before she hurried off.

'I guess, that's a no then,' Thomas called after her.

Alex found Elaine, Casey and Susan sitting at a small table at the front of their bus. Elaine had given the sanitary pads to Susan, whose eyes were red from crying. When Elaine saw Alex, she gave him a quick smile then made a place for him beside her.

'I can't do this,' Casey said. 'Thomas isn't going to stop. We need to escape.'

'You can't let him win,' Elaine replied quietly, putting her hand on Casey's arm to comfort him. 'He enjoys the torment. Every time you react it just spurs him on.'

'Those beady little eyes and that foul-smelling beard and rotten teeth. He's disgusting,' Susan said.

'And that's why he is allowed to harass us,' Elaine replied. 'The major knows we have nowhere to go, but he doesn't trust us either. And he doesn't want us hating his soldiers for watching over us and reporting our every move. Thomas is the perfect choice. He can keep a closer eye on us, keep us scared and report our every activity; and we can hate him all we like because he's already hated by everyone.'

'How do you know this?' Casey asked.

'I was talking to one of the soldiers this morning,' Elaine replied. 'The major only keeps Thomas around because he knows this area and knows how to survive on the surface. As soon as the major thinks he doesn't need him

46

anymore, he will be killed. He's more expendable than we are.'

Casey's face brightened at this.

'But you must be careful,' Alex added. 'Thomas is perfectly capable of killing someone. He thinks that these soldiers are the new Vikings and he and the major are their commanders.'

'We need to escape and warn Genesis,' Casey said resolutely, looking across at Alex for agreement.

Alex could not concur. 'We need to find a cure first,' he said. 'We have an armed escort who will do anything to protect us. We are the major's prized possessions. He will do anything to help us find this cure.'

'And when we do, won't we be expendable?' Susan asked.

'No,' Elaine said. 'Bacteriophages have to be grown in their bacteria hosts and purified before they can be administered to anyone. We will be needed to do this. Without us, the major has no cure.'

Casey dropped his eyes and lowered his head. Alex knew he was fighting back tears. In the few days Alex had known him it had become clear that he was close to breaking. Thomas had seen it too. Like a wolf circling a wounded animal, he had singled Casey out for special humiliation. Thomas had tried a few names out on him – hook nose, and crater-face referring to his acne scars – finally settling on Lurch from The Addams Family sitcom, mocking his height. Each time Thomas had said something his words had visibly shaken Casey – much to Thomas's delight. 'You mustn't let him get to you,' Alex said. 'If he sees his taunts are working it will only encourage him.'

'I know, I know.' Casey sighed. 'I shouldn't react, but I've never come across this sort of thing before.'

Alex nodded that he understood. 'When I was at school, I had an older brother who was brilliant at sports and dux of the school,' Alex said. 'I was Mr Average at everything and was teased about it constantly. I hated the taunts and always

47

reacted. The taunts only stopped when I stopped reacting. It's not fun if they can't get a reaction.'

'This is different,' Casey replied. 'It's more than taunts.'

'No, it's not different,' Alex argued. 'Thomas has also tried the same thing on the others in the second bus. He's probing for a weakness. Someone he can get a rise out of and he's picking on the Genesis people because he knows that anyone who has survived on the surface since the holocaust has seen too much to be even slightly upset by his antics. He's after a victim. You can't let him make you that victim.'

'What about Susan?' Casey asked. 'He's been propositioning her. Do I just stand by and let him do it?'

'That's exactly what you do,' Elaine said. 'He just suggested I could earn extra rations if I had sex with him.'

'I've seen his type before,' Alex said. 'Just after the holocaust, when nuclear winter had set in, I was interned at a labour camp. There was a corporal there who took delight in bullying the survivors. He worked many of the survivors to death and even killed those who opposed him. We waited and we planned. When we broke out, the corporal was repaid in full. Once we have the cure, we can do the same thing again.'

These words seemed to spark something in Casey. He looked across at Alex and nodded. The thought of revenge clearly etched on his face.

'Good evening, I hope I'm not interrupting.' A bald-headed man dressed in a military uniform poked his head around the door of the bus. 'I've met Elaine and Alex, but I don't believe I've met you two.' He stepped up into the bus and offered his hand to Casey and Susan.

'Adrian Holding.'

Casey and Susan leant over the table to shake his hand and introduce themselves.

'A present from the supplies.' Adrian placed two bottles of French wine on the table. 'I thought this might compensate for Thomas's behaviour. Compliments of the major.'

'The major?' Alex queried.

'No, not really. The Vikings had a warehouse stocked full of wine. They had been raiding cellars throughout this area for years. The leadership used cases of wine as a reward system. Best looters, murderers, torturers...that sort of thing. The major has a van stocked full of their best wines.'

'Won't he miss these wines?' Susan asked.

'A few bottles?' Adrian wrinkled his face. 'I don't think so. He's got far more pressing problems at the moment.'

'Such as?' Alex asked.

'That's what I came here to tell you. Our scouts reported back about half an hour ago. They came across a number of bodies about four hours drive south of here. A pack of dogs had eaten most of the remains, but from their clothing and belongings they appeared to be French and Spanish nationals.'

'Did they look infected?' Casey asked.

'It was hard to tell, but there did appear to be a lot of bloody faeces around and the people looked extremely thin, probably starving. They may have been too weak to fend off the dogs, or they could have just died from the disease.'

'These could be our first TB cases,' Alex enthused, looking across at Casey.

'Yes,' Adrian agreed. 'But what's worrying the major is that the dogs came back when they were inspecting the bodies. Normally they would avoid humans, especially if they have firearms and shoot a few rounds into the air. These dogs didn't care. They attacked the soldiers even though some were shot. Of the patrol of eight soldiers, one soldier was killed and five were bitten. The dogs were relentless; they just kept coming.'

'That is worrying,' Alex agreed. 'I've run into a lot of dogs over the years and I've never seen that behaviour. What sort of dogs were they?'

'A lot of smaller dogs mainly. Terriers, I think. Although the pack was led by some larger dogs that looked a bit like wolves.'

49

That at least made sense, Alex thought. He had always found that similar breeds stuck together in packs. He had often seen packs of terriers, sometimes up to 50 dogs, on his missions. These packs had thrived in the rat plagues. He had even seen them take on larger dogs, quickly dragging them to the ground and swarming over them. But he had never seen them attack humans before, especially when they had guns.

'Do the soldiers need treatment?' Susan asked.

'They need stitches. The doctors in the other bus are taking care of them,' Adrian replied. 'The major wants to go there tomorrow so you can take samples from the bodies. But be prepared; it's a horrible scene. If you want to know what to expect, you should ask one of the soldiers.'

The other bus was located a short distance away hidden among some trees. This was standard procedure to avoid any possibility of being spotted by an aerial drone from Genesis. Like their bus, the back of the bus had been refurnished with four beds, two on each side. A plastic partition separated this compartment from a mobile laboratory at the front of the bus which was equipped with biohazard hoods, centrifuges, fridges, incubators and plate shakers – everything required to grow TB bacteria and isolate bacteriophages.

Alex's group entered through the rear door while one of the doctors was in the middle of stitching up one of the injured soldiers. This soldier had a bandage over one side of his face and his left arm was heavily bandaged below the elbow. Both legs were also bandaged above the ankles, presumably where the dogs had torn at his legs above the boots. He looked a sorry sight, but a second soldier who was lying on the bed was in worse shape. This man was unconscious and was hooked up to a drip. His shoulders and neck region were wrapped in bloodied bandages, and, from the ragged sound of his breathing, it was clear that the dogs had attacked his throat.

A grey-haired man in his fifties was bent over the soldier's arm carefully sewing the sides of a wound together.

'Do you need any help?' Susan asked.

The doctor looked up hopefully. 'Have you got any plasma?'

'No, sorry,' Casey said.

'It probably wouldn't help anyway,' he said, glancing down at the prostrate body of the soldier before going back to his operation. 'I've stitched the bite marks around his neck, but the trachea has been punctured. He has lost a lot of blood into his lungs and he's probably still bleeding internally.'

'Mitch will be okay, though, won't he?' the soldier who was getting his arm stitched asked.

'I hope so,' the doctor replied, but there was no conviction in his voice.

The soldier sighed. 'It shouldn't have happened. They were on us before we could react. Mitch was kneeling down going through the pockets of one of the bodies. They swarmed over him before he knew what was happening. Tore his throat out. We shot so many of them, but they just kept coming.'

Alex had noticed there was a lot more dogs on the surface than a month earlier when they had attacked Genesis. No doubt thousands of dead bodies left to rot had attracted them. It was also possible they had acquired a taste for humans. Anything was possible on the surface.

That night, as the four of them settled into their beds in the bus, there was an added air of despair. At night, the barking and howling from packs of wild dogs was always the loudest. Now every howl or bark had a new meaning. Alex and Elaine shared a bed on one side of the bus while Susan and Casey had separate beds on the other side. Tonight, however, Susan and Casey climbed into the same bed. Alex had been noticing that they had been becoming increasingly close and had probably been wanting to sleep together before but had been too embarrassed with Elaine and himself in such close proximity. Not that it had ever stopped Elaine and him. Now apparently, as the situation seemed to grow worse

51

by the day, the need for reassurance and affection was greater than their embarrassment. The thin curtain that separated the two beds did little to mask the noise of their lovemaking. Alex was happy for them. There was little in this world to celebrate. Finding someone, amidst the tragedy, was something worth clinging to.

Chapter 6

Diego stood on the cliff watching the waves pound the rocky shoreline. The wind, laden with moisture from its travels across the English Channel, whipped at his hair, flinging it back past his shoulders. He closed his eyes and drew a deep breath, taking in the smell of the salt air. England was just out of sight – the land of his birth. Ever since the holocaust his thoughts had been drawn towards it. Much was still unknown. Who had survived? What was left? What were the radiation levels? Many of his relatives were in England when the missiles struck, including his girlfriend. All lost... He knew in his heart there was no hope; only sorrow waited for him there.

But this was not about the past. He looked to the future, as did the other 30,000 warriors who would accompany him. Together they would land at Dover and press westward. All who stood against them would either be destroyed or assimilated. There would be no other choice. For he and his warriors carried the plague with them in their blood and they would infect all they came in contact with – animal or man. Many would die, of course. A horrible messy death marked by vomiting and dysentery, and finally internal bleeding which ruptured all the major blood vessels. But there would be some that would survive. These men and women would be welcomed into the fold. For they had become Alpha, the next genetic evolution: resistant to all disease and able to bare the extremes of this world without succumbing to the scourge of cancer or disease. The land would finally be purged. A new world would be created.

He reached back and took a water bottle from his pack and drank deeply. This dream was still a long way off. There was much to do and many things that could go wrong. Their ultimate goal was the underground city at Box, near Bath. The city's drones had been flying over France and Spain for years and had not gone unnoticed, but the source of the drones had been unknown until recently. Then a scouting party in the south of Kent had come across a ragged, half-starved party of around 30 men dressed in military uniform. In exchange for food and clothes, they had told an incredible story of an underground city called Genesis that still retained much of the technology that existed before the war: advanced hydroculture and aquaculture, state-of-the-art science laboratories and medical facilities, even an underground rail system and underground forest. It sounded fanciful to say the least. But when they started talking about a recent battle between the dwellers of this underground city and the remaining survivors on the surface, the story started to have a ring of truth. Why would you make something like that up?

And how else to explain a band of military roaming the surface over three years after the holocaust? The story spoke reams about the resilience and resourcefulness of the survivors, who managed to drive the occupants of the city into submission, despite being clearly outnumbered and outmatched. Unfortunately, all the military party died within a week of being exposed to the scouting party. He suspected that only survivors that had been exposed to the high radiation levels of the holocaust had any chance of surviving the plague. Either way, the prize was too inviting to resist. The decision to invade had been taken soon afterwards. Even if this city didn't exist, it would not be a fruitless exercise. The intent had always been to cross over the Channel and occupy Great Britain – it was just a matter of when.

As he placed the water bottle back in his pack, he noticed a figure striding towards him. Long before he could discern his facial features, he knew who it was. Commander

Robison was one of Alpha's field commanders, identified by his half-shaven head. Tall, powerful and arrogant would sum him up pretty well, Diego thought to himself. His self-righteous fanaticism and intimidating style had catapulted him up the Alpha ranks. When he arrived, he punched his chest with a closed fist in a salute. Diego returned the salute without the vigour.

'We are almost ready. You are needed to sign off on the last of the supplies.'

Diego nodded. 'I'll be down in a little while.'

'We need you to do it now,' Robison insisted in a loud aggressive tone. 'We have to sign off all the supplies by sunset. The decision has been made to sail by first light tomorrow.'

'Okay.' Diego nodded, punching his chest in an Alpha salute, but he made no attempt to follow him back down to the encampment. After an awkward few moments, Robison punched his chest again, turned and strode off down the slope.

Diego watched him go. Robison's half-shaven head identified him as among the elite of the Alpha command. The unshaved part of his head was braided into a ponytail which swung from side to side as he trotted down the slope. His long, thick hair was the mark of an Alpha; the hair indicated that they were disease free and strong. Diego turned back to the horizon. The sun was starting its long journey through the dust particles in the atmosphere, gradually changing into an orange ball. He never got tired of watching the play of colours that danced across the horizon as the sun settled for the day. He stood in silence, just watching, until the creeping coldness of the coming night made him turn for home.

When he reached the encampment, he found the last of the supplies were still being loaded onto an assortment of rusted barrages, ships and yachts that were moored around the many wharves that lined the harbour. On land, lines of bonfires stretched off into the distance as thousands of soldiers – men and women alike – prepared for the night's celebrations. For this was to be a special celebration. The last feast in France before venturing into the unknown. Wild boar, pigs, cows and sheep were slowly turning on dozens of spits. The smell of roasting meat permeated everything and filled the air with a sense of excitement.

'Diego!'

Diego turned to face a tall man with a brown, bushy beard that stretched down to his chest.

'Still alive.' The man shook Diego's hand then embraced him warmly.

This was the normal greeting between Alphas. An acknowledgement that they had made it through another day alive. 'Still alive,' Diego repeated. 'Gerolf, great to see you.'

Gerolf stood back and looked Diego up and down. 'You look fit. Command must suit you.'

'As it does you. I heard we will be on the same ship,' Diego replied.

'Yes, they want a final strategy meeting while crossing the Channel. I don't know why they think we will be extra attentive with hangovers and throwing up over the side of the boat.'

Diego laughed at this. 'Is Ursula with you?'

'She's organising supplies for tonight. She won't be long. She's keen to see you.'

'And I her. We will celebrate our last night on these shores together.'

'Then we march toward our new beginning,' Gerolf said.

Diego smiled. It had been a familiar theme among the Alpha soldiers. The news of an underground city untouched by the holocaust had grown more extravagant with each telling. 'Don't get your hopes up,' he warned.

'But you have to admit it's intriguing. If they have the technology to produce radiation-resistant crops and genetically engineered animals... Well, who knows what else they could do?'

Diego saw the flicker of hope in his friend's eyes. This was the unspoken hope of Gerolf and Ursula. They had been together since the holocaust and were desperate for children. But most of the survivors were sterile. While the plague made them resistant to disease it had not made them fertile. Before the war, great advances had been made in stem cell therapy and in vivo fertilisation. In fact, any cell could be regressed back to the original embryonic stem cell then regrown into a new person. It was hoped that if this city was as advanced as the soldiers had said, these techniques would be freely available. The city offered more than just the skills and techniques for crop and animal production. It offered hope for the future. Otherwise, the Alphas, no matter who or what they conquered, would be the last to inherit this world. He patted Gerolf on the shoulder. 'We can only hope my friend.'

Gerolf nodded. 'Well, let's eat and drink tonight. Tomorrow we conquer England.'

'I will join you shortly. I just need to sign off on some supplies.'

They gave each other a parting salute and Diego walked down to the docks. Before the war this area had been an important trading port supplying goods for Paris. Like many of the towns in this region, most of the buildings had been destroyed by fire. The port facilities, however, had remained largely intact. Now, as Diego walked down to the docks, he counted five ships still taking on supplies – largely equipment. Several barges were still on a nearby beach taking on vehicles and some of their limited supply of armoured cars. A bevy of smaller craft were also lined up along the wharves being loaded mainly with food.

He made his way to the largest of the ships, a cross-channel ferry now sitting low in the water due to the large number of four-wheel drive vehicles and trucks that had been loaded. A lieutenant was standing on the wharf directing the last of the small arms supplies onto the upper decks of the ferry. When he saw Diego approach, he saluted. Diego noticed his clothes. He wore boots, woollen trousers and an oilskin top, all dyed black. Most of the soldiers were also dressed similarly. This was standard combat issue for battle. An air of excitement pervaded these final preparations. Diego could almost feel the energy. The Alpha army was finally mobilising.

'Almost there.' The lieutenant thrust a clipboard into his hands. 'You just need to sign off.'

Diego looked down the list of supplies. Sixteen armoured cars, 12, 10-tonne trucks, 10,000 assault rifles and 1,000,000 bullets. 'One thousand per rifle; not much.'

The lieutenant shrugged. 'It's all that could be spared.'

Diego nodded. Ammunition had always been a problem. Attempts to manufacture more from used casings had met with mixed success. The lead was not a problem because it could be melted down quite easily. It was manufacturing the gunpowder and hand assembling the bullets. The consistency just wasn't there. Too many misfires, too many missing fingers. Most people refused to use these bullets.

Diego went back to the list. Ten thousand mist pumps. This was their main weapon. Essentially it was a bicycle pump fitted with an adapter that could be attached to a syringe full of plague. When the plunger of the pump was pushed in, the liquid in the syringe was sprayed through a filter as a fine mist. Anyone breathing it in would be infected. Then it would only be a matter of time before they knew whether they would be welcoming a new Alpha or disposing of a body.

At the bottom of the list was 1250 boxes of bows and arrows. Every Alpha was taught how to use a bow and arrow. Indeed, it was regarded as one of the defining skills of an Alpha. Regular competitions reinforced this image. The people who could string the largest bow, aim and accurately hit a target at 100 metres were revered. Consequently, both men and women engaged in fierce competition to be crowned the best archer. He imagined it would have been a similar story in medieval times. The best killer gained the most accolades.

'Looks okay.' Diego signed his name at the bottom of the list.

'You know that everyone has to be in uniform for tonight's celebrations?' the lieutenant commented as Diego handed back the list.

'I do now.'

A faint smile raised the corners of the lieutenant's lips. 'You should know the regulations for dress before we go into battle.'

Diego noted the thread of sarcasm in his voice. 'Lieutenant Thornleigh, right?'

'Yes, sir.'

'I don't recognise your accent.'

'I'm from Rotterdam.'

'I hear most of it was flooded.'

'Yes.'

'And the rest was obliterated after a ground burst.'

The smile disappeared. 'Yeah.'

'Any of your family survive?'

'None.'

'Well, then we have that in common. We are all brothers in Alpha. Remember that the next time you seek to embarrass your superiors.'

The lieutenant's expression soured into thinly veiled annoyance.

Diego turned and strode off. He made a mental note not to trust him.

After he had changed, he found Gerolf and Ursula by one of the fire pits, greedily watching a pig turning on a spit. By this time the last of the twilight had dissolved into darkness. Floodlights lit the square and loud rock music pounded out of a series of speakers strung around the surrounding buildings. People were already dancing to the music and drinking beer, wine and any number of home-brewed concoctions distilled from whatever fruit or vegetable that was available at the time. The atmosphere reminded Diego of a rock concert, with lethal weapons and alcohol thrown in for good measure.

'Hi, Diego!' Ursula rushed up and gave him a big hug. She looked fantastic compared to the last time he had seen her just over a year ago. That was a terrible time. In many ways even worse than the holocaust. The plague had swept from the east, across Germany, decimating whole communities and leaving the streets littered with corpses. Finally, to stop the roving packs of dogs feeding off them, huge pits were dug and the bodies burned. He knew the smell of the acrid smoke and burning flesh would never leave him. For many, after all the survivors had suffered, it was the final straw. Suicides became common.

But the disease didn't make everyone sick. Some, like Gerolf, suffered little more than a cough and a mild fever. Ursula, on the other hand, lingered close to death for nearly a month. If it wasn't for Gerolf she would have died. He fed her when she was conscious, changed and cleaned her clothes when she soiled them, and bathed and medicated her to reduce the fever. With the world disintegrating around him, he stood fast when many fled in fear. It was a feat of devotion that few could match, and Diego admired him for it. Then one day, pale, skeletal, but wearing a beaming smile, Ursula sat up and asked for a beer. He would never forget that. He still remembered the look of sheer joy on Gerolf's face when he heard these words. After that, they were inseparable.

'Growing your hair out,' she said, laughing as she reached up and ruffled Diego's hair. 'Ready for when you are promoted to a half-head.'

'Not me,' Diego smiled. 'I like the freedom of the field.'

'Yeah, I second that,' Gerolf said, pushing a bottle of beer into his hands. 'Nothing like field operations to make you feel alive.'

'But you are a half-head,' Diego pointed out.

'Only because the Lion begged me.' Gerolf laughed. 'I didn't want to be, but he said I was the best commander he had ever seen. The Alpha army needed me.' He shrugged. 'What else could I do?'

All three laughed and clinked their beers, then drank deeply. Like all the survivors, they shared a deep camaraderie; they were bonded by the unspeakable trials they'd been through and the atrocious acts they had committed to survive. The three of them had each other's backs, no matter what. The bond between them could only be broken by death.

It wasn't long before calved portions of pig were handed around along with coal-roasted potatoes, piles of carrots and cobs of corn soaked in pig fat – it tasted fantastic. With the music turned up and the alcohol flowing freely, everyone was soon dancing and screaming to the music. Diego, like everyone else, was swept up in the primeval atmosphere – dancing, fist pumping, chanting Alpha!

Sometime later in the night, when the haze of alcohol had descended, the music suddenly stopped. Floodlights lit up a stage in the centre of the square as a bare-chested figure strutted onto the stage. He had blond-bleached hair trailing down one side of his head past his right shoulder. The other side of his head was bald and painted jet-black. He was an awesome sight; he was the supreme leader – the Lion. He pounded his chest then clenched his fists and raised them above his head. A roar of Alpha went up as everyone pounded their chests and raised their clenched fists in response. The figure paced the stage like a prowling cat.

He raised his hands again and the crowd fell silent. 'We are Alphas!' he boomed. 'The next evolution of humanity. We are stronger, smarter, more powerful than any human that has ever existed. Forged by holocaust and plague, we are the ultimate survivors, the new species of human. We are ALPHA!'

The crowd erupted in cheers and chants of 'ALPHA! ALPHA!'

He raised his hands again and the crowd immediately fell silent. 'Tomorrow we embark on a mission to take Great Britain for ourselves. But this is not just another campaign. It is a crusade. We will sweep across England and take Genesis and all its technology, then onwards to Wales, Scotland and Ireland. Nothing will stand in our path! Then we will take on the world! Alpha forever! Alpha forever!'

The crowd responded. 'ALPHA FOREVER! ALPHA FOREVER!'

The music came back on with the soundtrack from Led Zeppelin's 'Kashmir'. The raw rifts swept across the crowd, whipping them into a frenzy. Diego, like everyone else, was caught up in the euphoria. Like everyone else he beat his chest and yelled at the top of his voice. 'ALPHA FOREVER! ALPHA FOREVER!'

The sheer pleasure of the chant, the raw power of the music, the pounding of chests, built into a screaming climax. Like everyone, Diego screamed himself coarse, butted heads with Gerolf and pounded his chest till it hurt. Everyone was one in Alpha.

Chapter 7

Alex rubbed some of the condensation from a window of the bus and peered out. What little daylight that was left was quickly fading. It had taken the convoy – an armoured car, their bus and a four-wheel drive car – nearly nine hours of torturous driving instead of the predicted four hours to reach their destination. Rain had set in the night before and barely stopped all day, turning the already crumbling roads into long strips of mud. Added to this was the large number of swollen rivers which forced the convoy to backtrack and search for passable roads. They were now somewhere east of Reading in a sparsely populated area which seemed to consist mostly of old stone cottages and overgrown fields of brambles and thistles. The other bus and its occupants had remained back at their camp. Apparently, Harrow would not risk two buses going on a mission together.

They were parked on the side of a road that sloped down to a swollen stream that had already broken its banks and swept away most of the road ahead. On the opposite side of the road was a small stone cottage with a wooden barn next to it. The cottage was overgrown with vines that until recently had also covered the front door, which now hung partly twisted off its hinges.

'Thomas wants us to collect the samples tonight,' Elaine said, handing Alex a waterproof jacket and pants.

'Why not wait until tomorrow morning?' Alex asked. 'The weather may have cleared by then.'

Elaine pulled back her hair and tucked it in behind the hood of the jacket. 'He said we're behind schedule. I think he's trying to show us that he is in charge.'

'What about a military escort?'

'He said a few soldiers would go with us.'

The idea of being on the surface without a weapon felt like walking down a busy street naked. 'We should be armed,' Alex complained.

'No medical staff are allowed to carry weapons. Apparently, we're not to be trusted.'

'That's ironic coming from him,' Alex lamented. 'I've half a mind to refuse to go.'

Elaine zipped up her jacket. 'The cultures have all been prepared, the blood agar plates poured and the equipment has all been tested. We need to do this.'

Alex nodded. He knew what Elaine was referring to. The cultures and plates they needed to grow up the TB bacteria had only a limited shelf life before they became unusable. And there was also a deeper urgency he saw in her eyes. She wanted to help. She wanted this cure. It was the defining quality in her. She would even risk going out alone if it meant finding a cure. And he would not let that happen. He slipped on his jacket, pants and protective gloves. Susan and Casey were already geared up and waiting. Outside were two soldiers in wet weather gear carrying assault rifles. Much to Alex's disgust, the third figure, grinning at them stupidly through the window, was Thomas.

When they climbed out of the bus, Alex noticed that the rain had eased to a drizzle and the wind had dropped. In its place, a grey mist had descended that seemed to absorb the last of the daylight. Alex could hear the sound of dogs barking and there was also a smell he couldn't quite identify. Decay...rot...death. He had smelt it before when he visited the towns that had been swept clean by a rat plague in Scotland a year earlier. It had put him on edge then and he felt the same sense of terror rising in him now.

'Just small dogs?' Elaine asked, moving up beside him and was peering in the direction of the barking with her torch.

'Not all of them,' Alex replied. 'You hear those howls? Small dogs don't howl.'

Elaine grimaced but said nothing.

'Everyone ready? Got all your equipment?' Thomas's grinning face appeared, partially hidden under a hood, so all Alex could see was a broken row of yellow teeth and a scraggly beard.

'Of course, we have,' Elaine retorted, not caring to hide her irritation at seeing him.

'Good, good. Then we better be off. Don't want to spend any more time out here than we have to now do we?'

Two soldiers approached, fully kitted out with battle fatigues. 'I'm Mackinnon and this is Andrews,' he said, nodding toward the second soldier. 'Do what I say and you'll all be back in no time. Just collect your samples and go straight back to the bus. Understood?'

Everyone nodded.

'Good, I'll lead and Andrews will have your backs.'

The property was rimmed by a stone wall. Mackinnon casually kicked open an old rusted gate and strode through. They had not gone far, however, when he stopped and unslung his rifle. Their way was barred by a large black dog that was growling and snarling at them. Alex couldn't tell what breed it was, but it was powerful and had a broad head like a Rottweiler. When MacKinnon approached it began to bark.

Mackinnon pointed his weapon at it. 'Go away... Go on, shoo.'

More barking and growling could now be heard close by. Alex flashed his torch into the growing mist and many pairs of eyes stared back at him.

'Shoot it,' Thomas ordered.

Mackinnon shot a few rounds into the air and the dog jolted back then slunk off into the mist. Then the howling started. Deep mournful howls that seemed to coalesce around the party. Instinctively everyone huddled together, searching the mist with their torches. Alex spotted several pairs of eyes and sleek dark shapes that appeared and then faded back into the mist. A powerful smell of rot and disease permeated the air. The pack was unsure; it was waiting, probing for a weakness. Alex had seen this behaviour before – dogs circling some terrified animal or human, waiting for it to run so they could attack and tear it apart.

'Come on, let's get into the house,' Mackinnon called back.

Everyone broke into a run. It was a mistake. Immediately the howls stopped, replaced by hysterical barking and growls. Alex turned to see dozens of dark shapes pouring through the mist. Andrews and Thomas opened fire, cutting down the first line of dogs. But more sprang over their bodies. A wall of teeth closed around the fleeing party. Andrews stood his ground, spraying the pack, turning the growls into yelps of agony.

Alex grabbed Elaine's hand and together they sprinted along the path to the house. Behind them, the gunfire intensified in the direction of the bus, only matched by the hysterical barking of the pack. Mackinnon kicked open the front door and ran through, followed closely by Alex, Elaine and the others. There was no sign of Andrews.

Mackinnon shut the door and wedged a chair against it. The gunfire had now spluttered into silence. Alex shone his torch through a window and could see black shapes circling in the mist, but the pack made no attempt to breach the door.

'Don't you ever disobey a direct order!'

Alex turned in time to see Thomas grab Mackinnon by the arm and swing him around. 'You do what I say, understand?'

Mackinnon pulled his arm away. 'It was just a dog.'

'A dog? Is that what you think? Just a dog! Cute puppy dogs all got eaten in the first few months after the war. What was left will rip your throat out. That creature was the leader of the pack. If you had shot it, the rest of the pack would have retreated.'

Mackinnon shook his head slightly, a look of bemusement on his face. 'I don't think so.'

'What did you say?' Thomas pushed his face within centimetres of Mackinnon's. 'You think I'm joking? You think I say this for fun? This isn't a debate.' He pulled out his sidearm and pointed it directly at Mackinnon's face. 'If you disobey an order again, I will shoot you!'

'Hey, hey...' Casey yelled.

Thomas ignored him. 'Major Harrow put me in command of this mission for a reason,' he snarled. 'I know what it takes to survive on the surface, and you don't. If you disobey me, Harrow will have you shot when we get back, remember that the next time you decide you know better than me.'

'Yes, sir. Sorry, sir,' Mackinnon said obediently.

Alex watched genuine fear creep across Mackinnon's face at the threat of Harrow. In Mackinnon's mind, anyway, Thomas was not making empty threats.

Thomas glared at Mackinnon a moment longer then lowered the sidearm. 'Next time you do what I say.'

Mackinnon nodded. Relieved.

'What about Andrews?' Elaine asked.

'He's dog meat,' Thomas replied coldly. 'Now search this place and see if there's anything worth collecting.'

Alex returned to the window. Barking, growls and vicious fighting could be heard along the path they had just travelled, but there were no dogs circling the house. The pack was preoccupied. Alex knew instinctively what they were doing. The pack was feasting on Andrews and the dogs that had been shot. By morning there would only be a few scattered, gnawed bones left as testament to the night's horror.

'There are signs that someone has been here recently,' Mackinnon said. He had been inspecting the fireplace that was full of ash and fragments of furniture. When Alex looked around, he noticed that the rooms were largely stripped of furniture and a section of floorboards had been ripped up for firewood. Several food-encrusted pans, a cooking pot and a pile of utensils were also piled by the fireplace. Mackinnon stoked the ashes with a piece of charred furniture. 'Still warm,' he announced, holding his hand out to feel the heat. 'Someone has been here today.'

Everyone immediately focussed on a wooden staircase that led up to the second storey of the house. Muddy footprints could be seen trailing up the stairs to the floor above. Thomas nodded towards the staircase and Mackinnon immediately headed for the stairs.

Elaine slipped her hand into Alex's. 'We should go up with him,' she whispered.

Alex looked over at Casey and Susan. Neither had moved from the door. From their pale faces and vacant expressions, it was clear they were in no state to process what was happening.

As they climbed the stairs, Alex noticed that the air became putrid. At the top, the trail of footprints split up and led into five different rooms. Mackinnon pushed open the closest door. Inside was a double bed stripped down to the mattress. Lying on it was a corpse, half eaten and covered in maggots and flies. Mackinnon retched and quickly fled the room. Alex wasn't so squeamish. The corpse was a man with olive skin and dark hair. Much of the flesh on his arms and legs had been eaten. From the many faeces pellets around the body and the scurrying sounds at the back of the room, Alex concluded it was rats.

A backpack was lying on the floor by the foot of the bed. Alex emptied its contents onto the floor: a soiled T-shirt and torn jumper, a pair of glasses, a compass, some pens, a diary, and a map which was heavily patched with sticky-tape. Alex carefully unfolded the map. A route had been clearly drawn in black pen from the town of Toulouse in southern France to London. All along the route handwritten notes had been scribbled in French. 'Can you read French?' he asked Elaine.

'Can't speak it, but I can read a bit,' Elaine replied, crouching down beside him.

Alex pointed to some of the notes.

'The writing seems to be describing some type of person,' Elaine said.

'Alex, Elaine! I've got some live ones!' Mackinnon yelled from one of the other rooms.

In a bedroom down the corridor Mackinnon had one woman and two men bailed up against the back of the wall. All three were skeletal, and the room stank of urine and faeces. It was difficult to tell their ages. Maybe late twenties, Alex estimated, but like him, they could have been much younger.

'Do any of you speak English?' Elaine asked.

The woman stepped forward and nodded. 'Yes.'

She was dressed in a pair of jeans several sizes too large for her and a blue T-shirt crusted with blood and ripped down one side. Like most survivors who had lived on the surface, her hair was cropped short and only grew on patches down one side of her head.

'Stop pointing that thing at them. They're hardly going to attack,' Elaine said, pushing Mackinnon's rifle away. 'What's your name?' she asked the woman.

'Adele.' She gestured towards the man next to her. 'This is Leo.' She leaned over and pointed to a man who was sitting apart from them in the corner of the room. 'And that's Matthias.'

Leo nodded, but Matthias didn't react. He was either not interested in co-operating or he was incapable. From the glazed look and the stream of blood and mucus that trailed down one side of his mouth, Alex concluded it was probably the latter.

'I'm Elaine and this is Alex,' Elaine said gently. 'Would you like some food? Water?'

The woman nodded enthusiastically. 'Yes, please.'

Elaine took some energy bars from her pack – ground-up nuts and wholemeal moulded together with a glucose

69

mixture. Adele and Leo snatched them up, but Matthias only burst into a coughing fit that sent more bloody mucus streaming down his chin. Elaine pulled out a water bottle and gave it to Matthias.

'How long has Matthias been like this?' Elaine asked.

'Two weeks, maybe more,' Adele answered. 'He has a terrible cough and a high fever. He's coughed up a lot of blood.'

Alex watched Matthias accept the water but when he started to drink, he was consumed by another coughing fit.

'We need Casey and Susan to look at him,' Elaine concluded.

Alex was about to fetch them when they appeared with Thomas trailing behind.

'Where are you from?' Thomas demanded, pushing his way in front of Alex.

Adele looked up from eating. 'Leo and I are from France; Matthias is Spanish.'

Thomas looked over at Matthias, still gulping down the water. 'You're infected.'

'We need Casey to look at him,' Elaine said.

Thomas said nothing. He just stroked his beard as he watched Matthias. There was something about him that Alex couldn't quite define. A stance, a coldness in the lines on his face that he had not seen before. Thomas slipped his hand in the trigger of his assault rifle and in one fluid movement, he shot Matthias in the chest. Susan screamed. Adele and Leo barely had time to react before he swung the rifle in their direction and pulled the trigger. Leo jerked as the bullets sprayed up his chest then exploded into his face. Adele screamed then was blasted apart by a sustained burst to her chest.

No-one else had moved. The speed and horror of what had just witnessed had frozen everyone where they stood.

Elaine was the first to recover. 'What the fuck did you just do!'

'I can do what I like,' Thomas growled, sneering at her accusation. 'They were infected. I did you a favour. Now we can collect the samples without being coughed on.'

'You murdered them,' Susan spat. 'You just murdered them in cold blood.'

'I do what it takes. You tunnel people have no idea how to survive. You're on my turf now. You'll do what I say.'

'They could have given us information on the disease. How many people are heading this way. What the symptoms are. You've just shot our only way of finding out,' Elaine said.

'I prefer to be alive and wondering than knowing but dead.'

'We don't know even know if they were infected,' Susan said. 'They may have nothing to do with the disease.'

'Well, they looked pretty sick to me.'

'Only Matthias looked sick,' Alex pointed out. 'The others were fine.'

Alex watched Thomas as he glared back at the group. There was no remorse in those eyes; only a cold, calculating defiance.

'It's done, now do your jobs and get the samples. We will head out in the morning.'

When no-one moved, he pulled out his sidearm and pointed it at the group. 'NOW!'

No-one moved.

Grunting in frustration, he stepped across and grabbed Susan by the arm. She resisted, then there was a sickening thud. The next moment, Thomas had crumpled to his knees and his assault rifle had slid across the floor. Casey was standing above him with an iron poker raised above his head.

'KILL HIM!' Susan screamed.

Casey stood over Thomas motionless.

'KILL HIM!' Susan screamed.

The struggle of emotions played out on his face, but the poker remained raised, immobile. Thomas saw it too. The hesitation was all he needed. He kicked out viciously, jolting

Casey's legs from under him. Casey fell heavily, and the poker clattered across the floor in front of him. Thomas was on it in an instant, clutching it up then lunging across to plunge it deep into Casey's chest. But before he could deliver the blow, Alex kicked the poker from his hand then gripped him by the shirt and used all his strength to throw him against the wall. His head met the wall with a sickening thud, and he fell to the ground on top of Matthias's bullet-riddled body.

'FINISH HIM!' Susan screamed. 'FINISH HIM!'

Alex picked up the assault rifle and turned to Susan. Even in the dull light of their torches he could see the hatred smouldering in her eyes. The smartly dressed, inquisitive doctor he knew only a couple of weeks ago had turned into a wild animal, baying for blood.

'No,' he said simply.

'He was going to kill Casey.'

'Casey was going to kill him.'

'He killed three people.'

'I've killed a lot more, for less.'

'What?'

'Everyone alive today is only alive because they did things that would have put them in jail for life before the holocaust. All the good guys are long dead.'

Susan stared at him, her blue eyes like saucers as she tried to comprehend his words. 'He will kill us the first chance he gets.'

Alex understood her fear. 'He may try,' he conceded, 'but I don't think it's likely. He knows how important we are for finding a cure.'

'Alex is right,' Elaine spoke up. 'He won't harm us while we are still useful.'

'And we won't touch him while he is still useful,' Alex added. 'He knows what is out there and he knows the terrain. We still need him.'

'We have to go straight back to Genesis,' Casey said. 'We don't need him for that.'

'We can't risk going back the way we came. There are only a few passable roads left and Harrow will be guarding all of them. We still have the equipment and skills to collect the samples and find the bacteriophages. Nothing has really changed. If we head east to the coast to collect samples then follow the coastline back, we should be able to circle back.'

'Don't I get a say in this?' Mackinnon asked.

In all the chaos Alex had completely forgotten about Mackinnon. 'You're welcome to join us,' Alex replied. 'If you do and we make it back to Genesis, I hold a seat on the ruling committee. I will vouch for you and ensure that you won't get arrested.'

Mackinnon looked pleasantly surprised at this and was quick to nod. 'Okay.'

Casey was less convinced. 'What about the other soldiers who came with us?' he asked.

'If they are still alive, I will talk to them,' Mackinnon offered. 'Most of us regret leaving Genesis. A chance to return without being arrested would be gratefully accepted.'

'Then it's settled,' Alex concluded. 'We'll stay here tonight and see what has happened to the other soldiers in the morning.

Thomas regained consciousness several minutes later and seemed okay, apart from a large bump on his head and a headache. He was tied up and dumped in the corner of the downstairs lounge room. From there, he flung insults at Casey and Susan and only shut up when Mackinnon threatened to knock him out again. After some discussion, Casey and Susan headed back upstairs to collect samples from the corpses. Despite everything, the priorities hadn't changed. A cure for this disease was still their main priority. Hopefully the bus would be there in the morning and they could try to culture some bacteriophages and find a cure.

Alex, deciding that he needed to do some thinking, took the first shift by the door. There were still howls but they were distant. The fog had thickened to the point that when Alex shone his torch through the window, he could barely make out the steps leading up to the front door. He feared what waited for them in the morning. The pack that had attacked them had been huge and there had been gunfire from the direction of the bus. It could only have been the other soldiers trying to reach them. The fact that they hadn't, could mean that they had died in the attempt. Hopefully, that hadn't happened.

He was contemplating this when he noticed Susan watching him. She and Casey had returned from collecting the samples and were settling in next to the fire wrapped in blankets they had collected from an upstairs linen closet. When she saw that he had noticed her, she wrapped her blanket tightly around herself and walked over.

'Can I ask you something?' she said, settling into a chair beside Alex.

'Sure.'

'You said earlier that you have killed people. What do you mean by that?'

Alex studied her for a moment, noting the intensity with which she watched him. 'I have killed people... And caused the deaths of hundreds, maybe even thousands more,' he said quietly.

Her eyes widened at this. 'How? Why would you do that?'

'The how is much easier to answer than the why,' Alex said after a pause. 'I shot people, I knifed them, I've killed them with my bare hands and ordered people to massacre others. The why is more difficult to answer...and the reasons still haunt me.'

She pondered a moment on this. 'I'm sure you had good reasons,' she replied with confidence.

Alex nodded slowly. 'So, do you think that I am a good person?'

'Yes,' she replied confidently.

Her blind faith at his goodness was touching. 'I was a good person once, before the war. I can say that with confidence. I would never dream of offending anyone. I looked for the good in people and always gave them the benefit of the doubt. I even felt guilty if I thought that I offended anyone with a thoughtless comment. I wouldn't harm a fly. But that was then. That person doesn't exist anymore. He died when we locked out people who were slowly dying of radiation because we didn't have enough food to feed them... When I found out how my brother died... When I witnessed the horror of the work camps in the months after the bombs dropped and saw the remains of cannibalism. No-one can endure those horrors and remain unchanged.'

'I didn't know,' she said quietly. 'I can't begin to imagine what you must have been through. But you are still a good person,' she insisted. 'You and Elaine have helped Casey and me cope with Thomas. We couldn't have gotten this far without you.'

In the dim light of the fire, it was difficult to read her face, but there was a softness and sincerity to her words. It was born out of innocence, he knew. It was comforting all the same. 'There is no mercy on the surface, no compassion for the weak,' he continued. 'All that died when the first bombs dropped. The strong survive by their lack of compassion. Their ability to make the right choices despite the damage it might cause to others. And the right choice is always survival.'

'Elaine is not like that,' she protested.

'Elaine is not like me,' he agreed. 'She always wants to help. She still searches for the good in people and the best possible outcome. The laws that govern the surface have not penetrated to Genesis and she loved that. The idea of spending the rest of her life helping people in the medical centre inspired her and I love her for that.' He smiled grimly. 'She has the strength not to be twisted by what she has seen on the surface. But she has also survived for as long as I have on the surface. If necessary, she will make the same hard choices as I have. That much we have in common.'

Susan nodded. A contemplative expression crossed her features. 'I don't want to become like that,' she said after a pause. 'But these last few days, I've been so angry. I've never hated someone so much as Thomas; the way he acted, the cruelty, the enjoyment he got from inflicting pain...'

'Some people cannot handle power,' Alex agreed. 'It infects them, changes who they are. I've found that when there is no fear of retribution, the true psychopaths emerge.'

'Like Thomas?' Susan asked.

'Like Thomas,' Alex agreed. He will receive what is coming to him, I promise you that, but not yet. Not until I'm sure he is of no further use.'

'I can't think like that.'

'You will have to.'

'I can't.'

Alex studied her for moment. 'I thought that too. Once.'

She stared at him for a moment then dropped her head. 'I need some sleep,' she said quietly.

Alex watched her go. He liked her. Smart, curious, thoughtful. Not yet twisted by the surface. But what she would become would be another matter.

Chapter 8

'Nothing, just blood stains and ripped clothing,' Mackinnon said, shaking his head.

Alex glanced around at the two support vehicles. Both had their doors open wide. The four-wheel drive also had a shattered windscreen with a trail of blood leading out from the driver's seat. The armoured car looked almost intact, except for the blood splattered across the windscreen and bonnet. 'Anyone inside?' he asked.

'Lots of torn clothing, dog hairs, bone and blood, nothing else,' Mackinnon replied.

Alex turned back to examining the ground. Scattered around were all the signs of a horrific struggle; spent bullets, automatic weapons, blood and shredded pieces of army uniforms. He walked over and picked up one of the automatic weapons. The magazine was only half used, and the handle was sticky with blood. Yet there were no bodies – human or dog. The pack had eaten their own, along with their victims.

A short distance away, Thomas was shaking his head. He had the hood of his jacket peeled back revealing a swollen left eye where Casey had hit him, and his hands were tied behind his back. Despite this, he showed no signs of anxiety or depression.

'Dumb...really dumb,' Thomas said, shaking his head. 'Those cave trolls learnt the hard way not to take on a pack in a feeding frenzy. You just end up as part of the dinner.'

'They were trying to save us,' Susan said.

'But who was going to save them?' Thomas smirked.

'You would have done nothing. Just let us get eaten,' Susan replied in a voice thick with disgust.

'And I would still be alive, not halfway down some dog's digestive tract.'

'Did you know?' Alex asked. 'Is this why you told Mackinnon to shoot that dog?'

Thomas nodded. 'Take down the leader and the pack becomes confused. It would have given us time to reach the house.'

'And Andrews might still be alive,' Alex said.

'Maybe.'

Alex turned to Susan who was watching Thomas suspiciously, but there was nothing in his voice or expression to indicate that he was lying. 'I've never seen this type of behaviour before,' Alex said thoughtfully. 'There were dog packs in Wales, but they never hunted at night.'

'Yeah, it's a recent thing,' Thomas added. 'Probably to do with food. Humans are easy prey at night. We've lost a lot of good people at night. Fire and lots of bullets seemed to keep them away. But the dog packs are worse now. Nothing much seems to stop them. Best not to move around anywhere at night. Just head for shelter.'

There was a sense to this. Something Alex had not considered before. 'Will the packs get worse the further east we go?' he asked.

'Near London, for sure. South I'm not sure. Depends on the food supply, I guess...'

There was one positive from all this Alex thought – the bus was intact. At least their search for a cure to the plague could still be carried out.

***

'I don't understand.' Brigadier Metler, the operations commander, sat with his hands clasped tightly together as he leaned forward on the table, trying to comprehend his orders. 'You want us to kill all of them?'

'Yes,' Garrett replied forcibly. 'Our drones have detected thousands of survivors crossing the Channel from

France and heading westward. We need to stop them before they reach us.'

'But why kill them?' Metler asked.

Garrett paused for a moment. 'It appears that this plague doesn't kill everyone. Some survivors are naturally immune, but that doesn't mean that they can't still carry the disease and spread it wherever they go.'

'But how do you know if these survivors even have this disease?' Metler asked, frowning.

Garrett placed his two hands on the table and stared coldly at the brigadier. 'Whether these people are infected or not it doesn't matter; we don't have the resources to quarantine everyone. Our only choice is to eliminate the problem.'

'Has the committee agreed to this?' Colonel Johnson asked, shifting uneasily in his chair.

'Of course. The committee doesn't like it any more than we do, but there is no choice.'

'This is genocide,' Colonel Johnson blurted out.

'This is survival and your orders. You will take 5000 men and secure our borders. Any survivors who have crossed from Europe are to be killed. No exceptions.'

The two commanders looked across the conference table at each other, their horror plastered plainly across their faces.

'There will be women and children,' Johnson pleaded.

'Women, yes. The drones have not picked up children. For whatever reason, there does not seem to be any children. Maybe the plague killed them all, or like the survivors in England, most are sterile.'

'Do we have any intel on whether these people are armed?' Metler asked.

'Small arms mostly, some vehicles. They all seem to carry bows and arrows, so you won't have any problems there. We will equip you with tanks and armoured cars.'

'What about the two medical teams that have already been sent out to find a cure?' Johnson asked.

'We have lost contact with them. Our drones flew over their last reported positions several days ago and sent back footage of what looks like a firefight. We must assume that the mission was a failure, and they are all dead. It's not important now anyway.' Garrett waved his arms dismissively. 'There is no time to waste on finding a cure. We have to deal with these invaders directly.'

He unrolled a large map of England and spread it on the table. 'You need to be ready within 24 hours. The last drone footage from yesterday showed that many of these invaders have already started to move inland.' He pointed at the town of Haslemere in the South Downs National Park. 'You will head north to the M4. Take the Newbury turn-off and head south to Basingstoke along the A339. This route has been cleared, so progress should be rapid. From there you should proceed south to Haslemere then eastward to the coast. Try to stick to the arterial roads; the lanes are just about unpassable these days.'

Both commanders nodded their compliance.

Garrett knew that whatever reservations they had about their orders would not be voiced. An order was an order. 'Any more questions?'

'What do you want us to do once we have cleared these people?' Metler asked.

'When you have secured the coast along Kent, I want you to set up observation posts along the coastline. All boats or craft of any kind should be turned back to France.' He rolled up the map. 'This should have been done months ago and would have been done if we have not been attacked. I don't intend to be caught off guard again. Have a safe and successful trip, gentlemen. We will be monitoring your progress with drones.'

'Sir.'

'Yes, sir.'

The two commanders climbed to their feet and saluted then headed for the door. Garrett noted both wore decidedly stony expressions.

weren't stopped the whole of England could be infected within weeks. She also knew that with the surface people controlling the committee mass genocide would never be sanctioned. At least if the wave of immigration could be stopped at the coast then the remaining communities in England could be saved. There were no easy options. The thought sickened her to her stomach. She turned away, not wishing Garrett to see the tears that were welling up inside her.

Chapter 9

Lucas peered out through the shattered glass window of the hospital. Just beyond the outer perimeter fence were hundreds of black-clad soldiers, many also wearing black face paint. He swept away some glass from the windowsill so he could rest on his elbows while he studied these invaders with a pair of binoculars. Every last one had long hair, usually pinned back and tied into ponytails that trailed down their backs – men and women alike. He hadn't seen that much hair on anyone since the holocaust, let alone a whole army of them. They were fit too, almost glowing with health. He couldn't see any skin rashes or cancerous moles on their limbs or faces. They looked like they had just stepped out of a health clinic. But what really scared him was their arrogance. In small groups, they joked and laughed among themselves, like they were attending a street party, not about to mount a final assault on hundreds of people.

These invaders had come from the east during the night, travelling along the M20, and attacked just before dawn. Four bulldozers had been driven through the stone fortifications around the perimeter of the community. Behind each bulldozer was a stream of black-uniformed soldiers armed with assault weapons. The few dozen guards that were on duty were quickly dealt with. Once they were gone, and anyone wielding guns and rifles were killed, these invaders slung their weapons and resorted to bows and arrows. It did little to blunt the assault. They shot anyone within range with uncanny accuracy and used swords and knives at close quarters. No-one was spared; even the young were slaughtered.

Lucas had managed to grab a shotgun and probably wounded a few of them, but there were too many and the assault was brutally efficient. The survivors of the assault had managed to retreat to a nearby psychiatric hospital. Surrounded by a barbed wire fence, the building offered temporary respite from the inevitable. Now several hundred confused and terrified people crowded into several wards and stared out at the massing soldiers. Most people were still dressed in their pyjamas and few had weapons, other than hastily grabbed knives and farming equipment. In contrast, these invaders were armed with mortars, rocket-propelled grenades and assault rifles.

'Who the fuck are they?' The ginger-bearded man moaned, as he stood at the window next to Lucas looking mournfully out the window.

'They come from Europe,' a woman replied, still in her pyjamas. 'I heard them talking in French and Spanish to one another.'

'They're not surface people,' the ginger-bearded man added.

'Too much hair,' Lucas agreed.

'I also heard them talking,' another man added. 'They call themselves Alphas.'

'Alphas...' Lucas mulled over the word. 'Well, whoever they are, we can't stop them.' He slid down to the floor with his shotgun between his legs. He had one of the few weapons, but only two rounds left – one for each barrel. Enough to aggravate them as they charged in and ensure he would be one of the first to be cut apart by a sword or shot through with arrows, he thought sourly.

'LUCAS!'

At the sound of Emma's voice, Lucas's heart leapt. When their eyes met, she managed a weak smile, but he could see the tracks of tears down her cheeks. He strode across the room and embraced her.

'Your family?' he asked gently, not wanting to let her go.

'They shot Dad and Mum with arrows,' she said in a wavering voice. 'Didn't even give them a chance to surrender.'

He held her close again, trying to squeeze away the pain. Emma's parents were his adopted family. He had met Emma two years ago when he arrived, half-starved and injured, after his own community had been wiped out by raiders from the north. Emma's parents had taken him in, and Emma had been his constant companion and lover ever since.

'They don't know how many of us are in here,' the ginger-bearded man said. 'We could hide in the basement carpark. They mightn't even bother to search for us.'

'Well, I'm not running,' said a short, bald-headed man dressed only in an overcoat with no trousers and carrying a spade. Lucas knew him – a miserable man with advanced cancer. He didn't care if he lived or died.

'Me neither,' another man said defiantly, clutching a large kitchen knife. Lucas noted that the rest of the kitchen knife set was tucked into a leather belt pulled tightly around a pair of blood-stained jeans.

'Or me!'

'Or me!'

'Or me!' several others chimed in.

'Have you seen what we are up against?' Lucas asked, hoping to reason some sense into them. 'From what I can see, there are hundreds of them, and everyone has an assault rifle.'

'Why don't we try to barter with them?' Emma suggested. 'We could show them our food stores and hydroponic gardens in return for our lives.'

'Yes, that might work,' Lucas said after a moment's thought.

A murmur of hope passed through the surrounding group, with many nodding their approval.

'But how are we going to talk to them when they kill everyone they see?' a woman asked.

'I'll do it,' Lucas said. 'I can walk out unarmed with my hands above my head. They shouldn't shoot if I do that.'

'I'll come with you,' Emma said. 'They're less likely to shoot if they see a woman.'

Lucas wasn't sure if he agreed with her logic, but he wasn't going to argue.

'If we are going to die then I want to die with you. Not alone,' she added, staring up at him.

As he looked into her eyes, he knew he loved her more than ever. He collected her in his arms once again and hugged her hard. She returned his passion, wrapping herself around him. Whatever the outcome, they would face these monsters together, he thought.

***

When two bulldozers drove through the perimeter fence, Lucas and Emma swung open the front doors of the hospital and held their hands above their heads. Just beyond the perimeter fence stood hundreds of black-uniformed soldiers – men and women.

'WE'RE UNARMED. WE JUST WANT TO TALK!' Lucas yelled.

There was no immediate response from the soldiers who were gathering behind the bulldozers, so they kept walking forwards. When they reached within 20 metres an arrow flew past Lucas's head and embedded itself in a nearby wooden post.

'The next won't miss!' a voice yelled.

'We want to negotiate!' Lucas called back.

A powerfully built man, with half his head shaved and the other half braided into a ponytail, stepped forward. 'You have nothing we can't take,' he said in a thick European accent.

'We have hidden supplies of food and hydroponic gardens. I can show you where they are for our lives,' Lucas replied.

The man came up and stood in front of them. He was an imposing figure with high cheek bones, broad shoulders and tattoos down both arms. Lucas immediately thought of the image of a Viking.

'I'm Lucas and this is Emma,' Lucas continued in as pleasant a tone as he could muster under the circumstances. 'We were hoping we could do a deal with you. We have plenty of food hidden away and a glass house filled with vegetables.'

The man's face remained impassive. For a moment Lucas thought he had made a terrible mistake and the soldiers pointing arrows at them would unleash a volley aimed at their hearts. Instead, his features softened. 'Do you also have meat?'

'Chickens mainly; we have the eggs. Larger animals are too contaminated. But we have a large variety of vegetables and ground flour for bread,' Emma added enthusiastically.

'Good, and how far away are these stores?'

'Not far,' Emma said. 'Maybe 10 minutes' walk.'

The man turned his attention to Emma. 'Well, I think we have a deal,' he said, smiling for the first time. 'My name is Robison.' He shook both their hands, then signalled one of his soldiers. The man trotted up and Robison spoke to him in a language Lucas couldn't identify.

'No need to walk when we can drive,' Robison said as he led them through lines of black-uniformed soldiers. Emma smiled at some of them but received only blank stares in response. Parked along the street were rows of armoured vehicles and even tanks. Enough for a small war, Lucas thought. None of this armour had been used on their community; clearly, they were expecting a much larger battle. Robison approached one of the vehicles and spoke to the driver – a dark-haired man with tattoos down his arms. This time Lucas caught a few French words. The driver immediately started up the vehicle and Robison motioned them to climb into the back seats.

'So where is this food?' Robison asked.

'Who are you?' Emma blurted. 'And why have you attacked us?'

Her angry words hung in the air with neither the driver nor Robison reacting.

'We know you come from Europe,' Lucas added, hoping to prod a response.

'I thought that would be obvious,' Robison replied sarcastically.

'Why have you attacked us?' Emma repeated, her voice now filling with venom. 'We are peaceful farmers.'

Lucas watched as the two men glanced at each other in the front seat. 'You are weak and diseased,' Robison answered in a tone that suggested that was the only explanation that was needed.

'You call yourselves Alpha,' Lucas persisted. 'What are you? A cult?'

He saw Robison smile at this. 'Yes, we are a cult, an army and the next version of humanity all rolled up in one.'

'What are you saying?' Emma asked.

'We have evolved to adapt to this world, and we plan to take it,' Robison said simply.

'Where does that leave us?' Lucas asked, suddenly scared. 'You said that if we showed you where the food is you will leave us alone.'

'And we will. We still have a deal if the food you promised is there.'

With little choice, Emma gave them directions to the community's food stores. After several minutes of driving along a winding dirt road they arrived at a vast greenhouse hidden in the fold of a valley. Nothing had been said during the drive. Their complete lack of interest in anything other than the food stores made Lucas feel uneasy. Emma felt it too. Although she said nothing, Lucas could see the fear rising in her eyes.

The greenhouse doors were locked, as the early morning attack had happened before daybreak. Robison shot through the lock and kicked the door open. Before them were rows of hydroponically grown tomatoes, cucumbers, peas, lettuces and potatoes that stretched for over 100 metres down the valley.

'And where are your food stores?' Robison asked, walking over to the nearest row and inspecting the tomatoes.

'At the back,' Lucas replied.

'Show me.'

Lucas led them through the glasshouse to a sliding door that opened onto a large storage area. Inside, were hessian bags full of corn and barley for grinding into flour, and steel racks full of rows of glass jars containing pickled vegetables and fruit.

Robison walked up to the closest shelf and picked up one of the jars full of cucumbers. After unscrewing the lid, he used his fingers to pull out a cucumber and bit into it.

'Nice,' he said, munching through the rest. 'Is this all the stores you have?'

'Yes,' Emma answered.

He nodded to the driver, who pulled out a walkie-talkie and spoke into it. Only seconds later, a series of distant explosions could be heard coming from the direction of the hospital. At these sounds, a faint smile crossed Robison's face.

'What have you done?' Emma gasped. 'We had a deal.'

'We did,' Robison replied with a slight nod of his head. 'Now we don't.'

'You said if we showed you our stores you wouldn't attack,' Lucas said, reinforcing Emma's point. But from the look on Robison's face, it was pointless.

'Those who remained in the hospital have been given a choice,' Robison replied, like he was reciting a well-worn mantra. 'They can surrender, and we will give them life as an Alpha. Or they remain and die. Some have joined us, many did not.'

As Robison stood there arrogantly, cold laughter in his eyes, Lucas felt his rage quickly building. He clenched his fists and Robison responded by unbuttoning his sidearm, as though daring him to try something.

It was Emma who did. In one swift action she lunged forward and tried to pluck Robison's revolver from his holster. The driver, only metres away, reacted by pointing his automatic weapon in their direction, but there was no clear shot. A second later, Lucas crashed into the driver, sending him sprawling into a stainless-steel shelf, which buckled and sent dozens of pickled cucumber jars down on his head. Lucas turned to see Emma desperately trying to wrench the revolver from the Robison's holster while Robison had one hand on his holster and another round Emma's neck as he tried to peel her off. For several seconds they remained locked together, but Robison was too strong – there could only be one result.

Lucas ran at Robison, driving his full body weight into his chest. The three of them crashed to the ground with Lucas on top of Robison and Emma thrown clear. For a second, Lucas stared into Robison's eyes, now lit with rage. Lucas knew where Robison's gun holster was but when he reached for it, he found it was empty. Two shots rang out. Lucas felt a searing pain in his stomach and chest. Robison gripped him by the shoulder and pushed him aside. Lucas's breathing became incredibly difficult and when he touched his chest his hand came away slippery and wet. Robison climbed to his feet and stood over Lucas. His eyes were filled with insane rage. He aimed the revolver directly at Lucas's head and pulled the trigger twice more.

Emma screamed and crawled over to Lucas, cradling his bloody body in her arms. The bullets had blown away much of his face, leaving only an unrecognisable bloody pulp. The horror of her lover's face reduced to smashed bone and blood shuddered through her, snatching her breath away.

The driver, now back on his feet, wiped away the last fragments of broken glass from his face then aimed his automatic weapon at Emma.

'No,' Robison ordered. 'She has spirit... She will make a fine Alpha.'

Chapter 10

In the fading light Alex, Elaine and Mackinnon stood on a hill overlooking the town of Crawley with Gatwick airport in the distance.

'I don't know who they are, but they're organised, and they appear to be dressed in some type of uniform.' Mackinnon handed his binoculars to Alex.

Alex adjusted the focus and carefully scanned the train of vehicles that were steadily making their way down the A2011. At the front of the convoy were several bulldozers with their trays down, ploughing through thick vines and thistles that criss-crossed the highway. Behind were several armoured cars, a number of four-wheel drives and trucks carrying troops. But more disturbing was the trail of fires that these people seemed to be leaving behind them wherever they went. They had been perched on a hill watching the advance of this army for nearly two days. Any fortification that looked like it could burn was set alight either with mortars or burning arrows.

The occupants of these communities had fought hard, but it was clear that they were outmatched by sheer numbers and armaments. A large community in the centre of Crawley had been attacked in the early hours of the morning by a wall of four bulldozers that had been driven right through a two-storey house to reach them. Two armoured vehicles with mounted machine guns had quickly dealt with the main pockets of resistance, then soldiers with bows and arrows had picked off the rest. The battle was over in less than 30 minutes. It was too far away to know if there were any survivors, but one thing was clear – these people were not here to make friends.

'They have to be from Europe,' Mackinnon said. 'The communities around here are small and peaceful. Such a force just can't exist in England, especially this close to London.'

'But how can they be from Europe?' Elaine asked. 'They all look healthy. Not like the ones we found in the house.'

'And they also have war paint on.' Alex sighed. 'One thing's for sure, they're not open to negotiation.'

Alex felt a hand on his shoulder and turned to see Mackinnon pointing at an object in the sky. When he adjusted the focus on his binoculars a drone plane came into focus. It was slowly circling to the west only a few kilometres away. When he scanned the ground beneath it he saw a convoy of tanks and army vehicles heading directly towards them. The insignia on the tanks was unmistakable – Genesis.

'Should we warn them?' Mackinnon asked.

'I'm sure they already know what's waiting for them,' Alex replied. 'That's why they're here. It's us who could be in trouble. We could be caught in the middle of this.'

'We should head for the coast,' Mackinnon said, 'and wait out whatever this is.'

Alex nodded. 'It will be dark in around an hour. We can head south then.'

The rest of the group was shocked when they heard the news.

'We should go straight to the Genesis army,' Casey said.

'They will protect us,' Susan agreed.

'But not now,' Mackinnon said. 'If they are preparing for a battle tonight, we would more than likely be shot at.'

'And considering what we have seen in the last few days there is no guarantee that Genesis will win,' Alex added. 'They have no combat experience, and they are facing an enemy that has no qualms about killing. The best course of action is to just get out of here and see what happens next.'

There was general agreement with this. The only dissenting comment was made by Thomas, who wanted to stay and watch the Genesis army get smashed by these new invaders.

As soon as darkness fell, they headed south along the A23, towards Brighton. Progress was slow. Rusted cars and trucks littered the road and forced them to stop frequently to push them to one side. There were disturbing noises too. Distant explosions and gunfire and a growing smell of smoke. After several hours, the road widened, and houses started appearing.

'According to the map, this is Sayers Common,' Elaine said.

Alex had noticed that over the past few kilometres the road had been cleared of vegetation and several fallen trees had been cut up and neatly piled beside the road. Many of the houses, however, were little more than burnt-out shells. They rounded a bend and Alex immediately noticed a glow coming from behind a cluster of houses.

Elaine pointed toward a gap between the houses. 'I can see flames and smoke.'

Alex pulled into a carpark and switched the engine and headlights off. The flames could clearly be seen leaping above a row of houses. The smell of burning wood and rubber was almost overpowering.

'I don't like this,' Elaine said. 'Maybe we should turn around.'

Alex pointed towards a house at the other end of the carpark. 'There's a light on over there and I think I can see movement.' He looked in the rear-view mirror and noticed four shadowy figures creeping towards the bus carrying what looked like assault rifles. A powerful beam of light suddenly found them. Immediately there were shouts; some in English, others in a foreign language.

'What do you want to do?' Mackinnon called from behind them.

If they opened fire, they could quickly destroy the bus and everyone in it. 'Nothing,' Alex said. 'We'll see what they want.'

As they came closer, they fanned out and surrounded the bus. To Alex's dismay, he noticed they were wearing the same uniforms as the advancing army they had seen earlier. They also had bows strapped to their backs.

'S'ils bougent, tirez sur eux.'

'French,' Elaine whispered. 'I think one of them told the others to shoot if we make any sudden moves.'

'Okay, we are just medical doctors who are going to help some sick people,' Alex called to the back of the bus. 'Mackinnon get rid of your weapon. Casey and Susan, we are heading to the coast to help some sick people. Understood?'

'Yep.'

'Okay.'

One of the soldiers came forward and waved his rifle at Alex. 'OUT!'

Alex and Elaine climbed out while a second soldier came across and tapped on the door to the main cabin. 'OUT!'

Mackinnon, Casey, Susan and Thomas climbed out and lined up next to Elaine and Alex. One of the soldiers came forward and quickly frisked everyone, while another two soldiers searched the bus.

After a few minutes, the soldiers emerged carrying three assault rifles and two handguns in a plastic bag. They showed the arms to a powerfully built man with thick black hair tied into a ponytail that trailed past his shoulders. The man inspected these weapons then disappeared into the bus. When he emerged, he slowly walked down the line of captives, stopping in front of Mackinnon. 'You're military?'

Mackinnon met his stare but said nothing.

'He's protection,' Alex said. 'We are a group of doctors who are heading to the coast.'

'To do what?'

'Treat the plague.'

95

The man came up and stood in front of Alex. He was taller, with deep-set eyes and a neatly trimmed beard, threaded with grey hairs. 'Are you in charge?'

'Yeah,' Alex replied.

The man paused, and Alex felt his eyes slowly searching him. 'And you are a doctor?'

'I'm the guide. Mackinnon is the protection.' Alex pointed to Casey and Susan. 'Casey and Susan are medical doctors and Elaine is a microbiologist.'

'I had a look inside the bus. What's all the laboratory equipment for?'

'We plan on isolating whatever this disease is,' Elaine replied.

'So, you think you can find a cure?'

'We're going to try,' Elaine replied.

The man gave a lopsided grin at this. 'You think you can stop a plague that has already swept through Europe. If there was a cure don't you think someone would have found one by now?'

'Have you tried?' Casey asked.

'The plague cannot be stopped. Just as we cannot be stopped.'

'And who are you?' Alex asked.

'Where do you come from?' the man replied, ignoring his question.

'West of here, near Horsham,' Alex lied.

'There's a large community there?'

'Yes, and we are worried what this plague will do. We have been sent to collect samples and find out more about this disease.'

The man nodded slightly then walked slowly back along the line of captives and stopped in front of Thomas. 'And who are you?'

'Their prisoner,' Thomas replied mournfully. 'They kidnapped me.'

The soldier straightened at this and turned toward Alex. 'Is this true?'

'It's true we don't trust him because he has already tried to kill Casey,' Susan replied.

'She's lying,' Thomas interrupted. 'They're not going to find a cure and they're not from Horsham. They're from an underground city called Genesis. They're spying for their army, which is only a short distance from here. They were heading back to report your position.'

'That's a lie,' Susan spat. 'Don't listen to him, he's a compulsive liar.'

'Am I? Check out their bus. What's written on the side?'

The soldier shined his torch on the side of the bus. In bold red letters was the word GENESIS.

'We come from a small community called Genesis. That's all that means,' Alex said.

'They are keeping me prisoner because I come from the surface and they think I can help them find their way,' Thomas said in the same pleading tone he had used so effectively when Alex first met him. 'I can tell you all about their underground city. It's full of amazing technology and lots of food. I even know where it is.'

The soldier shone his torch directly in Alex's face. 'The thing is...we have also heard about Genesis. We heard it is an underground city and has advanced technology. And several months ago, it was attacked by survivors from Scotland and Wales. We know what happened.' He stepped up to Alex. 'You are not from Genesis. Your skin is rough and discoloured. Your hair is thin and patchy. You are from the surface.' He shone his torch on Casey and Susan. 'But these two. Well, they have beautiful clear skin, full bodied hair, although a bit dirty. They are not surface people. You can't hide what you are. The question is how much of what you have been saying is the truth.'

'Told you so,' Thomas said triumphantly. 'These two.' He pointed at Alex and Elaine. 'Are from up north, but they're now with Genesis. They're here to spy on you.'

'Yet their bus is full of medical equipment,' the soldier replied.

'It's just a cover in case they were stopped.'

'So, Casey and Susan aren't doctors?'

Thomas shook his head. 'No.'

The soldier walked up to Casey. 'Can you name the bones in the arm?'

'Humerus, radius and ulna.'

'The skull?'

'Cranium, mandible and maxilla.'

He stepped up to Susan. 'And you. What are the bones in the leg?'

'Femur, tibia and fibula. The ankle bones are the talus and calcaneus.'

'Enough,' he said angrily.

'As parting with the truth appears an impossibility, I have someone I want you to meet. No-one can hide the truth from him.' He stood back and turned to his men. 'Take them to the Lion.'

Alex glared at Thomas, who catching him looking at him, smiled. Alex knew then he should have killed him.

Chapter 11

The soldiers led them down a laneway and past the burning remnants of a large two-storey house. The house was a solid stone structure and had its windows reinforced with iron bars. In front, were three smouldering vehicles with their tyres still alight. Beside them, in pools of their own blood, were several bodies. Alex noted, with some satisfaction, that they wore the same uniform as their captors. As they passed, one of the internal walls collapsed, sending thousands of orange sparks spiralling into the night sky.

'What happened here?' he asked the woman who was walking beside him.

'They resisted,' she replied in a thick French accent. 'They shot at us, so we burnt the house down.'

Alex looked back at the house. The front door, which appeared to be made of some type of metal, lay bent and twisted on the ground, and the walls were riddled with bullets.

'Couldn't you just have left them alone?' Elaine asked.

'They were given a chance to surrender. They didn't,' she replied without a trace of emotion.

Past the house, they came across a sports ground filled with armoured vehicles, trucks and tanks. In the centre of the field a blazing bonfire roared into the night; its flames fed with broken-up dining tables, chairs and paintings plundered from nearby houses. A crowd of soldiers – men and women – were gathered around laughing and drinking. All had full heads of hair down to their necks or shoulders, but a small number had even longer hair. As the music pounded out,

After a few moments there was a brief knock on the door and Adriana entered. 'How did it go?' she asked.

'As well as can be expected. They don't like their orders, but they are soldiers, they will obey.'

'No awkward questions then?'

'Some,' he conceded. 'But I only gave them enough information to complete their mission. Any more information would have invited unwelcome speculation.'

'So, you didn't tell them what the drones saw?'

'And what did those drones see?' Garrett said, not bothering to hide the note of sarcasm in his voice.

'They saw dozens of large craft heading across the Channel.'

'They saw some larger boats heading across water, but they may not have been heading towards England. Without GPS we can't be sure.'

'They shot down the drones.'

'We can't be sure the drones were shot down.'

Adriana shook her head. 'Those boats shot down three drones. You can't do that with rifles. They had to have had some sort of artillery.'

'There was no sign of that in the footage. You're just guessing. For all you know the drones could have malfunctioned.'

'All three?'

'Yes, all three. It was windy, and we have lost drones before. I'm not about to brief my men based on a rumour.'

'I hope you're right. We're going to have enough trouble explaining our actions to the committee when they find out without having to explain a high casualty rate as well.'

'We will be in contact with them at all times and monitoring their progress with drones. I assure you the situation is well in hand.'

Adriana folded her arms. The situation wasn't in hand. It was spinning out of control and there was nothing she could do about it. There was no doubt that there was a sizeable wave of survivors coming across from the continent. If they

they all danced and gyrated, flinging their mops of hair from side to side. There were others too, gathered in small groups quietly talking in the shadows of the fire. These soldiers, all dressed in black uniforms, had long knives in sheaves strapped to their belts, long bows and quivers full of arrows. When they passed by, they stopped talking and watched in silence. Their stares made Alex uneasy. There was a malevolence about these people. This wasn't a dishevelled bunch of raiders who would dissipate as they maundered across the country. They were organised, disciplined – someone's army.

Diego, the soldier Alex had spoken to, stopped in front of an old English pub, complete with a red-tiled roof and towering chimney stacks, but also with smashed windows and a broken door that had been patched up with planks of wood. The sign in the front, still hanging on one hinge, read 'Duke of York Inn'. Diego disappeared inside. After a few minutes, he reappeared and waved them through.

They were bundled through the door into a large, carpeted room stripped bare of all furnishings, except for two pool tables lying flat on the floor, stripped of their legs, which Alex assumed had been taken for firewood. Two blazing fires at either end bathed the room in a warm flickering glow. In one corner, next to the fire, were the only pieces of furniture – a table with accompanying chairs. The table was spread with papers and plates of half-eaten food. Seated on one side of the table were two of the most extraordinary people Alex had ever seen. Both looked healthy with clear skin. The man had half of his head shaved. The other half was covered in thick, sandy-coloured hair that tumbled down one side of his face and hung in plaited tails past his shoulders. The woman had blonde hair neatly plaited past her shoulders and wore black eye-liner that accentuated her blue eyes. She was a lot younger than the man and greeted them with a half-smile. Alex couldn't work out if it was a friendly or a mocking smile.

When they approached the table, the man leaned back in his chair and studied the assembled group for a moment. 'A soldier...some surface people and most intriguing of all...three people who have no signs of radiation exposure,' he said, stroking a neatly trimmed beard. 'All found driving around in a very sophisticated medical bus. Sounds like you have a lot to tell us.'

'It's like I said,' Thomas said, stepping in front of Alex. 'They're from Genesis and they are here to spy on your forces.'

The man's gaze settled on Thomas. 'You're Thomas?'

'That's right. I'm their prisoner.'

'And you say they are not doctors?' the man queried.

'No, it's just part of their cover.'

The man raised an eyebrow. 'In case they got caught?'

'Yeah.'

'Seems a little far-fetched,' the woman waded in. 'If they were spying on us, I hardly think they would be driving around in a bus with "Genesis" written on the sides.'

'We've seen the drones flying over our forces,' the man added. 'Genesis already know our strength. Why would they need spies?'

Thomas's mouth opened slightly, and he pulled at his beard – a sure sign he was struggling for an answer. 'I know this area really well. I can guide you to Genesis,' Thomas replied, changing tack.

The man appeared unimpressed and turned his attention to Alex. 'You are also from the surface,' he stated. 'We know Genesis was attacked by surface people months ago. I assume you must be one of them.'

'How do you know that?' Elaine asked.

The man looked across at Elaine and his eyes wandered the length of her body. Alex got the impression of someone carefully studying every aspect of her appearance. He could see Elaine felt it too. She crossed her arms in a defensive gesture, as though suddenly realising what she must look like.

101

'We visit England periodically to look for equipment and food to take back to Europe,' he said finally. 'One of our scavenger parties came across a unit of rather ragged looking ex-military from Genesis that had escaped an attack from the north. I would have to say they told an incredible story that was hard to believe. It was only when I had a chance to talk to one of them myself that I realised they may be telling the truth.'

'Is that why you are here,' Mackinnon interrupted, 'to attack Genesis?'

'I'm sure you must realise that in a world that is struggling to rebuild itself, a technologically advanced city such as Genesis is of great interest,' the man replied, his tone almost condescending, implying the answer was self-evident.

'They know you are coming. You can't defeat them,' Mackinnon replied.

The man smiled at this. 'How can you say that?' he said, waving a hand in a dismissive gesture. 'You don't know who we are, or what we are capable of.'

'Are you the leader of this army?' Alex asked.

'Yes, they call me the Lion, but my real name is Pierre Dubois. And this is Adelene.'

Alex looked across at the woman, who acknowledged them with a slight nod of her head but there was no discernible expression, only watchfulness.

'I'm sure you have many questions,' Pierre continued.

'Who are you?' Alex asked.

'We are many things. A movement...a philosophy...a disease, all wrapped up in one.'

'You're an invasion,' Mackinnon stated.

'Invasion is only what we are doing now. Our movement aims to sweep away the old world and replace it with a much better one.'

'I've heard this before from the mouths of lunatics. The mantra is always the same,' Alex replied.

102

'I'm sure you have. It's been a common theme since the holocaust. But those people were talking only from ego. We have something much more substantial.'

'Uniforms and funny haircuts,' Alex replied snidely.

Pierre raised an eyebrow at this, and Alex instantly regretted his comment. He did not want to appear angry. This was not the time.

'That is only window dressing,' Pierre continued. 'It is merely a way of inspiring loyalty. In a world as broken as this one everyone is looking for a reason to exist. We have provided that reason. Haircuts, and bows and arrows and uniforms are merely the hook that identifies who we are.'

'I just see people with war paint killing everything in their path,' Mackinnon replied, taking up Alex's theme.

'Yes. That's all you see now, but I will show you something far more powerful. First, I need to understand who you are and what you are really doing here.' He nodded at Diego who was standing quietly next to Alex. Before Alex knew it, Diego had his arms around his neck dragging him backward while two other soldiers grabbed his legs. Alex lashed out, kicking, and tried to scream, but Diego had him in a choke hold. Mackinnon and Elaine rushed to intercept but soldiers brandishing assault rifles quickly moved to block their path.

'You won't be hurt,' Pierre said quickly. 'I just need you seated and restrained. I can't have you breaking contact once we begin.'

'Begin what?' Elaine demanded.

'Everyone calm down. Just watch and listen,' Pierre instructed, rising to his feet and striding around the table to where Alex was being tied to the legs and arms of a chair.

Alex pulled at the ropes that bound him and twisted in the chair. 'You're wasting your time. We don't know anything.'

Diego pulled out a roll of masking tape and covered his mouth. Pierre gripped both of Alex's arms and brought his face close to Alex's. 'Look into my eyes,' he ordered.

When Alex turned his head away, Pierre gripped his head and forced Alex to look at him. 'Remember where you are. I will order one of your group shot if you don't obey.'

The threat was enough. Alex turned his full attention to a pair of eyes that were as dark as coals. Once engaged, he found that he couldn't turn away.

'That's it. I want your full attention,' Pierre said, resuming his grip on Alex's arms.

Pierre's face was now only centimetres away, his eyes locked on Alex's with an intensity that Alex had never felt before. He felt exposed by something he couldn't understand, let alone resist; it was becoming increasingly hard to think – to reason. And there was something else, a presence at the back of his mind. Images of his past started to appear like pages from a picture book. His childhood, school in Australia, travelling through South-East Asia with his brother Jason. Their arrival in London, then the horror of the first detonations. Jason's blood-splattered face; people dying of radiation; the black blanket of snow that covered the land; Tina, the workcamp and the horror of her death. More images flicked by rapidly: the discovery of the Welsh mine, the mission to the Scottish community, the craziness of Samuel and the first time he had seen Elaine. When the images came to the discovery of Genesis, they slowed down as though someone was carefully examining every detail: the tunnel system leading into the city, the rooms, the domed central business complex and subterranean forest with light flooding in from the surface. The brutal battle on the surface for control of the city. Alex saw through his own eyes the men he had killed, the battle, the firefights in the tunnels as the survivors hunted down the last of the military. Then everyday life at Genesis. The committee meeting where he was asked to lead the mission to find a cure to the plague. Their capture by Major Harrow…Thomas…the fight with the pack of wild dogs. Then there was nothing.

Alex found he could focus again. Pierre was still staring at him, but his eyes had lost their intensity. His face instead was creased with a smile. 'Excellent, excellent. Alex Carhill. Once a science teacher. But now you are so much more.'

'You okay?' Elaine called, pushing off one of the guards and walking over.

'Yeah.' Alex stared back at Pierre who hadn't taken his eyes off him. 'What just happened?'

Pierre drew away, flicking back some of the hair that had fallen down when he was leaning over Alex. 'Your boyfriend is fine,' he said casually over his shoulder to Elaine. 'More than fine, in fact. A rare find. A journeyman of courage and endurance. Untie him.'

'You could have told us what you wanted to do instead of attacking him like that,' Elaine said, glaring back at Pierre.

'You're right,' Pierre conceded with a slight nod. 'I do apologise; sometimes the urgency of the situation overrides my manners.'

Alex massaged his wrists when the last of the ropes had been removed, frowning to himself. He felt violated. This person had not only peered into his life but into his most private thoughts. More than that, his emotions. The emotions that had driven some of his most important decisions and some of his darkest acts. Emotions he never wanted to surface again, yet alone revisit.

Pierre had not stopped watching him. Alex felt like a caged animal who had just been freed from a science experiment. 'What just happened?' he asked.

'I opened a window into your past,' Pierre replied, casually leaning on the table and stroking back some of his hair that had fallen across his face.

'That's impossible,' Alex said.

'Is it?' Pierre questioned, smiling broadly. 'I know about your brother, how the death of Tina nearly destroyed you. The Welsh and Scottish communities. How you and Elaine were tortured by the military at Genesis and how you escaped. I know your history, the decisions you made and most importantly why you made them.'

Alex looked over at Elaine who was watching him with a mixture of surprise and fear. 'How could you know that?' she asked.

'A question I ask myself every day,' Pierre replied, this time addressing the whole group. 'But there is no answer. All I can say is that when the plague swept through Spain and France everyone was struck down, most died. The ones who survived were different. Their cancerous sores disappeared; their hair grew thick and strong. Sickness was almost unheard of. It was almost as though our immune systems had been supercharged. We formed small groups, which coalesced into larger camps. And among these new survivors were those of us who had a connection – a sixth sense. Gradually word spread and we all came together. It was then that we realised what we had become.'

Alex looked around the room for some sign of disbelief among Pierre's soldiers; some snigger or wry smile. However, there was nothing but earnest and sincere expressions, even nods of agreement.

'So... What have you become?' Elaine asked.

'The next step in human evolution,' Pierre replied.

Alex looked over at Elaine and recognised the twisted smile of disbelief on her face. 'So, are all of you some type of superhuman?' she asked.

'Not superhuman. Humans who have adapted to a world which is still killing off the last of the old order,' Pierre replied. 'We are the result of natural selection and some among us have this new ability. We can look into a person's mind and see their past. Understand why they made the decisions they did. They say that our decisions define the person. Understand them and you know the person.'

'Can you make people do things against their will?' Susan asked.

'No nothing like that. It's about connection. Seeing images from people's past. Understanding what drives a person to do what they do.'

'How many of you are there?' Elaine asked.

'Not many, but I'm sure that we will find more.'

'You said everyone was sick but then became stronger,' Casey said, frowning. 'Are you the carriers of this disease? Are you all still infectious?'

'No, I don't think so, but we have isolated the organism that infected us. We have vials of it stored away.'

'So what? You plan to infect everyone at Genesis...kill them?' Casey said, his voice beginning to shake with anger.

'We don't want to kill anyone,' Pierre said mildly. 'But for a new order to rise, the old has to be swept away. I believe your military had a similar mantra.'

'What they were planning to do was criminal. No-one in the civilian population knew their plans,' Susan replied.

'But would you have stopped them if you knew? Scientists, medical experts, administrative staff... I don't think so. They would not have taken up arms against their own military. People rarely revolt against injustice unless it directly affects them. Your military had the will and the arms to carry out their plans with or without your approval. It was only Alex and Elaine's determination and bravery that stopped them. Otherwise, there would be no survivors left in the whole of United Kingdom today.'

Susan frowned at this and looked across at Casey, who looked equally confused.

'Ah...you didn't know,' Pierre smiled, watching their reactions. 'Alex and Elaine found your underground city. They were captured. Tortured by your military, then escaped. When they reached the Welsh and Scottish communities, they told them of your military's plans. It was their efforts that triggered the attack on Genesis.'

Casey and Susan looked across at Alex for confirmation.

'He's right,' Alex said after a moment, searching their faces. 'Considering all that has happened, it's not something I was willing to talk about.'

'You acted to stop Genesis wiping out the survivors. There was no other course of action if you wanted to live,' Pierre commented in a tone that reminded Alex of a

107

schoolteacher giving an ethics lesson. 'Yet only months later, we find ourselves in the same situation. Genesis's forces are grinding towards us, planning to wipe us from the face of the earth.'

'The situation's different; you invaded,' Mackinnon replied.

'The situation is the same. They think they are wiping out the diseased survivors; although we carry disease, we are not diseased. We are the new order.'

'Your disease will kill off most of the population,' Casey said.

'We are not mass murderers,' Pierre replied, for the first time with a sharp edge to his voice. 'When we reach Genesis, we will do our best to save as many of Genesis's population as possible. We have found that type 0 rhesus negative blood donors can give partial immunity to the disease – enough immunity to significantly increase survival. We have spent a great deal of effort to identify these people among our soldiers. They will happily give blood to any person we choose. We will use the blood from these donors to save as many of Genesis's population as possible.'

'And what about the army that is heading this way?' Mackinnon asked.

'We are prepared to fight but we have no wish to,' Pierre stated firmly. 'It will only happen if negotiation fails.'

'You are planning to talk?' Elaine asked with sudden hope in her voice.

'Yes, but until now I could not see a way of approaching an army intent on destroying us without it ending in chaos.' He turned his attention to Alex. 'But it appears now there is a way.'

The implications of his words were not lost on Alex.

'You want us to negotiate…what? Genesis's surrender?' Alex asked.

'No. I want you to make them understand. We have the means to survive on the surface. We are strong, we don't have any disease. Cancer levels among us are almost zero.

We can eat contaminated food without getting sick. We have these abilities, but we don't understand them. The technologies that Genesis possesses can help us understand.'

'You want Genesis to help you understand what you have become?' Elaine asked.

'Yes. If what we have heard is true, you have the facilities to do this. But even more importantly, the one thing that we cannot seem to do is have children. Most of us are sterile. We need Genesis's technical and medical help to have children.'

Alex looked across at Adelene, who was watching him intently. Now he understood. What was the use of a new generation of humans if they couldn't reproduce themselves?

'So, you don't want to just take over Genesis's technology?'

'We want to build a new society with Genesis. We have the means to survive on the surface; you have the technology to help us understand and use what we are. But none of this could happen if we go to war. The last thing I want is to renew the cycle of war and retribution. We need to stop this now. If you can talk to the leaders of this army and make them understand the benefits of combining what we have with their technology...' Pierre raised his hands in an almost pleading gesture. 'We can stop this slaughter.'

Alex looked across at the others. The cynicism was sliding from Mackinnon's face and Casey and Susan were even nodding agreement. However, Elaine had crossed her arms and was staring back coldly at Pierre. 'I don't understand what you mean,' she started. 'You say you want to collaborate with Genesis's scientists. Is this before or after you infect everyone with the plague and kill off most of us?'

Pierre nodded thoughtfully. 'I want to be completely honest with you. Our policy until now has been to take no prisoners: we fight, we infect, and the survivors of the plague become us – Alpha. But this rule is not set in concrete and I see now that it should not apply to Genesis. You are all too valuable. With your resources we may quickly be able to understand this disease, even genetically alter it so it will infect people without the loss of any life.'

'People may not want to be infected by this disease,' Elaine replied. 'They need the choice.'

'And they will get it. Once people understand the benefits, they will want to become Alpha. That I am sure of, but that is for the future. If your military agree to a truce, all this can be discussed later. The main thing now is to stop another pointless war.'

'And you can do this?' Elaine asked. 'You can order your army not to kill?'

'Of course. If we can negotiate peace, we will live up to our end of the deal.'

There was silence as everyone absorbed this.

'We want our bus back,' Susan said. 'And I want some of your stored plague bacteria so we can have a preliminary look at it.'

Pierre frowned for a moment, then nodded. 'Of course. Diego will give you some vials from our stores and he will also go with you. I want you to persuade whoever oversees this Genesis army to meet me, then we can discuss how to work together.'

'And if they don't listen?' Mackinnon asked.

'There can only be one outcome,' Pierre replied, walking over and stopping in front of Mackinnon.

'We also have drones; we know Genesis's strength. They have only a few thousand men and little armour or support equipment. We are 30,000 strong and growing every day, with heavy armour, rocket launchers, tanks and hardened fighters.'

Alex looked across at Mackinnon. His expression said everything. Most of the military's armaments had been destroyed in the previous battle against the combined Scottish and Welsh communities. There would be precious little in the way of heavy armour left, only small arms and limited ammunition. They would not have been expecting to encounter a well-organised and well-supplied army of this size.

'Alright,' Alex agreed. 'We will see if they are willing to talk.'

'Excellent.' Pierre glanced back at Adelene and for the first time Alex saw her smile warmly back at him.

'Now.' Pierre turned his attention to Thomas. 'I know Alex's story, but I still don't understand where you fit into all this. I think it is time that I have a closer look.'

'No, no, you're not doing anything to me. You're not getting into my head.' Thomas backed away but was quickly grabbed by Diego and another soldier and bound to the same chair Alex was tied to.

When Pierre approached him, Thomas let out an enormous howl then screamed expletives until Diego taped up his mouth. As with Alex, Pierre placed both hands on Thomas's arms and stared into his now terrified eyes. Once they locked eyes, however, like Alex, Thomas seemed mesmerised and stared back, barely blinking. They remained locked together for more than a minute before Pierre broke contact.

'Right.' Pierre shook his head and stared at Thomas for a moment, a look of disdain spreading across his face. 'Now I see the real Thomas and you are not what you seem.'

'I'm the only one here who will co-operate with you fully. I have nothing to hide,' Thomas said, with a look of complete sincerity.

'You were married young, in your early twenties, and had two young children, a boy and a girl, I believe.' He paused and began pacing the floor in front of Thomas. 'You worked as a sales assistant in a large department store, but this wasn't your main source of income. You sold drugs on the side, largely party drugs in nightclubs. You were out most nights, barely spending any time with your wife, who was struggling to cope. When the bombs hit you abandoned them, choosing instead to roam the streets with armed gangs and taking what you wanted, whenever you wanted; drugs,

111

food, women. You loved your life. I saw the images of what you did.'

'I did what I needed to survive.'

'No.' Pierre stopped and waved his finger in his face. 'You wanted to do the things you did. Rape and murder. You prayed on the weak. You killed for pleasure. There is a huge difference.'

'We all did those things.'

'I didn't, Alex didn't. No-one here did those things. You betrayed people, you killed those you didn't like.'

'I don't know what you think you saw,' Thomas said after taking a nervous glance around the group. 'But I did none of those things. You're just making up stories to impress everyone, but I can tell everyone that is not what happened; he's making this stuff up.'

Pierre stared coldly back at Thomas then looked across at Diego. 'I've seen enough.' He walked up to Alex and offered his hand.

Alex saw the warmth in his smile and understanding in his eyes. Without thinking, he shook it. Pierre then walked up to Elaine and hugged her, then repeated the procedure with Casey, Susan and Mackinnon.

'Together we can all build a better world,' he said with confidence. Finally, he turned to Thomas. 'But Thomas doesn't deserve to be part of it.' He paused, his eyes narrowing on Thomas as he considered his options. 'You say you are an expert at survival. Here's your chance to prove it. Leave now. If my soldiers find you in the morning, I will order them to shoot you.'

Thomas's eyes widened. 'NO! I know things. I can tell you all about Genesis. Where all the communities are around here. I'm valuable.'

Pierre turned away. 'Go now!'

Chapter 12

Early the next day they set off in their medical bus for Haslemere, a town south-east of London. The town itself no longer existed. Abandoned soon after the holocaust, it was now overgrown by the forest. Scouts from the Alpha army had sighted the smoke from Genesis's army encampments just south of the abandoned town. The Alpha army was gathering near Loxwood some 20 kilometres to the east. The concern was that Genesis's army would soon close the distance and engage the Alpha army. At this point there would be no turning back. Not even Pierre could stop the inevitable.

Alex estimated that the almost 50-kilometre trip would take them the whole day, if they were lucky. If the road was blocked it could be longer. Pierre, Adelene and Diego and a contingent of Alpha soldiers would be riding in two armoured cars equipped with winches, ropes and chains, and heavy-duty chainsaws to clear any road blockages.

Alex felt good to be back in the bus again. It felt like home after what had transpired over the last 11 hours. But the future was still as uncertain as ever. He felt like he was in a car without a steering wheel, spinning out of control around a sharp curve. The thought terrified him. He longed for certainty. Something solid he could grab onto that wouldn't disintegrate in his hands the minute he touched it. These depressing thoughts were interrupted by Casey and Susan holding a small, round plastic culture plate up to the light and chatting animatedly at the back of the bus.

'Something interesting?' Alex asked, hoping for some good news.

'There certainly is!' Susan flashed a smile at him. 'Diego gave us some samples of their Alpha bacteria last night.'

'Alpha?'

'That's what we nicknamed it. It's their superbug they claim gives them special powers. They must have stored it in human body fluids, which makes sense as it clearly infects humans. We thought that if we culture the bacteria and the body fluids together, we might find bacteriophages.'

'And?' Elaine asked eagerly.

Susan held up a small circular agar culture plate covered in a brown lawn of bacteria. 'See the clear spots?'

Alex peered hard at the plate and could see places where the brown bacterial lawn had clear, circular spots in it.

Susan pointed to one of these spots. 'That's a bacteriophage plaque,' she said excitedly.

'You got them?' Elaine cried. 'Bacteriophages?'

'Yep, we just need to grow them up and we may have a cure for this Alpha plague after all,' Susan replied, flashing a grin at them.

'And that's not all,' Casey said, holding up another plate. 'This is a culture of the samples we collected from the people at the house.'

Alex peered at the plate. The bacteria lawn was the same colour, but the spots were different. 'They're larger.'

'Yes, and the shape is different too. They may be different bacteriophages.'

'What does that mean?' Elaine asked.

'Bacteriophages are very specific,' Casey replied. 'They only infect a particular strain of bacteria. We could be dealing with multiple strains of the same organism.'

'Different strains?' Alex asked.

'It's not unusual,' Casey replied. 'Pseudomonas, Staphylococcus, E. coli…they all have a huge number of strains of the same organism. Each strain is remarkably similar but varies in certain aspects; for example, resistance to antibiotics. This is good news because it means that we have bacteriophages against different strains of this Alpha plague. We can combine these bacteriophages into a cocktail that can treat multiple forms of the same disease.'

'We just need to purify these bacteriophages from these plaques and confirm their identity by sequencing,' Susan said.

'How long will that take?' Alex asked.

'To grow up the bacteria and purify the phage will take at least 24 hours.' Casey pursed his lips in thought. 'The sequencing will take a few hours, then analysing the data should be quite quick…maybe another hour. Then we'll know what we have.'

'Of course, we don't have the culture flasks or liquid media to grow these bacteriophages up in bulk, but Genesis does,' Susan added. 'They could grow hundreds of litres.'

'We need to get back to Genesis as soon as possible with this news,' Alex said thoughtfully. 'No matter how the negotiations go with Genesis's army, we must continue on to Genesis.'

There were nods of approval all round. For the first time Alex felt inspired. An enormous weight seemed to lift from his shoulders. There was a clear path, they had a plan and a purpose, and they may even be able to stop another war.

***

'What have you done?' Peter asked, standing with his knuckles on the conference table, his face creased into a grimace.

'Saved your lives,' Garrett said defiantly. He sat sullenly in a chair facing the rest of the committee members. Either side of him stood a soldier making sure he stayed firmly seated.

'More like, sanctioned the slaughter of thousands of people,' Arthur shot back. 'I knew you couldn't be trusted but sending out an army to kill everyone from here to Kent.' He shook his head. 'You should be taken out and shot.'

115

Garrett's response was a sneer. 'I knew that would be your attitude,' he scoffed. 'This disease is marching across the surface. It can't be cured or quarantined. I ordered the only possible solution. Something you are all too weak to do.'

'You have a strange definition of weak,' Peter replied angrily. 'Trying to slaughter the problem was never a solution. What happens if your soldiers get infected while they are busy killing all the refugees from Europe. What happens then? Do they start killing each other?'

Garrett raised an eyebrow then shrugged slightly. 'I would hope they would use their common sense.'

'These are not surface people,' Arthur shot back. 'They won't make the hard decisions. This disease is contagious. You have probably doomed thousands of your people to a horrible death.'

Garrett frowned, and a look of confusion momentarily crossed his features. 'Well, your bright idea has come to nothing,' he countered. 'You lost contact with Alex and his medical buses in less than two days. You have no cure, and you don't even know what's out there. All you have done is waste time we don't have.'

'It was the right decision at the time,' Peter replied, 'which we all debated and agreed to. You have acted without consulting anyone. Now we have to decide how to contain this disaster.'

'You need to call them back,' Martin interjected, staring across at Garrett.

'I've given them orders not to come back under any circumstances. Don't you think that I haven't anticipated your reaction? They know that any order given by me will be under duress. It won't be me speaking but you are forcing me to call them back.'

'You get on the radio and order them back now,' Arthur ordered. 'Tell them that we will shoot you if they don't come back.'

Garrett laughed. 'Shooting me won't help.'

116

'It would help me,' Arthur spat.

'Enough!' Peter shouted. 'Shooting Garrett will not turn his soldiers around. I suggest we focus on more constructive suggestions.'

'We should go after them,' James suggested. 'Send a small contingent of soldiers, maybe 50 of our people. And travel light so we can catch up with them quickly.'

'But where are they?' Arthur asked.

'Yes, where are they?' Garrett repeated with a shrug. 'I just gave them general instructions to head east. They could be anywhere now.'

'How long has it been since they left?' Arthur addressed Peter.

'They left in the middle of last night, so they have at least 12 hours head start.'

'And how long would it take to gather a force of 50 soldiers?' James asked.

'At least another six hours,' Peter replied. 'But the main problem will be the transport. They have taken most of the mobile armoured cars and trucks and left the tanks. The remaining vehicles need to be checked and fuelled. They may even need some maintenance to ensure they are roadworthy.'

'How long?' Arthur asked.

'Another 12 hours,' Peter said after a moment's thought. 'Does anyone know how many drones are operational?'

'There should be a few,' Arthur replied.

'And their range?'

'About 200 kilometres per round trip.'

'Okay. In the meantime, we should send out the drones and try to locate where this army is.'

There were general nods of agreement at this.

'And can I also suggest that Garrett should come with us?' Arthur added. 'If they see him in handcuffs it may act as an additional incentive for them to turn back.'

Peter nodded. 'Agreed. Let's aim to leave at first light tomorrow.'

'And Adriana should also go with some medical staff,' James suggested. 'We need to check anyone who has been exposed to the refugees.'

Peter nodded again. 'Arthur, can you organise the drones?'

'Sure.'

'Then we are all agreed,' Peter concluded. 'Let's bring them back and hope that we are not too late to save them from the plague.'

Chapter 13

It took over 20 tortuous hours to reach the Genesis encampment. Alex shared the driving with Mackinnon and Elaine as they slowly weaved their way north across weed-invested fields and roads cluttered with fallen trees. As they came closer to the London blast zone, damage to buildings and infrastructure became more evident. Many houses had collapsed, and their contents had spilled out onto the narrow laneways, forcing diversions across fields and through overgrown hedges. If it wasn't for the two armoured cars that accompanied them and the frequent use of chainsaws, many roads would have been impassable. Alex was just thankful that the bus hadn't broken an axle or burst a tire on the journey.

The convoy eventually stopped among a clump of trees less than a kilometre away from the lights of the Genesis encampment. There was around three hours of darkness left so it was agreed that they would try to snatch some sleep before dawn. Alex climbed into the bunk next to Elaine and stared blankly into the bunk above. He had a pounding headache and his body felt like someone had given him a massage with a sledgehammer. He wished he was back in Genesis and could clean his teeth with running water, have a shower and eat hydroponically grown food from the canteen. Genesis had been a brief glimpse of heaven before being thrust back into the harsh reality of the outside world. And as always, he thought miserably, although there was a plan the way ahead was still murky. The worst nightmare would be if Garrett was leading this army. If that was the case, there would be no compromise. If he somehow had managed to convince the committee to carry out this slaughter, nothing would stop him. If, however, his mission was not sanctioned by the committee then he would be leading a renegade army with nothing to lose. Either way, it would be like negotiating with a circling wolf.

Elaine hadn't moved since climbing into her bunk. She too was exhausted, but it wasn't Garrett who was keeping her awake. When she wasn't driving, she had been talking to Casey and Susan and discussing their latest results. They had been testing the bacteriophages they had found in cultures of the Alpha bacteria. The results had been nothing short of spectacular. A culture flask full of the Alpha bacteria could be completely lysed in under 30 minutes. Each phage multiplied a hundred-fold in their bacteria host before bursting out, so they now had millions of bacteriophages. The next step was to purify the bacteriophages away from the bacterial debris – all that was left of their bacterial hosts. Failing to do so would cause a severe immune reaction if the bacteriophages were injected into a human. The purification, however, would require more specialised equipment back at Genesis. There, DNA sequencers, culture facilities and advanced gene editing equipment could be used to produce an injectable bacteriophage treatment for the Alpha strain.

She turned on her side and watched Alex relentlessly turn over in his bunk. They had barely spoken since the meeting with Pierre the previous day. With everything that had been happening there had been no time to talk. Still, even though they had barely spoken, she had noticed a change in him. More emotion, she decided. Alex was like an impenetrable tank grinding through life, ploughing down every crisis with cold logic that was honed by horror and grief. But there had been a change in him since meeting Pierre; a hope for something better.

'Can't sleep?' she whispered.

'Not really.'

'Are you having doubts about Pierre?'

'No... I'm worried about who is in charge of this Genesis army. What happens if it's Garrett?'

'From what you tell me, it would be hard to convince him to back down.'

'Impossible...'

'Well, then... If he is in charge, and the committee has agreed to this attack,' Elaine said thoughtfully, 'we must ask to use their radio to talk to Peter and the other committee members. They must know what we have found. We need Peter to stop this madness.'

'And if Garrett doesn't let us use the radio?'

'Then we leave for Genesis. It can't be more than a few days drive.'

There was silence for a moment. 'Yes...' he agreed. 'Hadn't thought of that.'

'Pierre will understand,' Elaine continued. 'If we tell him what we have found and the potential to save lives, he will let us go. We should tell him about the bacteriophages first thing tomorrow.'

Alex realised Elaine was right. If negotiations did not go well with whoever was in charge of the Genesis army, they couldn't just give up. They had to continue on to Genesis so that a possible cure could be developed. There was a clear path after all. 'Maybe Pierre should come with us to Genesis.'

'My thoughts exactly. If we have Pierre confirming everything we say, we stand a lot better chance of stopping this madness.'

'Yep,' Alex agreed. The path forward had suddenly crystallised. He closed his eyes and felt all the tension and anxiety seep away. A wave of exhaustion quickly swept him into a deep dreamless sleep.

***

Alex woke and rubbed the sleep out of his eyes. He felt cold and hungry. When he peered out of the window, he noticed that the ground was wet and a thick fog had settled. This was common for the time of year, and he figured it was probably good news. The fog meant that Genesis couldn't fly their drones and the poor visibly would make any engagement with an unknown enemy dangerous. He was sure that since the defeat of Genesis's military only four months ago they would not be eager for a repeat dose.

Elaine was already sitting in the front of the bus munching through their supply of muesli, nuts and dried fruit with a cup of hot herbal tea by her side. Alex climbed to his feet and padded over to her.

'Sleep well?' she asked, between mouthfuls.

'Okay. Better than I thought I would.'

'You look better,' she replied, studying his face for a moment. 'You should eat something. Pierre has already been to see us and wants us to meet his field commanders before we talk to Genesis.'

Alex pulled out a packet of cereal bound in waxed paper and poured some into a bowl. 'What about Casey and Susan?'

Elaine brushed some of the hair from her face and took a sip of tea. 'Didn't mention them. I think he wants to keep things simple. I told him about the bacteriophages we found and the possibility of developing a cure.'

'What was his reaction?'

'Hmmm... Good, I think. More than anything he wants to understand what has happened to him. Why he seems to have this ability while others don't.'

Alex wasn't surprised. There were few people he trusted these days, but Pierre he numbered among them. There was a connection between them now. He had peered into Alex's private memories without his permission, but somehow that didn't matter. The transference of knowledge had not been all one way. He had sensed something of Pierre's mind. Not specific memories but a sense of understanding. His motives were not self-serving.

Pierre arrived in an armoured car with Diego as Alex was finishing his cereal. Unlike the previous day, he was dressed in full Alpha uniform complete with leather boots, a black overcoat and revolver strapped to his belt. His beard was neatly trimmed, and he wore a beret that had the word Alpha sewn into it.

'I have decided to relay the change in plans in person,' Pierre replied after warmly embracing Alex and Elaine. 'I've been thinking through everything last night. The future could be very bright...very bright indeed. But we will have to proceed carefully. My commanders have orders to subdue all resistance. This is the Alpha way. It will not be easy to persuade them otherwise.'

'Won't they just do as you say?' Alex asked.

'We are not like the armies that existed before the war,' Pierre said. 'My word is not the law. We are a new breed of human. The previous world was run by dictators, some elected, some not, but all corrupt and only interested in their own power. We are Alpha and we are strong, but we are not like them. With our new abilities we can understand each other. Detect the lies. Important decisions like this need to be discussed.'

'So, this is not settled?' Elaine asked. 'You may still attack Genesis's army?'

'I'm sure they will see sense. Our change in plans may just cause a bit of a stir at first, so expect some rather difficult questions, particularly from Robison my second in charge, who we are going to see now. A good man, but he does have...let's say some very rigid beliefs.'

Pierre's army was camped several kilometres to the north in a small hamlet cradled in the fold of the hills. The army headquarters was not hard to find. Numerous armoured car and tank tracks had carved a path through fields and across laneways to a large Tudor-style house set back from the road.

The place had an energy to it, Alex thought, as he climbed out of the vehicle and looked around. A makeshift workshop had been set up in the garden where a group of soldiers were now busy repairing tyres and tinkering under the hoods of trucks and armoured cars. A row of gas cookers

123

with simmering cooking pots had been set up along the front verandah of the house, along with trestles piled with vegetables that were being sliced up and thrown into pots. The air was alive with activity and the smell of beef stew mixed with engine oil.

'I've asked Diego to mind the car while we go and talk,' Pierre said, placing a hand on Alex's shoulder. 'Follow my lead and remember Robison will not be happy with the change in plans. He's all about adrenaline and conquest. We need to explain the advantages of working as a partnership with Genesis. How destroying their army would not be a good start.' He smiled. The smile was good humoured, reassuring, but there was an unease in his eyes that Alex had not seen before.

Inside they found themselves in a large foyer with a broad staircase that curved to the upper floor. Like every house, the furniture had been stripped out, but the floors were polished stone and the walls solid brick. Nothing to steal or burn. A guard moved quickly to intercept them but stopped when he saw Pierre and pounded his chest in what Alex assumed was an Alpha salute.

'Where's Robison?' Pierre asked, tapping his chest with a closed fist in return.

The guard stood back and pointed towards a doorway that had a grey blanket draped across where the door had once been. Alex could hear the hum of a generator and a harsh artificial light seeped out around the edges of the blanket. Pierre took a deep breath and swept away the blanket and walked inside. The room was lit by a portable floodlight which was centred on a large fold-out trestle table. Plates of half-eaten food, wine glasses, empty bottles and cutlery were liberally scattered across its surface as though a great number of people had once been gathered around the table. But now only one person remained: a tall man, bent over a creased and partly torn map of Greater London. Like Pierre, he was a half-head, a top-ranking Alpha. And like Pierre, his blond hair was swept back into a neat ponytail which trailed past his shoulders. Although they made no effort to be quiet, he did not look up until they were assembled at the opposite side of the table.

'Robison,' Pierre said warmly.

The man rose to his full height, towering over Pierre and Alex, and stared directly at Pierre for a moment without speaking. Pierre gave the Alpha salute which Robison responded to in kind. He then said something in French.

'Please,' Pierre replied, gesturing to Alex and Elaine. 'Speak in English.'

Robison nodded slightly and turned his attention to Alex. He smiled but there was no hint of warmth in his eyes.

'Alex and Elaine are from Genesis,' Pierre continued addressing Robison in a very formal tone. 'This is Field Commander Robison; he oversees all the ground operations.'

Robison nodded but made no attempt to shake their hands.

'We are here to discuss a proposal with you,' Pierre continued.

'Proposal?' Robison nodded to himself as if expecting this. 'Please take a seat. We have tea and even some coffee...only instant, but it's very drinkable with some fresh milk we managed to find in the last town we liberated.'

Pierre shook his head. 'No thanks. I will just have water.'

Robison turned to Alex and Elaine.

'Water's fine,' they both said, following Pierre's lead.

'Okay then.' Robison walked over to a kettle that was simmering on a portable gas burner and poured some boiling water into a mug then added a spoon of instant coffee. After adding some sugar, he gestured to a row of chairs tucked into the table. 'Please be seated.'

'May I congratulate you on your progress so far,' Pierre said, taking a seat opposite Robison.

'There have been a few minor problems but overall,' he added some milk to his coffee, 'it's been a successful campaign. Recently, we have even found a greenhouse stocked with fresh fruit and vegetables and a storehouse full of pickled vegetables two days ago. Plenty of food for the troops.'

'And have you added many new recruits?' Pierre asked.

'We've been selective, but we have found some good candidates.' He sat back in his chair and took a tentative sip of his coffee.

'What do you mean by selective?' Pierre asked.

'I don't want people who are crippled or have bad attitudes.'

Alex saw a flicker of anger cross Pierre's face. 'Wasn't it agreed that the offer to become an Alpha should be open to everyone?' Pierre replied. 'Anyone who is still alive today must have the right attitude.'

'I'm building the strongest army the world has ever seen,' Robison replied casually. 'You can't build a house out of sand. The building blocks have to be strong.'

'Our aim isn't to build the strongest army. It's to build a strong vibrant society.'

Robison shrugged. 'The army comes first. A society can't be strong if there is no army to control and guide it.'

'That is old world thinking,' Pierre countered. 'The same thinking that created the war in the first place.'

'Yes. It's also the same thinking that built armies that conquered nations. Isn't that what we are doing?'

'All you are doing is following the same path that led to the last war.'

'We are Alpha, a new order, we are nothing like the old world.'

The two men glared at each other, neither willing to concede the point.

'Let's not get bogged down in philosophy and ethics,' Robison said finally, breaking the deadlock with another sip of coffee. 'Debating the ethics of what I am doing is not why you came here. What is this proposal that is so important that you have called a halt to our progress?'

Pierre took a few mouthfuls of water to cool his anger and restore his calm. 'What we have been talking about does matter; that's why we are here. We came across Alex and Elaine and a team of doctors in a medical bus two days ago. They have been collecting samples for Genesis to develop a cure for the Alpha plague and have told me all about the advanced medical facilities that Genesis possesses. With these facilities we can finally understand what has happened to us. And they are willing to help.'

'So, what are you proposing? A collaboration?'

'Alex is a member of the committee that governs Genesis. He can talk to them. They have much to offer. Highly advanced technical facilities that can make our people fertile again. Together we can understand what has happened and use this knowledge to build a better world. There is a window of opportunity to talk to their leaders. If we attack their army there will be no negotiation. It will become the same cycle of war and slaughter. No-one wins.'

'Hmm...' Robison took another sip of coffee and his gaze settled on Alex.

There was a coldness and calculation in those eyes that Alex had seen before in the brutality of the work camp after the holocaust. Deep within him, his sense of danger began to stir.

'This is not the Alpha way,' Robison replied.

'The Alpha way is only a dream we sell to the masses. We shape the Alpha way. And the best way is to talk to Genesis, not destroy them.'

Robison sat across from them, his bushy eyebrows knitted together as he stared first at Pierre, then at Alex and Elaine. 'I think we need a second opinion on this,' he said finally, waving his hand at a doorway behind him.

Alex felt like he had been punched in the stomach when he saw who walked through the doorway.

'What is he doing here?' Pierre demanded.

'Advising me,' Robison said casually, a faint suggestion of a smirk on his face. 'And it appears what he says may be true.'

Thomas walked up beside Robison, clearly enjoying the looks of horror on their faces. 'Hi, Pierre... Alex... Elaine. Nice to see you again.'

Robison leaned forward on the table, focusing his full attention on Pierre. 'Thomas turned up late yesterday with a strange story of how you are now colluding with Genesis to stop our army's advance. Of course,' he leaned back in his chair and opened his arms in a magnanimous gesture, 'I didn't believe him.'

'Don't trust anything he says,' Elaine blurted. 'He's a liar and a murderer.'

Robison gave Elaine a look of complete disdain before focussing back on Pierre. 'He said you would try to convince me not to attack Genesis's forces. You would instead urge me to strike some deal with Genesis's army and that's exactly what you have just suggested. The Lion wants to negotiate.'

The last words were said with such contempt it felt like Pierre had been physically slapped.

'This man is not what he seems,' Pierre replied angrily. 'I looked into his memories and saw a history of lies and cruelty. He is a master at switching sides...of lying and taking advantage of any situation. And that's exactly what is happening here.'

'I'm not interested in your witchery,' Robison replied caustically. 'I deal in facts, not your fake mind probes...'

'It's not fake,' Alex interjected. 'He knew things from my past that he couldn't possibly know.'

'Of course, you would say that.' Thomas smirked. 'I tell you this whole mind probe thing is just a performance. Pierre just guesses something then waits for a reaction. If it's positive he continues, if negative he switches to some other topic. I've seen it done hundreds of times. It's a cold reading. A cheap fortune tellers' trick.'

Robison was nodding agreement. 'Yes, that's more like the truth.'

'Pierre has probably already worked out a deal with Genesis,' Thomas continued. 'They're just here to stop you attacking so they can bring up reinforcements. Alex and Elaine have probably already relayed information to Genesis about your strengths and weaknesses.'

'This is ridiculous!' Pierre pounded the table with is fist. 'I've had enough. Why would I betray the Alpha movement? I'm one of the people who started it! You would take the word of someone you have only just met over me. I am in command here and I say that we should talk to Genesis's army first. Not start another bloody war.'

'But you are not in charge. I command the army. You are just a figurehead; the entertainment for the troops.'

Robison's voice had a cold edge to it that even Thomas sensed, his inane grin dissolving into a look of unease.

'I will call a meeting of the other commanders,' Pierre replied angrily. 'Then we will see who is in command.'

'No.' Robison shook his head in a slow deliberate fashion. 'You won't be calling any meeting.'

Alex saw Robison's right hand shift from his coffee cup down to his sidearm. Pierre saw it too. Immediately he tried to draw his sidearm, but two shots sent him sprawling backwards, sending his revolver spinning across the floor.

At first Alex didn't move. The shock welded him to his chair. Elaine wasn't so slow; she dived across the floor and picked up the revolver, but before she could turn and aim Thomas was on her. Brandishing a large knife, he stabbed her in the stomach. The impact jolted her backwards and she dropped the revolver. Thomas pulled his arm back for a second thrust, but the blow never arrived. Alex gripped his arm and bent it behind his back while his left arm tightened around Thomas's throat in a strangle hold. Alex summoned all his strength to squeeze the life out of Thomas. The knife dropped to the floor as Thomas tried desperately to loosen the stranglehold that was crushing his windpipe.

Two shots rang out. 'Off him!'

Alex turned to see Robison aiming his revolver directly at him. 'Let go, or you're dead!'

Alex held his grip for some seconds, assessing what he saw in Robison's eyes. There was no emotion, just cold calculation. He loosened his grip and Thomas immediately disentangled himself and scrambled away, gasping for breath.

Elaine was sitting on the floor gripping her stomach, her hands covered in blood. The sight of her immediately swept away all other thoughts. Alex crawled over to her and placed his arm around her shoulder to support her. 'She needs a doctor,' he pleaded.

Robison holstered his revolver. 'I didn't tell you to attack the woman with a knife,' Robison said over his shoulder to Thomas. 'We need both for questioning.'

Thomas looked momentarily surprised by the comment. 'I was just making sure she didn't shoot you.'

'I had the gun pointed on her,' Robison replied casually. 'The situation was under control. All you have done is create a mess.'

'I'm so sorry,' Thomas replied in his most sincere tone. 'I didn't realise. I just reacted without thinking.'

Robison grunted. 'Better get a doctor. I want them both alive so I can question them.'

One of the soldiers that had rushed in after the shots left to find a medic. The other two soldiers stood motionless, staring at Pierre's body and the growing pool of blood that was spreading across the floor.

'The Lion was shot by this woman,' Robison said, addressing the soldiers. 'This is the type of people we are dealing with at Genesis. Mark my words, this treachery will be repaid in full.'

Chapter 14

'Couldn't stem the bleeding.' The medic tensed his shoulders in a shrug. 'Lost too much blood.'

Robison scowled at him, not bothering to hide his annoyance. He had been watching the medic's frantic efforts to save Elaine's life. It looked rather like someone trying to plug a leaking roof with toilet paper. Instead of applying pressure to stem the flow of blood he had just thrown bandages on the spurting wound. Even his face was smeared with her blood where he had continually wiped away his own sweat. 'Clean up the mess,' he growled. 'Every last drop.'

The man swallowed, a momentary pulse of fear contorting his face. 'Of course... And the body?'

Robison crouched down and studied Elaine's body for a moment. Moments earlier her face was a series of contorted lines as she struggled against the pain. Now the lines had gone. She looked like a window mannequin, staring glassy eyed at nothing.

'Bury her alongside Pierre. They are both traitors. They deserve each other,' he ordered.

The great shame of all this is that it would make the interrogation much harder, he thought miserably. He had planned to question them separately then compare their answers. Now he would have to bluff.

***

Alex was being held in the servants' quarters at the rear of the house. Robison led Thomas down a narrow, winding flight of stairs to a wooden-beamed room with a low ceiling. The room was once the servants' dining area and had an open gallery at the far end. Now it was strewn with broken cutlery and pots, littered with rat droppings. It smelt of shit, damp and mould. In the centre, tied to a chair with his head bowed, was Alex. A soldier stood either side of him and immediately gave the Alpha salute when he approached.

Alex looked up anxiously when he saw Robison. 'How's Elaine?'

'Fine for now.' Robison threw him a smile. 'How well she remains will depend entirely on your answers to my questions.'

Alex frowned. 'We were trying to help. Instead, you shot Pierre.'

'Elaine shot Pierre,' Robison replied mildly. 'That's why Thomas stabbed her.'

Alex's face flushed red with anger and he strained against his ties. 'That's a lie!'

Robison paused to study Alex for a moment. Not much affected him these days, but when he locked eyes with Alex, he felt a shudder of pure hatred sweep through him. 'I need you to tell me everything about Genesis. Its exact location, its defences, where the tunnel entrances and vents are...everything.'

'You want to destroy us?'

'I want to capture Genesis with the minimal loss of life – ours and yours. If you tell me how to enter the city undetected then casualties will be kept to a minimum.'

'What will you do once you have Genesis?'

'They will become like us. Alphas.'

'Your disease will kill thousands of my people.'

'Only the weak. The strong will survive and welcome us.'

Alex bowed his head and remained motionless.

'I know a lot more about you than you think,' Robison went on, when it became clear Alex wasn't talking. 'Thomas has explained your history. Caught in the holocaust a long way from home, the death of your brother, the work camp, the death of your girlfriend and the struggle for survival at the Welsh community. We share so much tragedy.'

Alex looked up. A good sign, Robison thought. 'Before the bombs dropped, I was a defence lawyer with my own practice in Amsterdam,' he continued, keeping his voice calm and appealing. 'I had a beautiful wife and two young girls, six and eight years old. Life was good. All that changed in an instant. I wasn't there when a bomb denotated in the middle of the city. By the time I reached my home it was in ruins. The windows were blown in, the door smashed and the place ransacked. There was no sign of my wife and two daughters.' He paused in front of Alex, ensuring eye contact. 'To this day I still don't know what happened to them. There is not a day that passes when I don't think of them and wonder. I searched of course, but in the chaos that followed there was no-one to ask. No authority to search for the missing. Every day was just a struggle to survive. I became like an animal, roaming the streets with others, fighting for food and shelter. I'm sure you know the story...'

Alex nodded grimly.

'My life was a living nightmare until the Alpha plague arrived. It changed everything. Cleared away the weak and gave strength and vitality to the survivors. The sickness brought on by the contaminated food and water disappeared, our hair grew again. We became strong, we could think and plan ahead. We began to organise ourselves into small communities; we set up farms, collected material to rebuild, and started to grow food again. We realised that we were the new generation that would inherit this earth. You and I are alike. We have both struggled against terrible odds, made tough decisions, fought to live, hoping for a better world. Now with the technology that Genesis possesses we can build that world.'

Robison crouched down in front of Alex. 'All you have to do is co-operate.' He was hoping for some spark of agreement but there was none. Just the same smouldering hatred. 'I'm not a patient man,' he went on, the sharp edge of

133

steal creeping into his voice. 'Elaine is alive now, but that can easily change if you don't co-operate.'

'So, after telling me how you and I are so alike, you are threatening to kill Elaine. You and I are nothing alike.'

The last words were almost spat at him. Robison felt his own temper rising. 'Don't doubt that I am a man of my word. Elaine will die if you don't answer my questions. All I need to do is order her treatment to stop and she will die in agony.'

His last words were delivered with such venom that Alex felt compelled to look into Robison's eyes to judge their worth. There he only saw a cold calculation and a willingness to carry out every threat. Alex held his gaze a moment longer then dropped his eyes. 'What do you want to know?' he muttered under his breath.

Robison smiled at the resignation he heard in Alex's voice. He nodded to Thomas, who came forward and laid out a detailed map of the village of Box on the floor.

'If I give you this information, what is to stop you killing Elaine and myself afterwards?' Alex asked.

'You still don't understand, do you?' Robison shook his head like someone chastising a small child. 'I am offering you a new life as an Alpha. Stronger, fitter than what you are now. Free from disease, able to walk on the surface knowing that the radiation from contaminated food won't kill you. And with Genesis's technology we can rebuild a better world. We need people like you and Elaine in this world. The last thing I want is to kill you.'

For the first time Robison saw the hatred in Alex's eyes recede. He dropped his eyes and stared at the floor, his forehead pinched in thought.

'Have you got something to write with?' Alex asked.

Robison pulled a pen from his coat pocket while one of the soldiers untied Alex. Alex marked the main entrance to Genesis and several positions of ventilation shafts. He also gave numbers of people in the city, information on the medical and agricultural facilities, and an estimation of the armaments, although he could not offer information on the forces that currently faced the Alpha army.

'Good,' Robison said, when Alex had finished. 'Very useful information.'

'Can I see Elaine now?' Alex asked, handing the pen back.

'Elaine...' Robison said, accepting the pen and placing it back into his coat pocket. 'Unfortunately, she died just before we came down here. Couldn't stem the bleeding, you see.' He watched impassively as Alex's eyes widened and his pupils dilated in horror. 'Sorry for your loss,' he added as an afterthought.

Alex tried to stand but was immediately set upon by the two soldiers. A flurry of punches knocked him off his feet, then one of the soldiers pinned him to the floor while the second soldier tied his hands behind his back.

Robison watched the struggle with a look of detached boredom, then glanced around the room. 'I like the look of this place,' he said aloud. 'It has a rather rustic look, cosy. I bet the servants loved this place.'

'What shall we do with him?' the soldier who had pinned Alex to the floor asked.

'Take him outside and dispose of him,' Robison ordered, dismissing him with a wave of his arm. 'The people who killed the Lion don't deserve life.'

'YOU KILLED HIM!' Alex screamed, but Robison was already heading for the stairs.

Alex and Elaine were always going to die, Robison thought, as he climbed the stairs. There could be no witnesses to what had happened to the Lion. The message would have to be managed carefully. Pierre was popular with the troops, which would prove very useful. His death at the hands of Genesis spies would galvanise the troops to a great victory in the coming battle.

'Got you.' Thomas giggled as Alex was hauled to his feet. 'I bet you never saw that one coming.'

Blood was pouring from Alex's nose and his left eye was cut and swollen. Thomas's words barely penetrated. The collapse of his world was complete.

***

The two soldiers dragged Alex up the stairs, through the front door and past all the vehicles and activity to an open field a short distance away. Here, in a paddock overgrown with thistles, two fresh graves had been dug. One of the soldiers cut his bonds then pointed to a shovel lying on one of the freshly dug graves. 'Dig.' He pointed to the ground next to the grave with his automatic weapon.

'Whose graves are those?' Alex asked.

'Whose do you think?' one of the soldiers replied with a smirk.

Alex felt a wave of nausea sweep through him which threatened to reduce him to a sobbing wreck. This would be fatal. He would more than likely be shot out of annoyance. Instead, he willed himself to pick up the shovel. If they shot him now, they would have to dig the grave themselves. If he started digging at least he would have a shovel. Something that he could kill them with if they dropped their guard. He didn't care if he died but maiming or killing someone beforehand had a certain appeal. He picked up the shovel and began slowly shovelling away the dirt. The soldiers stood their distance – watchful. They were both young, well-muscled and in their teens, he estimated, with short sandy-coloured hair pushed back behind their ears. They had the look of arrogance about them, like they were taking out the trash – something not quite human.

'Keep digging,' the shorter of the two ordered when Alex stopped to observe them. 'Don't want the dogs digging you up in the night and gnawing on your bones.'

The second soldier laughed; a loud, cruel laugh filled with self-importance and malice.

'What's going on here?'

Alex recognised the voice immediately.

The two soldiers turned then and gave the Alpha salute when they saw the approaching stranger's long hair spilling past his shoulders.

'Carrying out orders of Commander Robison,' the taller of the two soldiers replied.

'What orders?'

'To execute a Genesis spy,' the shorter soldier replied.

Diego pushed past the two soldiers and looked directly at Alex. When their eyes met, Diego's features remained unchanged, but Alex saw the nod, barely detectable; it was all that he needed.

'Why does Commander Robison think he is a spy?' Diego asked, his tone casual.

'He was with a woman who shot the Lion,' the shorter soldier replied eagerly. 'Straight through the chest. I saw the wounds. He deserves everything he gets.'

'So, you have him digging is own grave.'

'Saves us doing it. Can't just leave his body out here, it will just attract packs of dogs.'

'Well, then you better hurry up,' Diego said, turning to Alex. 'Make sure its deep and wide.'

Alex started digging in earnest, shovelling out the dirt and squaring up the hole so it could accommodate two bodies. The soldiers seemed impressed by Alex's sudden burst of enthusiasm, even commenting that he was keen to get into the ground. He only stopped digging when he heard two shots and the bodies of the soldiers nearly toppled onto him.

When Alex turned around Diego was returning his revolver to its holster. 'So sorry.'

Alex could only nod a reply. Any display of sympathy he knew would send him into uncontrollable sobs. Together, they stripped the bodies of their weapons and ammunition, pushed them into the hole and filled in the grave.

'I still have the car,' Diego said when they had finished.

Alex took one last look at Elaine's grave and the tears began to flow freely. He was still alive when he didn't want to be, and Elaine, who had so much to offer, was dead. It wasn't right. She deserved life. What would he do now? The woman who had showed him how to forgive, how to embrace the future, was gone. He felt the darkness closing in on him again.

Chapter 15

She couldn't remember much about the trip back to the psychiatric hospital. There was laughter...lots of excited talk in French as Robison talked to his driver, but that was just background. Her mind just kept replaying the death scene. The choking pressure on her neck as Robison tried to squeeze her life away. The look of insane rage as he aimed his revolver at Lucas's head and pulled the trigger. The blood... Lucas's shattered face as she held him in her arms. The images poured through her brain in an endless loop of nightmares. Her clothes felt wet, cold and sticky. When she looked down, they were dark crimson with congealing blood.

When the car stopped, she was pushed out past a line of tanks parked with their muzzles pointing towards the hospital. Past the shattered front doors and broken walls, the smell of blood and shit almost overpowered her. Bodies cut to pieces with bullets or riddled with arrows stared back at her as she passed by. She was pushed down several flights of stairs, then led into an underground carpark filled with terrified people. Hands reached out to greet her...to pull her into their midst. Questions were thrown at her, but she ignored them. Instead, she crawled into a space between two cars and curled up into a ball. Time passed. Hands reached out and shook her.

'Emma...Emma. Look at me, Emma.'

A fair-haired woman with deep shadows under her eyes and a large cancerous mole on the left side of her forehead came into focus. 'You have to snap out of this,' she urged, gripping Emma's chin and forcing her to look into her eyes. 'Don't give them an excuse to shoot you, you understand?'

Emma recognised her. Kate. She had worked with her for the past two years mending clothes for the community. She was a confidante and had been like a mother to her since her own mother had died a year earlier.

'Here, take off that top,' the older woman ordered as she peeled off her overcoat and handed it to Emma. 'That's better,' she said, when Emma had put on the overcoat. 'You have to snap out of it. They are walking around and examining everyone. The people that look sick or disabled they are taking away. Don't give them an excuse to take you off somewhere and kill you.'

Emma nodded that she understood.

'Now get up and walk around. They won't pick on you if you can walk.'

Emma climbed to her feet and began moving among the remaining survivors. She recognised many, but many more were missing. 'What happened here?' she asked.

'After you and Lucas left, they offered us a deal,' Kate replied, putting an arm around her. 'Those who didn't want to fight should move away from the windows and doors and they wouldn't be harmed. Those who remained would be attacked and killed. About a third decided to stay and fight, even though they knew it was hopeless. The rest retreated down here.'

'So, this was straight after we left?'

'Pretty much. We assumed that whatever deal you made with these people was a lie. You were being tricked.'

Emma nodded. 'When we finished showing them the stores, this man Robison ordered the attack. We tried to stop him, and Lucas was shot.'

Kate stopped walking and turned to face Emma. 'Is that Lucas's blood?'

Emma nodded but couldn't speak. Instead, she burst into tears. Kate hugged her hard, drawing her into her bosom and rocking her like a small child. Death was never far away in this world, she thought sadly, but it was always more tragic when one person was taken from a couple who were meant for each other.

'What's wrong with her?'

Kate looked over Emma's shoulder at a thin pockmarked-faced youth with a long goatee beard and lines of black face paint streaked across his cheeks. 'You killed her boyfriend,' Kate replied coldly.

'Uh...' The youth frowned slightly. 'Well, he shouldn't have resisted.'

Kate didn't reply.

'It's all for a good cause. You wait and see,' he continued enthusiastically. 'We have an exciting future planned for you all.'

Kate had to restrain herself from slapping him in the face. He reminded her of the type of mindless stupidity that permeated the world before the war. When politicians lacking all sense of morals and ethics spouted meaningless words to legions of admirers. Their actions caused massive deaths in the COVID-19 pandemic and directly led to the global conflict which devastated the world. She would not listen to more of the same mindless bullshit. 'Just go away, get out of my sight. I don't want to hear your meaningless babble.'

The youth looked mortally offended. He pointed to a line of soldiers carrying in boxes full of food and what looked like medical supplies. 'Look, we are taking care of you.'

Kate noted with disgust that the food supplies were pickled vegetables from their stores. 'You stole our food and slaughtered us, and you have the nerve to tell us you care.'

She could see the soldier was going red even under his black face paint, but he appeared incapable of stitching together a rational response. 'I hope you die, lady,' was all he could come up with before stalking off.

When the last boxes had arrived, a soldier with shoulder-length hair and a bow slung across his torso stood on a box and raised his arms for quiet. 'You have all been selected to

141

become Alphas!' he shouted before pausing to watch the sea of miserable faces staring back at him. 'You will soon realise that this is the best thing that has ever happened. Look at us; strong, fit, disease free!'

'What are you planning to do?' someone asked.

'We were all infected with a plague that made us stronger. You will be sprayed with this plague. Some will become sick...some extremely sick...but those of you who recover will become like us!' He paused and looked around the group. 'Now, I want you all to sit down while we come around and spray you!'

This set off a round of heated discussion and anger among the gathered crowd of over 200. The bulk of the people, however, seemed to accept their fate and began to quietly sit down in groups.

The soldier nodded to a line of soldiers that had assembled in front of the crowd. Each one appeared to be armed with some type of aerosol spray. Immediately they began walking among the groups and deliberately spraying each person in the face. Screams went up and some struggles started but they were quickly subdued with threats and the occasional butt of a rifle.

Emma sat down with Kate as a woman wearing black face paint came up and sprayed both of them in the face.

'What do we do now?' Kate asked the woman.

'You wait,' she replied. 'If you are lucky, in a few days you will be Alpha.'

After the spraying had finished, food and water were supplied. The carpark was half full of abandoned cars, all of which had long since been smashed open and ransacked for their contents. Kate and Emma, after grabbing some food and water, quickly claimed a spot in an old Volkswagen. Its windows were smashed and the tyres were missing, but the seats were still intact and could be folded back into comfortable beds.

As night approached, blankets and foam mats were brought in so people didn't have to sleep on the cold concrete. As the group settled in for the night, the carpark fell silent, except for the many tonal snores and occasional coughs. Emma and Kate stretched out in the car and ate some of their supplies of pickled cucumbers and dried tomatoes, then wrapped themselves in blankets and fell asleep.

The morning of the second day it started. Emma noticed an increase in coughing and people started complaining of nausea and fever. By the afternoon, diarrhoea and vomiting were widespread. The soldiers moved among the group selecting the worse cases and moving them to a separate quarantine area at the other side of the carpark. These poor souls could barely move without breaking into coughing fits or retching their already empty stomach contents. As the day progressed, the number of severely infected people grew until more than half the group had been transferred across to quarantine.

Like everyone else, Emma and Kate developed coughs and fevers and lost their appetites, but they were spared the diarrhoea and vomiting. That night, the carpark echoed to the sound of coughing and the smell of sewage and vomit. By the morning of the third day the first deaths occurred. The soldiers ordered the strongest of the group to carry the bodies out and dump them in pre-dug graves near the entrance of the carpark. Kate's cough got worse and she developed a high fever. By the afternoon she also had diarrhoea and a splitting headache that drove her to tears. The soldier with the long goatee beard returned and ordered her to move into quarantine.

Emma was left alone with only the horrors of the last 48 hours for comfort. As the afternoon wore on, her body started to ache, and chills and stomach cramps set in. By late afternoon she had also developed a headache and her cough had evolved into wracking fits that drained all the air from her lungs and left her gasping for breath. Night was punctuated with fevered dreams of Lucas's mangled face and Robison's insane rage.

In the morning, the soldier with the long goatee beard appeared and ordered her to come out of the car. When he saw her pale clammy face and smelt the stench of diarrhoea on her clothes, he immediately ordered her into quarantine. Wrapping her blanket tightly around herself, she slowly dragged herself across the carpark. The number of mattresses in the quarantine area had grown significantly during the night. But many were empty. Only brown stains and congealed vomit marking that they had ever been occupied. Soldiers were constantly walking among these rows of mattresses and checking patients for vital signs. When there were none, the soldiers would cover the head of the patient with their blanket. A burial detail would then wrap them tightly in their own blanket and carry them outside for burial.

Emma scanned the lines of mattresses for Kate and found her lying next to an empty mattress; she was still wrapped in the blanket she'd been wearing on the previous day. Her lips were blue and her face had a sickly grey pallor. Emma sat down next to her and held her hand. The skin felt damp and cold and there was no response to her touch. 'Kate. Kate, it's Emma,' she whispered.

Kate blinked then slowly turned her head toward her. A faint smile crossed her lips when she saw Emma. 'Still alive,' she said in a rasping voice. 'Where's Lucas?'

Emma squeezed her hand. 'He died.'

'Oh,' she said. 'That's right, now I remember.' But there was no understanding in her eyes.

'Do you need some water?' Emma offered.

Kate stared at her but didn't respond. Emma felt her forehead and realised she was burning up. She rearranged her pillows so that Kate was sitting upright, then tried to encourage her to drink. But the minute she took a sip she was consumed by a coughing fit.

A short distance away a man carrying what appeared to be a medical kit was checking patients. He wasn't dressed like a typical Alpha. He wore khaki trousers and a matching shirt and had a short, neatly trimmed beard. When he looked

144

her way, Emma called, 'Can you give her something to lower her temperature?'

The man came over and studied Kate for a moment. He had large hazel-coloured eyes and a reassuring smile and smelt of disinfectant. 'What's her name?' he asked with a French accent.

'Kate.'

He crouched down and said, 'Kate... Kate, can you hear me?'

Kate blinked but did not respond. He felt her forehead, then took her pulse.

'Sorry,' he said, slowly shaking his head. 'We only have limited resources. I have to save them for people who will survive.'

'How do you know she won't survive?' Emma asked.

'Her fever is very high, her pulse is rapid and she's unresponsive.' He tucked some of his dark hair behind his ears as he leant over. 'She's also severely dehydrated. These are all bad signs.'

'Of what?'

'The terminal stages of this disease. I'm sorry,' he said quietly. 'All I can do is offer an electrolyte drink. If you can get this down her, it may help.'

Emma wanted to scream, to yell abuse, to call him a murderer, but there was a sincerity in his voice, and empathy too, which was something she had not detected in any of these people before. It gave her pause. It made her face what she knew in her heart was true. She meekly took the bottle and watched as he rose and moved onto the next patient. She tried again to get Kate to drink, but this time she would not even open her mouth. And when she tried to force the drink down, Kate only spat it out again then burst into another round of coughing. In the end, Emma was reduced to holding her hand and putting her arms around her as she lay next to her.

As the day wore on, Emma drifted in and out of sleep. Her dreams were fevered and strange. She saw Kate as a young teenager wearing a low-cut red dress and going to the movies with her girlfriends and a group of boys. One boy in particular she liked. He had short, cropped ginger hair, dazzling blue eyes and a wicked sense of humour. Kate was flirting with him, touching his arms, laughing, preening her hair whenever he came close. She could feel her excitement, her thoughts about him and her arousal when he put his arms around her and gave her a quick kiss. The scene switched to a more intimate moment where they shared long passionate kisses in the back of a car. She could feel each desire and emotion as it surged through her body. Then the scene switched again. A blinding flash was followed by a searing heat and gale force winds that ripped up trees and blew in doors and windows. She could see through Kate's eyes the growing mushroom clouds as the first bombs hit London. The confusion, the panic, people running for cover. The look of terror on Kate's husband's face and the confusion on the faces of her two girls. Then there were more scenes. The death of her husband in a street fight over food, the sickness that took her two children. The horrors piled on top of each other, finally jolting her out of her sleep.

She still had hold of Kate's hand and her other arm was wrapped around her body. Kate, still asleep, was thrashing her head back and forth as though she was gripped by the same nightmares. When she released Kate's hand the images in her mind stopped. It was weird. Some side effect of the plague, she pondered. Maybe they shared each other's thoughts because she had such a strong connection to Kate in this fevered state. Still there was a strangeness to it; it was an intrusion into Kate's personal thoughts that should not have happened. She pushed the idea to the back of her mind and concentrated on Kate. Her brow was still extremely hot. She placed her head on her chest and listened. Her breathing was coming in long ragged breaths accompanied by a wet crackling sound deep within her chest. Her face was grey and sweaty and her lips blue. Bad signs, Emma thought miserably. She huddled up close to her and prayed that whatever happened, Kate would not suffer for much longer.

Sometime in the late afternoon the rhythm of her breathing changed. She started taking long ragged breaths…pausing…then exhaling the air in a long rattling sound. This continued for what seemed like hours until she drew one last ragged breath then exhaled, like air whistling from a balloon. Her chest failed to rise again. Emma held her hand: there was nothing, no images, no memories. Kate was gone.

It didn't take long for one of the guards to notice. The same guard who have given her the electrolyte drink earlier came and knelt by the body. He took her pulse and when he found none, he covered her face. 'I'm sorry for your loss,' he said, turning to Emma.

'Don't bother with comforting words,' Emma spat. 'You did this. This is like apologising while drowning someone.'

Her words seemed to bite.

'You're right, of course,' he replied, a sincere note of remorse creeping into his voice. 'We did this, but it was necessary if you are to become an Alpha.'

'No-one wants to become an Alpha,' Emma pointed out. 'We had no choice in the matter. It was become an Alpha or die.'

'I know it's hard to see now, but in time you will come to understand,' he offered.

'Aren't you afraid that the people who survive will hate you for the death of their love ones?'

'Yes… I know that is true now, but in time you will understand.'

'Don't just repeat the same story to me,' she replied, the anger stirring in her once more. 'Nothing changes what you have done – my boyfriend, my best friend and my family are all dead. We were a peaceful community. You destroyed us.'

'You also had no future. Maybe not this year, or the next, but you would all die from disease or radiation. Now you have a future as an Alpha.'

'If I live,' Emma replied sarcastically.

'You will live,' he said firmly, a smile for the first time touching his lips. 'You already have the signs of someone who will survive. The colour has come back into your cheeks, your coughing has stopped, and you are arguing with me.'

Emma realised he was right; she did feel better. A few hours ago, she would barely have had the energy to speak, let alone vent her anger.

The soldier opened his medical kit and pulled out a bottle of orange-coloured liquid. 'You thirsty?'

Emma realised she hadn't drunk anything for several hours. She nodded.

He handed her the bottle then shook out some tablets from a second bottle. 'These will help with your headache.'

'How do you know I have a headache?' Emma asked.

'You all have headaches. It's part of the disease. When the headache starts to go, you know you are getting better.'

'Why couldn't you give us these pills before?' she asked.

'The fever needs to run its course. If you are medicated in any way you may not receive all the benefits of being an Alpha. We can only administer medication when a patient shows signs of recovery.'

He smiled and leaned over and took her hands in his. 'You are now part of us.'

Emma looked into his eyes, but it wasn't he attempt to console her that she was seeing. Images immediately started flashing through her mind. His name was Sebastian, and he was in the second year of university, studying to become a doctor, when the first bombs dropped on Paris. He had survived by using his medical skills to treat members of a gang that roamed the streets of Paris, often preying on the weak and vulnerable. He wasn't bad. She could see the mental conflict in him as he struggled with decisions that cost lives. The Alpha plague was a release. A way out of the nightmare. He embraced it like a lost child does a mother. He was part of something greater now. She saw his need, his dedication to the cause. She pulled her hand away and the images stopped. 'Are there any side effects to being an Alpha?' she asked.

'Side effects?' he queried, frowning slightly.

'Yeah... Other abilities that you haven't mentioned.'

The soldier's eyebrows creased together. 'What abilities?'

'I saw a woman call you Sebastian. Is that your name?'

A look of pure astonishment crossed his face. 'Who called my name?' he asked.

'A woman... She was small with dark, shoulder-length hair, and she was wearing a brightly coloured dress and glasses.'

The soldier didn't speak for several seconds. Emma watched the play of emotions on his face – confusion, comprehension and finally fear. 'My name is Sebastian and only my sister calls me by my full name.' His eyes dropped to her hands. 'When we touched. That's when you saw my sister?'

Emma nodded.

He leaned closer so his face was level with Emma's. 'You can't tell anyone what you have just told me,' he said in a voice not much more than a whisper. 'You are what we call a Witcher. Some people, after they have been infected, have these abilities. We don't understand them, but they are not allowed.'

'Not allowed?'

'People who have spoken of these abilities after they have recovered have disappeared.'

'Disappeared... You mean they were killed?'

'Yes, no-one ever sees them again. But you will be alright,' he added quickly, viewing the horror in her eyes. 'When you recover, you will be asked a series of questions about how you feel. Any unusual experiences you have had. Tell them that except for feeling stronger, you don't feel any different. Even better, act as if you don't even understand the question. Make them explain it to you. That way they will not suspect anything.'

Emma nodded again, reading deep concern in his eyes. 'Won't you get in trouble if they find out what you have just told me?'

Sebastian closed his medical kit. 'Yes,' he replied. 'So, please don't say anything.' He climbed to his feet. 'Make sure that you finish the drink and take the pills. It will help you recover. I will see you tomorrow.' With a quick smile, he was gone, quickly moving to the next patient, who was in the middle of a coughing fit.

Emma watched him go. She had the impression that her abilities somehow disturbed him. He didn't want to be seen with her. No...it was more than that. She scared him. There was fear in his eyes, but she was at a loss to know why.

A few minutes later two soldiers arrived with a stretcher. Kate's body was quickly lifted onto it and carried off. Only an empty, stained mat remained as testimony that she ever existed.

Emma finished the drink and swallowed the pills. It was late afternoon, and the light was beginning to fade. As she looked around, she realised there were less people now. Only half of the beds in the quarantine area were full and the area where they had originally stayed was nearly empty. Overall, maybe 80 of the original 200 people remained. Were all the rest dead? The question haunted her. These people were her life blood. They had survived the bombs, flu, a rat plague and countless other disasters, only to be slaughtered by some cult army. She knew dwelling on what she couldn't change was a bad idea. She had seen too many survivors dig themselves into mental holes they couldn't escape from. Lucas had taught her there was always something to strive for. You just had to dig deep enough to find it. No matter what the situation, there was always hope. He always had a plan, a way ahead for every problem. A focus. She searched her soul for one. All she could come up with was her hatred for Robison. The man who took her life away. That's what

150

she would latch onto, she decided. She would track him down and kill him. That would be her goal. Revenge. Immediately her heart felt lighter.

That night was the first night that she slept soundly without waking up with a coughing fit or stomach cramps. In the morning, Sebastian was back checking her temperature, pulse and listening to her chest.

'You're good,' he said, putting away his stethoscope. 'I'll be recommending you for processing. You will be given new clothes, asked about your life and what you would like to do as an Alpha. But remember...don't say anything about what you have seen.'

Emma nodded. 'Thanks.'

He rose to his feet. 'Hope to see you soon,' he replied before waving over some soldiers who were standing a short distance away.

The soldiers led Emma upstairs to one of the wards where a man was waiting beside a metal stool. Next to him was a trolley arranged with hair clippers, scissors and razors. Emma noticed the floor either side of the stool was covered in piles of human hair.

'Why do I need my hair cut?' she asked after being directed to sit on the stool.

'All Alphas start with no hair,' the man replied, selecting a pair of scissors to start cutting her shoulder length hair. 'You will find that your hair will grow back thicker and stronger after it has been cut. It will be a symbol of your new strength. How long it will be permitted to grow will depend on the rank you obtain in the future. I'm sure a young girl like you will soon have very long hair.'

Emma smiled at his smooth talk, but there was also logic to this, she thought as she sat on the stool and felt him swiftly shear through her hair. New hair, new life...it sort of made sense.

Next Emma was taken to the communal shower area of the hospital and ordered to strip off all her clothes. Two buckets of water, a bar of soap and a flannel were placed in front of her. One bucket was for washing and sponging away the filth of the disease and the other for washing off the soap. When she had finished, a pile of black Alpha clothes was provided.

The next stop was the delivery dock where a small coal fire was burning in a cut-down metal beer barrel. A soldier with dark curly hair was gently rotating a metal poker among the coals. When Emma realised what was about to happen, she backed away, only to be held fast by her escort.

'You're branding me?' she gasped.

'We have not been formally introduced,' the soldier replied in a smooth, calm voice. 'My name is Mario.' He smiled. 'And what's yours?'

'Emma.'

'Emma... Lovely name. Don't think I've met an Emma before. This is a little...let's say, ritual, that all Alphas have to endure. It's something that we try not to tell new recruits. Saves a heated discussion about the merits of branding.' He shrugged. 'It seems rather barbaric at first, but you will come to accept it and even love this symbol.' He held a red-hot poker up in front of her. At the end of the poker was the small Greek letter α. 'See, it's only a small symbol,' he continued with a smile. 'Once you have this brand you are officially an Alpha. Without this brand you are not.'

Emma looked at the glowing α symbol, barely the size of a five pence coin. 'Where do you want it?'

'All Alphas are branded on the right shoulder.'

Reluctantly, Emma rolled up her shirt sleeve. The searing pain made her flinch, but it was over in seconds.

'There,' Mario smiled again. 'That wasn't so bad. Now you are a fully-fledged Alpha with a sparkling life ahead of you.' He pulled a small tube from his pocket. 'And I would like to offer you some cream to ease your pain. May I?'

Emma nodded.

He squeezed some onto his finger then dabbed it over the burn. 'Just rub it on whenever the pain gets bad. In a few days you won't even notice a thing.'

'Where to now?' Emma asked.

'Now you will be interviewed. We want to know all about you.'

Emma was escorted to a glass-panelled office which had the sign 'Dr Maurice Denton, Head of Psychology' on the door. The office at one time must have been beautifully detailed and decorated. Now there were turned over filing cabinets and folders scattered across the floor and smashed photo frames hanging at various angles on the walls. One photo caught her attention. A man in his forties with a receding hairline had his arm around an attractive dark-haired woman and clinging to their legs was a small boy and girl, both laughing. It was a classic picture-perfect family photo. She wondered vaguely if any of them were still alive.

Against the far wall, at a wooden desk, was a woman scribbling something on a document. Emma did a double take when she saw her. She was huge. Her massive arms protruded from the shirt like two slabs of meat and were heavily tattooed with pictures of tigers and lions, and the image of a wolf was tattooed on her upper arm. Like Sebastian, she was not in Alpha uniform; instead, she wore a mauve shirt which was several sizes too small for her and consequently it stretched around her like an elastic band.

Her eyes must have lingered on this woman too long because she suddenly stiffened in her seat and returned her stare with a look of mounting hostility. 'Sit down.' She motioned to a wooden chair opposite her.

Emma sat down and dabbed some more cream onto her α brand.

The woman continued to stare at her for a moment. A look full of disdain and cold calculation. 'Your name?' she asked, picking up a pen and holding it over the document.

'Emma Hudson.'

'Age?'

'Twenty.'

'Occupation before the war?'

153

'I was in my final year of high school, so I don't have any occupation.'

The woman grunted and kept writing. 'Any living relatives?'

The question stirred up a deep burning resentment in Emma. 'I had a family and a boyfriend until you killed them.'

The women stopped writing and raised her eyes. Her glare slammed into Emma like a fist in her face.

'I guess that's a no then,' she replied with no sign of empathy or pity in her voice. She continued to stare until Emma responded with a shake of her head.

She wrote some more then turned over to the back page of the document.

'Where do you think that I will be assigned?' Emma asked.

'Our army is on the move eastwards towards a place called Genesis. An underground city I believe,' she replied, still writing. 'This is our goal. You are untrained as a soldier, but you will be useful as support staff. We are heading out soon. If you are fit enough, you can join.'

'Will Robison be there?' Emma asked.

The woman looked up in surprise at this question. 'How do you know Robison?'

'I met him when the hospital was attacked.'

The woman grunted then went back to her writing. 'He's leading our army, so I imagine he will be there. Now...' she looked up. 'I want you to think carefully before you answer the next question. During your illness did you experience anything unusual?'

The question was clearly meant to provoke some type of revelation or confession. Emma wasn't biting. She shook her head. 'I don't know what you mean.'

'Did you see anything when someone touched you? Images...visions?'

Emma made sure she frowned deeply in confusion. 'No nothing.'

'Hmm...now I want you to hold out your hands.'

'Why?'

'Just do as I say,' she ordered.

Emma, after some hesitation, held out her hands. Abruptly the woman grabbed both hands and held them in a vice-like grip. Images immediately flooded into Emma's thoughts. Snow-capped mountains, beaches with thundering surf, the bustling streets of Piccadilly circus, Big Ben, the Houses of Parliament all flowed through her conscious in a constant stream of thought. Then there was nothing. The woman's hands were gone and she was staring at her again. This time with an expression of surprise.

'Enjoy the picture show?' she asked.

'What do you mean?'

The woman gave a long, despairing sigh. 'I saw you stare at me when you first came in,' she started. 'Not a typical Alpha, you thought: old, fat, a bit of a train wreck really. And you would be right. But I do have a unique talent that sets me apart from the average Alpha. I can spot Witchers.' Her fat sausage lips parted in a smile. You steal people's memories. Mind-robbing, I call it.'

Emma saw the look of delight in her eyes and felt like a fly caught in a web. 'I didn't see anything.'

'Of course not, dear.' The woman leaned back in her chair and her eyes flicked to the two guards standing behind Emma. Before she realised what was happening, she was lifted out of her chair and pushed towards the door.

'Where are you taking me? I didn't do anything,' she pleaded.

'Witchers can't be Alphas.' The woman's voice trailed off as Emma was led down the corridor. 'They need to be culled from the pack. Nothing personal. Just orders.'

***

After they left the hospital, they had to walk a long way to find a secluded spot. Somewhere away from prying eyes. All the way the two guards chatted and joked. Emma didn't know much French, but she understood enough. They had done this before – taken women who were deemed unworthy of Alpha status into the woods to dispose of them. But first they would rape them. Emma plucked the key words from their conversation. As they walked on, they turned their attention to her body. She heard the French words for arse, tits, pussy, frequently mentioned in between frequent laughter.

Whenever she slowed down the larger of the two, with thick hairy arms and a bushy beard, pushed her in the back. Eventually they came to a laneway enclosed on either side with hedges and blocked with fallen trees. After some heated discussion, they called a halt and the soldier with the beard laid down his weapon. Emma assumed he was first in line.

'Take off your clothes,' he ordered.

Emma didn't move. 'You will have to take my clothes off yourself.'

The suggestion clearly appealed. The soldier gripped her by the arm. Immediately images started flowing. She saw a different girl, small, also shaven, the look of sheer terror on her face as her pants were ripped off her by a man twice her size. Emma could feel his excitement, his sense of power over the weak and defenceless as he fumbled to undo his belt. The scene disgusted her. There was no pity, no empathy in his thoughts, only the excitement of crushing a life. As the scene went on, the girl managed to grab a knife from his quickly discarded clothes and plunge it into his left side. The knife went deep, thrusting into her attacker with all the hatred of someone who knew her fate.

The images vanished as the soldier threw Emma to the ground and pulled down her trousers, then began frantically unbuckling the belt of his own trousers. Emma estimated that the wound was just above his hip. She waited as he pulled off his trousers and started moving up on her from behind. When he dropped to his knees she kicked out at the same spot, driving the hard heel of her shoes directly into his soft underbelly. The effect was immediate. His eyes bulged and he crumpled into a heap. As she had hoped, the wound was

156

recent. Her heel had split it open again and a fresh stream of blood poured from his side. Emma quickly pulled up her underpants but made no attempt to escape. The second soldier still had his rifle aimed at her. Instead, she watched as the second soldier ran forward, responding to the flood of harsh French words pouring from his comrade. Indecision played out on his face – should he help, or should he shoot her?

'Tire lui dessus. Tire lui dessus. 'Tirer sur la chienne.'

The larger soldier screamed as he clutched at the blood pulsing from his wound.

Emma recognised the words. He was ordering his comrade to shoot her. She saw the confusion clear from the soldier's face as he raised the weapon to his shoulders and took aim. There was nothing she could do. The nearest cover was over a dozen metres away. There was no time. She closed her eyes, not wishing to see the shots that would rip through her. Two shots rang out but she felt nothing. No searing pain. She opened her eyes to see the soldier drop to his knees, a look of complete confusion on his face. Blood spurted from his mouth as he fell forward on his face. Behind him stood an Alpha soldier holding an automatic weapon. Emma recognised him immediately – Sebastian.

When the bearded soldier heard the shots and saw his comrade fall, he immediately started to crawl over to his weapon. Emma was on him like a flash. Sprinting past him, she picked up his weapon and aimed it at him. When he looked up at her, she saw the look of defeat in his eyes. But there was no remorse or sense of pleading for his life – only smouldering contempt and hatred.

'You English bitch,' he spat out.

Emma pumped the rest of the clip into him, feeling a sense of satisfaction for the first time.

When it was all over, and her brain had time to think, not merely react, she turned to see Sebastian by her side. The sight of someone who actually cared enough to save her was almost overwhelming. Before she knew it, she had her arms around him and her head buried in his chest.

'How did you find me?' she asked, finally releasing him from her hug.

'I followed you and waited to see what would happen.'

'You didn't know?'

'Not for sure. There were rumours, but no-one knew for sure what happened to people who have your abilities.'

'I didn't tell them,' Emma replied, shaking her head vigorously. 'A woman held my hands and I saw pictures in my mind. Somehow she knew I had seen them.'

Sebastian nodded. 'Her name is Margot, and she is what we call a seer. She can detect people like you. When I found out that she was interviewing you I knew you were in trouble.'

'I owe you my life.'

Sebastian dipped his head slightly in acknowledgement. 'You can thank me when we are safely away from here,' he replied. 'There is an attack planned against the Genesis forces in the next day or two and troop carriers are moving out in a few hours. We need to be on them and as far away from here as possible.'

'Okay.' Emma nodded, pulling on and straightening her clothes. She was an Alpha now. She had her α brand and her head was shaved. She would join the battle and find Robison, then wait for her chance.

Chapter 16

'You can't win,' Alex said doggedly. 'They are too well equipped and trained.'

Brigadier Metler was unmoved. 'Our drones have not picked up this phantom army of yours. All we can see is a general movement of bands of men and women heading west, killing and burning villages as they go.'

'Of course, it exists,' Diego cried, a tremor of frustration permeating his voice. 'I've given you the numbers of soldiers, the military hardware they have and the types of weapons.'

'Yeah...' The brigadier flicked through the notes he had taken. 'But our drones haven't picked up anything like this. And quite frankly, bows and arrows? An army that uses bows and arrows doesn't really sound like much of a threat.'

'Depends how they use them,' Diego replied sarcastically. 'At close quarters arrows are lethal and it saves on bullets.'

Metler looked across at Colonel Johnson, who smirked, not bothering to hide his mirth.

'How many drones have you lost in the last few days?' Alex asked, deciding to try a different tact.

'Three in the last two days.'

'Don't you find that strange?'

'Unusual, yes. But the weather has been bad. They probably got caught in wind shear or there was an electrical problem.'

'Or the Alpha army shot them down,' Diego added. 'We made a point of shooting down your drones so you couldn't see what was coming.'

'Hmmm...' The brigadier looked bored. 'I find the simplest explanation is probably the correct one,' he carried on in his annoying, monotone voice. 'The electronics on these drones are old and we don't have replacement parts. It's likely they just failed.'

Alex placed his hands squarely on the desk and studied the man. He was clean shaven and dressed in a smart woollen khaki-coloured jacket buttoned up to a matching woollen tie. His thinning hair was neatly combed back and greased, so it remained in place regardless of the weather. The picture of privilege and arrogance. Alex could even smell the faint hint of aftershave. 'Do you think Diego got dressed up in a black uniform just to fool you? What would be the purpose? Why would we risk our lives to tell you this? Do you think we have gone over to the other side and are trying to stop you attacking the Alphas?'

Metler pulled out a handkerchief and wiped his nose. 'All I can tell you is that we have our orders,' he said calmly, seemingly totally oblivious to the implications of Alex's words. 'You have said nothing that would cause us to change them.'

'Your orders?' Alex repeated, his anger rising. 'From Garrett? Did the committee know about this?'

'Yes, he assured us they were behind this action 100 per cent.'

Alex knew the committee would never sanction such an action. Either Garrett was lying or the brigadier was. Given what he had seen over the last half hour, it could be either. 'I don't believe you,' he said bluntly. 'Why don't you ring Peter, the chairman of the committee, to confirm? I would also like to talk to him.'

'That won't be necessary, we know what we have to do,' Metler replied airily. 'Tomorrow, once this fog clears, we will be moving out to engage this supposed Alpha army.'

160

'Do you want to repeat the same mistakes you made only months ago?' Alex asked, his anger now spiking into rage. 'You thought we were nothing more than a rabble of filthy survivors, easy prey, fit to be crushed underfoot. And with all your tanks and weapons you were no match for us. Well, the Alpha army is much worse.'

'That's enough! We have our orders and you have said nothing to change them,' Metler replied with a look like he had just sucked on a sour lemon.

Alex slammed his hands on the table. 'I gave you a chance. If you don't pull back your army your corpses will be feeding the dogs within days.'

Alex could see the cold glint of arrogance in their eyes and he knew that his words had been futile. Nothing was going to puncture their bubble. 'So be it.' He turned to Diego. 'I'm not wasting any more time on the walking dead.'

Mackinnon was anxiously waiting outside the tent. He took one look at the thunderous expression on Alex's face and gasped. 'They don't believe us.'

'They not only don't believe us, but they are also preparing to attack at first light tomorrow,' Alex replied. 'I would have had better success talking to a wall.' He looked up at the night sky. The stars were bright tonight, and the moon was nearly full. There would be no fog to stop them, nothing to impede their slaughter.

'What do we do?' Mackinnon asked.

'First light, we leave,' Alex replied resolutely. 'But in the opposite direction, back to Genesis. Leave them to their battle and hope they come to their senses.'

Their bus was located a short distance away on the motorway where they had been stopped and held at gunpoint until they convinced their capturers that they weren't a threat. As Alex trudged back to the bus, the enormity of the day's events started to pound at him. By the time they reached the bus he was so choked with his own emotions he could barely speak. After the disastrous meeting with Robison, he had informed Casey, Susan and Mackinnon of

161

Elaine and Pierre's deaths without a shred of emotion. He remembered the horror on their faces. Yet he had delivered the news like he was reading from a newspaper article. It was all he could manage. Any emotion would had broken him down into a quivering heap. Something that couldn't happen. Not when the very existence of Genesis was under threat. But now, with yet another defeat and the knowledge that Elaine was not waiting for him, he felt a deep ache within himself. She would have seen a way through this mess. An angle he hadn't thought of. He desperately needed her advice and words of encouragement. He longed for her comforting smile and embrace to show she understood his pain. He was lost. He felt like a knife was slowly being plunged through his heart.

When they reached the bus, Casey and Susan came out to greet them. He knew they wanted guidance – strong words, a direction – but he could muster none. They were facing an enemy that would only become stronger as they slaughtered their way westward. New Alpha recruits would swell their ranks before their forces washed against Genesis.

'They're not going to retreat, are they?' Casey said, reading Alex's slumped shoulders and downcast face.

'No, they didn't believe us. They only believe in themselves.'

'We'll go back to Genesis then,' Susan replied, her face full of determination as she searched for confirmation among the others. 'We will grow up these bacteriophages so we can treat the whole of Genesis.'

Alex nodded. 'Yes, that's right,' he said quietly, his voice barely above a murmur. 'We will get some sleep and head off in the morning.' But there was no conviction in his voice. He simply couldn't see a way to defeat them. His headache felt worse; all he wanted to do was to go to bed and sleep.

***

Alex woke up with a start. Mackinnon was vigorously shaking him out of his sleep.

'There are soldiers crossing the road,' he whispered urgently when he saw that Alex's eyes were open.

Alex was in a deep sleep and took some moments to realise where he was. 'What road?'

'The motorway. There's hundreds of them.'

Alex dropped his legs over the side of the bunk and rubbed his eyes. 'You better show me.'

Outside, the night was cold with a stiff wind blowing from the west. The moon was full but periodically concealed by fast-moving clouds.

Mackinnon pointed down the road. 'There.'

At first Alex couldn't see anything, but the moment the cloud cover thinned, hundreds of black-clad Alpha soldiers could be seen creeping across the motorway towards the Genesis camp. There was something odd about them. Their faces were elongated, and they were carrying bows with arrows strung, ready to fire. 'Their heads look strange,' Alex commented.

'Night vision goggles,' Mackinnon replied. 'It's a surprise attack.'

'Have we got any weapons?'

'No, they were all taken off us when we arrived.'

Alex was wide awake now, trying hard not to panic. He looked down the road in the opposite direction. It appeared to be clear.

'But we do have flare guns and some military grade flares,' Mackinnon continued after a moment's thought.

Alex caught his drift. 'Get them. I'll wake everyone. When I give the order, fire the flares.'

Alex quickly woke everyone and told them what was happening while Mackinnon found the flare guns. When Alex reached the driver's seat, he gave the signal. Two flares shot up into the air and burst, then bathed the motorway in an orange incandescent glow as they drifted back to earth. The light revealed hundreds of black figures, as far as the eye could see, creeping across the open space of the motorway. The reaction in the Genesis camp was almost immediate.

163

Shouts rang out, followed quickly by gunfire. Alex started up the engine and jammed his foot on the accelerator. Within seconds they were speeding down the motorway, leaving the carnage of the battle behind.

Chapter 17

Alex had been awake for a while staring into the darkness. The problem was setting his feet in motion to face the day. It had been over nine weeks since they had arrived back at Genesis. So much had happened, yet there had been so little progress. He stretched across the bed and switched on the bedside lamp. Today was the key decision day for the committee. There was no more time for procrastination. The Alpha army would arrive soon, robbing them of any possibility of stopping their advance. Already the main entrance to Genesis had been sealed by their advanced forces and other exits would probably soon follow.

As he had predicted, the Genesis army had proven no match for the battle-hardened Alphas, and they had been overrun within days. Apparently, the flares had helped blunt the surprise attack, but many soldiers were quietly despatched with arrows or swords before they had fired the flares. The remainder were not mentally prepared for the brutality that followed, and capitulation was swift. Remnants of Genesis's army had been trickling back for weeks, relaying graphic stories of the battle.

One soldier, who was on guard duty near the brigadier's tent, relayed what had happened to him. The noise of the first engagements had woken Metler and he had exited the tent, still in his underwear, to see what the commotion was about. He died with an arrow in his chest. Alex found it hard to feel sympathy for the man. He still remembered the look of complete disdain in his eyes, the yawning and drooping eyelids, as though he was more interested in bed than listening to their pleas about the tsunami of soldiers that was about to wash over them. If he had only listened and placed more guards around the camp – done something proactive – more soldiers may have been saved.

Alex climbed to his feet and pulled on his clothes. Ever since the defeat of the Genesis army they had been using drones to watch what was happening. The Alpha army were taking their time moving westward. All the settlements in their path were being overrun and then slowly absorbed. This is what Diego said they would do: subdue, infect and convert as they marched westward. This army was now larger, better equipped and growing more potent with each day. The bravado and confidence of the committee members had quickly evaporated when they realised what they were facing. The initial thought had been to mount a second surface attack, assuming the Alpha army had been weakened by engaging the Genesis army. But it soon became obvious from the drone footage that the Alpha army was much larger and well equipped than previously thought. The focus had then switched to negotiation. Diego and himself had argued against this. They weren't dealing with someone who was interested in compromise. Robison had a lethal force at his command, and he had every intention of hammering it home.

The committee meeting was scheduled for 9 am. Alex finished dressing and shaved, then dropped by the canteen for breakfast. The food, as always, was delicious. Hydroponically grown fruit and vegetables, manufactured meat grown in the laboratory, and breads processed from genetically modified grain crops that grew in subdued lighting conditions. Agriculture and farming had made huge advances since the holocaust. But none of this really mattered. Each day he woke up and for a moment he felt happy. Then the memories would flood back. The visions of Elaine's death would hit and the ache in his stomach would start. Only the imminent threat of the Alpha army allowed him to block out those memories. He channelled all his waking thoughts into destroying Robison and convinced himself it was all that mattered.

He ate quickly and then headed for the conference room. When he entered, he found Peter with his hands wrapped around a mug of hot tea, quietly sipping it as he stared out of the glass-panelled windows at the underground forest beyond. Alex paused to watch his friend. His tall frame seemed more withered these days, and his grey hair was thinning. His skin, mottled with sunspots, now formed permanent creases around his eyes. His appearance was in stark contrast to the clothes he wore; a smart tweet jacket and matching trousers gave the impression of business-like authority. Alex remembered Peter had been in finance before the war, some type of banker. Smart clothes were his comfort zone, he figured. A semblance of control where there was none.

'Are you just going to stand there?' Peter asked, still staring out of the window.

'Sorry,' Alex apologised. 'I didn't want to interrupt your train of thought.'

'Ha... You know what I was thinking about,' he said, turning to Alex and offering a grim smile. 'A football match before the world imploded. Barracking for the Celtic Football Club. The raw noise of the crowds, the cheering and the heated debates about a referee decision over a beer in the pub afterwards. I miss that. I miss the excitement...the mindless banter. It was a time when nothing else mattered but who scored the goal. All that meaningless pleasure is gone.' He took another sip of tea and went back to staring at the beautifully manicured forest, which formed the centrepiece of the shopping and business district of Genesis.

Alex wasn't much into sports. That was Jason's thing. But he understood. The carefree luxury of indulgence was gone. 'Those days will come back, you'll see,' he said, putting on a comforting smile.

Peter didn't respond, instead taking another sip of tea. 'Beautiful, isn't it?' He sighed. 'It's so ironic that the most

167

beautiful forest and gardens in the whole of the United Kingdom exists underground.'

'Someday that will change,' Alex said, trying to instil some reassurance into his voice. 'We just need to deal with this Alpha situation.'

'Yes, the Alpha situation. Let's hope someone has come up with a solution because at the moment our options are very limited.'

'Hopefully... I know there are a few ideas floating around.'

Alex heard movement and turned to see Diego enter the room followed by the rest of the committee members, who shuffled in and took up their regular seats around the conference table. He noted their general mood seemed very subdued. The usual chatter was replaced with downcast faces and grim looks. Lastly, Garrett entered and took up his seat directly opposite Peter. Not surprisingly, he looked notably thinner, as he had spent six of the past nine weeks in jail after his treasonous act of ordering the Genesis army onto the surface. He had not been pardoned for his actions and he was still officially under arrest. But he was the only person who had intimate knowledge of the tunnel system, and the command and respect of the remaining military forces. His skills would be essential if there was a decision to mount some type of military action in the tunnels leading to the city.

Peter drunk the rest of his tea, then sat down at the head of the table. 'Morning, everyone. I know these are unprecedented times, so I thank you all for your hard work in trying to find a way forward through this crisis.' He paused and his eyes settled on Garrett. 'I think we should start proceedings with an update of what the drones have seen recently.'

Garrett stretched across the table and pressed a button on a remote control. An image appeared on an overhead screen behind him. 'These images were taken yesterday, around 100 kilometres to the east.'

Columns of tanks and armoured cars were slowly snaking along an arterial road. On either side of the convoy were hundreds of black-uniformed soldiers, many armed with assault rifles and bows and arrows slung over their shoulders. The drone dropped down to within a hundred metres of the convoy so the faces of the soldiers could be clearly seen. Many had hair past their necks and some past their shoulders, but large numbers, usually at the rear of the column, had shaved heads. These soldiers moved forward with a sort of sullen resolve, like they had accepted their fate and were determined to make the best of it. The longer-haired soldiers often looked up when the drone passed and pointed, laughed and even raised their arms and cheered.

'Aren't you worried that the drone will be shot down?' Arthur asked.

'At first we kept our distance but there was no attempt to shoot any of our drones down. We soon realised they wanted us to see them. It's good propaganda. They want us to know just how outnumbered we are. The other drones have similar footage. We found a second army to the north and third heading up from Portsmouth. All three armies seem to be converging on the town of Newbury some 80 kilometres to the east.'

'How many soldiers are we talking about?' Peter asked.

'We can only guess at the true numbers but based on the drone data to hand, I would say there could be upwards of 50,000 soldiers when all three armies merge. If we assume the drones only saw part of these armies, there could be twice that number. And the worst part is that their numbers are growing rapidly as they absorb the communities in their path.'

'Is there any good news?' Arthur asked.

'Some...if you can call it good news. I don't believe they are in a hurry to attack us. Their progress has slowed in recent weeks and it will take time for the other two armies to reach Newbury, as every time they absorb a new community, they stop for at least a week. They are being very thorough. Nothing, or no-one, is left behind.'

'So how long do you think we have before they arrive?' Peter asked.

'It's weeks away,' Garrett said confidently, 'maybe even a couple of months.'

'But we can't be certain of that.' Peter sighed. 'We need to plan for the worse scenario; that is, we can expect their arrival within weeks.'

Garrett nodded. 'That would be wise...yes.'

'And how many of the original 5000 soldiers you sent out to slaughter everyone on the surface made it back?' Arthur asked.

Alex saw Garrett flinch at the sarcastic tone of Arthur's voice.

'Around 1000.'

'That means 4000 are either dead or now fighting for the other side,' Arthur commented. 'And you can bet that Commander Robison knows every detail about Genesis. How many people are here, our tunnel layout, our defences. He probably knows the name of everyone on this committee and has given orders to hunt us down. Thanks to you.'

Garrett eyes narrowed on Arthur and his face distorted into a snarl. 'My only regret is that I didn't do this sooner,' he shot back. 'If we had moved sooner, we could have stopped these Alphas from ever reaching our shores. It was the reluctance of this committee that has caused this crisis.'

'You sanctioned killing on a mass scale,' Arthur spat, leaning forward and pointing an accusing finger at Garrett.

'The infection was everywhere. It needed to be stopped,' Garrett countered, raising his voice and going red in the face.

'You ordered the killing of innocent survivors!'

'Both of you. Stop it!' Peter shouted. 'I will not let this meeting degenerate into a slanging match. We all know what has happened; restating it will not change anything.' Peter glared at Arthur until he shrunk back into his chair.

'There is no doubt that bad mistakes have been made in the past,' Peter continued in a more conciliatory tone. 'It's the job of this committee to correct these mistakes without causing further harm. Now...what can the scientists do about this?'

Adriana quickly opened a folder and shuffled through some papers. 'So far, we have produced around 30,000 of the bacteriophage treatments, but we need probably twice that number to treat everyone in the city. And of course, we haven't had time to assess the correct dose, so we really have no way of knowing if the treatment will work.'

'And how long would it take to manufacture enough treatments for the whole city?' Peter asked.

'Another month at least,' Adriana replied after a moment's thought. 'We have also started safety trials to check if there are any side effects of the treatments. So far, all subjects have remained healthy.'

'Do you know how effective the treatments are against this plague?' Martin asked.

'No. We have confirmed Susan and Casey's results that the bacteriophages kill the Alpha plague bacteria on culture plates, but as we don't have any people in the city who have been infected, we can't tell how effective the treatment is in a person.'

'We can only hope and pray that it will be effective,' Peter replied.

'So, what is the plan?' Alex asked. 'Does everyone who takes the treatment become immune to the Alpha plague?'

'No,' Adriana replied. 'It's not a vaccine. That will take a lot longer to develop and we don't have the time. The bacteriophage treatment is a virus that will directly attack the bacteria. If it doesn't completely eliminate the bacteria, it will severely reduce its effect and hopefully save many lives.'

'So, when will you use it?' Diego asked.

'If we can't stop this Alpha army, we may have to surrender the city. If that's the case, we will need to negotiate the use of this treatment,' Adriana replied.

'That path would only lead to disaster,' Diego interrupted. 'Robison will not permit any drug to interfere with the effects of the Alpha plague. If he enters the city, he will spray everyone. He won't care how many die.'

'Surely he will listen to reason,' Adriana answered, her eyes widening in horror. 'Most people in the city haven't been on the surface for years. They have no immunity. The plague will kill them.'

'It won't matter,' Diego replied, shaking his head solemnly. 'In his mind, the Alpha plague is everything. It's creating the new breed of humans that will inherit the earth. We either convert to an Alpha or we are unworthy and die.'

His words rattled around the room; their impact was etched on the surprised faces of the committee. Many looked to Alex for some kind of solace, but Alex could only nod his agreement.

'But only the scientists in Genesis have the skills he needs. Surely, he will not want to put their lives at risk,' Martin said. 'He needs us.'

His last words were almost a plea for help and Alex heard the panic rising in his voice. But they needed to understand what they were facing. 'He will not compromise,' he said firmly. 'He is creating a new human. Nothing will stop him, even if it means that most of the population of Genesis will be sacrificed.'

'Alright,' Peter said despairingly, breaking the morbid atmosphere that had descended on the room. 'What other alternatives do we have? Garrett, what preparations have you made to defend the city?'

Garrett stood up and clasped his hands around his back, something Alex had seen him do before when he was about to deliver privileged information only he knew. 'We have finished laying explosives in all the tunnels leading to the surface from the city,' he began. 'Motion monitors have also been installed. We have also finished digging a new tunnel which surfaces in a warehouse in the village of Box. As it is a new tunnel, no-one will know of its existence, except us.'

'And how wide is it?' Martin asked. 'I mean, if we have to leave in a hurry, will we be able to move a large number of people quickly?'

'It's wide enough to allow three people to pass through at a time, and we have trucks and supplies already stored in the warehouse.'

'And where would we be going?' Arthur asked.

Garrett shrugged. 'The Welsh mine is one possibility.'

'I don't see the point of escaping,' Arthur said, looking over the top of his glasses at the rest of the committee. 'We would be on the surface, exposed, with no protection against a well-equipped Alpha army. We would end up as just another one of their conquests.'

'It's a last resort.' Garrett agreed for the first time with Arthur. 'But it was felt that we should have an option of escape if things went pear-shaped.'

'Like if this Robison decided to exterminate everyone?' Arthur added.

Garrett nodded. 'That's one possibility.'

'What about defending the city?' Peter asked. 'Is there any hope of withstanding an attack?'

'Realistically, we couldn't hold out long against a determined effort,' Garrett answered. 'The city is built inside a concrete shell that could withstand a nuclear blast, although not a direct hit. But we have many vulnerable areas. The main problem would be our ventilation system. If an attacker knew exactly where it was, he could cripple it. They certainly have the heavy equipment and armaments to do that.'

'Have you repaired the damage from our attack several months ago?' Arthur asked.

'As much as we can. The section that was blown up has been evacuated and sealed off but is remains a weakness in our defence. If they targeted this area we may have a problem.'

'Assuming that they don't have all the intimate details of the city's plans, how long could we last?' Peter asked.

'We can last indefinitely underground,' Martin replied.

'Okay...if Robison doesn't allow us to protect ourselves from this Alpha plague, we may end up in a siege situation,' Peter summarised.

'And that could work to our advantage,' Martin replied. 'We have been conducting experiments injecting wild dogs with the Alpha plague to see what effects it would have. When a dog catches this disease, it appears to lose all fear of humans. They become more vicious. We realised that this could be used to our advantage.'

'How so?' Peter asked.

'A few months ago, we had a locust plague on the surface, this was followed by a rat plague – both standard occurrences this time of year. Normally this is followed by a spike in dog numbers as the rats become plentiful. But this year, the dog numbers really took off after the battle for Genesis. Many of the dead were eaten by dogs before they could be buried. So, we decided to inject rats with the Alpha plague and see if by eating these infected rats the dogs became infected with the plague. Sure enough this disease was transferred to the dogs, who became more aggressive...almost rabid. Since then, we have been breeding these infected rats in large numbers. If we have your permission, we will start releasing them on the surface.'

'A biological weapon,' Arthur gasped.

'Essentially yes,' Martin agreed.

Alex didn't like the thought of using dogs like this and it was clear from the many frowns that the committee members shared his reservations. However, he reminded himself, the dogs that exist on the surface today were not the cute pets that existed before the war. They were more like roaming packs of wolves.

174

'If we can infect the local dog population,' Martin continued, 'it would make things very difficult for any army camped on the surface. They would have to fend off attacks from packs of wild dogs day and night.'

The committee members looked at each other, searching for a consensus.

'Well, I think it's a great idea,' Arthur said. 'Anything that would make life on the surface more difficult for these Alphas, the better for us.'

His words were quickly met with a series of affirmations and nods of agreement.

'Alright,' Peter said. 'That's one more bit of positive news that has come out of this meeting: we have an escape tunnel and we have a bio weapon. But what do we do now? There are too many to fight, so do we lock down and hope that they don't try to blast their way in? Are you sure we can't negotiate some compromise and try to reason with this Robison person?' he asked Diego and Alex.

'I think we should at least try to reason with him,' Adriana interrupted.

'I agree.' Alison Weaver from the Scottish community spoke up for the first time. 'We must talk to him. Ultimately, we all want the same thing, to rebuild this world and make a future for our children. Our technology will do this. He needs us. Without us, his Alpha army will die.'

Nods and mutterings of agreement echoed around the room. Alex looked over to Peter and saw the same sentiment inscribed on his face. Alex shook his head.

'It does seem our best option,' Peter said. 'Nearly four years after the holocaust and we are still killing each other. Surely this must stop. Robison must also be sick of this. If we can offer him our technology and a treatment to reduce the death rate, surely he will agree.'

'He will agree alright, but he won't keep his word. It will only be a means to enter Genesis without a fight. Once in, he will do what he wants,' Alex snapped.

175

'It's true,' Diego said, backing him up. 'He can't be trusted.'

'Look, we all know what happened to you and it's a terrible tragedy about Elaine,' Alison replied. 'But that doesn't mean that once Robison understands what we can offer, he won't accept. We can offer them new agriculture methods that can improve crop yields on the surface, IVF methods for sterile women, advanced electronics…the list is endless. If we make our case, he will see that collaboration between the Alphas and Genesis is preferable to another bloody conflict which could end up in the destruction of large parts of Genesis.'

'You think you are dealing with a rational man,' Alex replied, his voice strained with the sharp edge of anger. 'The argument you have just presented is exactly the same argument that was presented to him by Pierre, and he was shot dead.'

'But from what you were saying there was a power struggle going on,' Adriana replied. 'Pierre's death was a result of that struggle.'

'It was more than that,' Diego continued, clearly exasperated. 'It was a clash of ideals. Pierre wanted to understand what had happened to us, why we can survive on the surface better than anyone else. He wanted to use the technology at Genesis to understand this. Robison doesn't care. He is raising the cult of Alpha. Everyone must become an Alpha, no exceptions. He's only interested in the power that it gives him.'

'I agree we have to be very careful in dealing with this man,' Peter said, breaking an awkward silence, 'but we can't pass up the opportunity to try to negotiate a compromise. We are willing to accept these Alphas if they genuinely want to work with us, but we can't accept the deaths of our citizens if they just want to spray us with this Alpha plague. It that a reasonable summary of what we have been discussing?'

There were general nods of agreement around the conference table except from Alex and Diego. Martin also shook his head in solidarity with Alex.

Peter leant back and adjusted his tie. 'Those who are in favour of negotiation with the Alphas raise their hands.'

Nine out of the eleven committee members raised their hands with only Alex and Martin disagreeing.

'The motion is passed,' Peter said formally. 'I will put together a draft document laying out our terms and submit it for discussion at the next meeting. In the meanwhile, it seems that preparations for our defence, should we need it, are well underway under Garrett's direction. Are we all happy about our defensive situation?'

Again, there were nods of approval.

'Good. I think we have made some excellent progress. If there are no further items, I think we should conclude this meeting and convene again in two days' time.'

The meeting broke up in a light-hearted mood amid mutterings of approval and smiles as the committee members moved off to their next meetings. Alex and Diego, however, did not share their good humour. Alex had been dreading this outcome. He was now left with little choice.

***

An hour later, Alex and Diego met in Alex's apartment. In the bathroom, Alex had laid out a pair of scissors and an electric razor and he had packed a backpack with food supplies, a portable shortwave radio and spare clothes in the form of an Alpha uniform. Diego also had a backpack full of supplies and a shortwave radio and an additional item – an iron poker with the end bent into an α symbol.

'Are you sure you want to do this?' Diego asked a final time.

Alex nodded. This plan had been fermenting in both their minds for weeks, ever since the drones had shown the enormity of the Alpha forces sweeping towards them. The committee still didn't understand that Robison could not be trusted. Any agreement that allowed him to enter the city

177

would result in a staggering death toll. There was only one path left. Alex took off his shirt and presented his right arm to Diego, while Diego lit a portable butane lighter and slowly rotated the end of the poker in its flames. When the symbol was red hot, Alex nodded then looked away as the searing hot poker burnt into his upper arm. The room filled with the smell of burning flesh as Diego placed an ice pack on the wound.

'How does it look?' Alex asked.

'Passable,' Diego replied, taking the ice pack off and examining the α symbol carefully. 'All the branding irons are handmade, so the symbols are quite variable. No-one is going to question the authenticity.'

Next, Alex sat in a chair while Diego cut then shaved his head. When he had finished, Alex looked in the mirror. Two grey eyes stared back out of the weather-beaten mask that was his face. Like so many other survivors, the lines under his eyes were now permanent; like the α symbol, they were burnt into his skin as a reminder of who he was and where he had been. 'Do I look like an Alpha?' he asked, slowly rotating around in the mirror.

'Yes,' Diego said, flipping back some his shoulder length hair that had fallen across his face. 'You look like a sickly surface person who has recently survived the Alpha plague.'

'Good.' Alex placed a cap over his bald head and put on an overcoat to cover the Alpha uniform, then picked up the backpack.

Diego strapped on his own backpack and gave the Alpha salute, which Alex repeated.

Diego nodded his approval. 'Good; it's time to go hunting.'

Chapter 18

The journey to the surface took nearly three torturous hours. To avoid human traffic and cameras, Alex had chosen the same route he had used to escape from the city six months earlier. The route involved trudging through a series of side tunnels riddled with partial cave-ins and deep pools of water. To compound these problems, Alex's memory was somewhat rusty and several times they had to turn back because of cave-ins. They finally emerged in a disused quarry caked in mud and soaked from constant drips and water that flowed like sheets of rain through parts of the tunnel system. Alex had taken the precaution of parking a four-wheel drive a street away, laden with supplies and weapons just in case the committee couldn't be persuaded to abandon their plans of negotiating with Robison. The plan was to travel north to the M4 motorway, then east along the M4 until it intersected with the A34 road heading south. This road bypassed Newbury to the east and continued south until it reached Winchester where the third arm of the Alpha army was slowly making their way north to Newbury.

Alex would leave Diego when they were close to Newbury and travel on foot to the Alpha army. If he was stopped, his story was simple. He was still feeling ill after being infected with the Alpha plague and had stopped by the road to recover. After falling asleep, he had woken up alone and had been walking around ever since. The drone footage showed many new recruits wandering aimlessly next to the armed convoys, so this story made sense. Once he found Robison, he would report his location back to Diego, but that was all. Diego was very clear on this point. Diego would continue on and intercept Gerolf and Ursula, who were leading the Alpha army to the south, sweeping along the coast of Kent before joining up with Robison at Newbury. He would explain how Robison had killed Pierre and try to convince them to arrest Robison and put him on trial. Only if something went wrong with his plan would Alex act on his own.

The trip along the M4, as before, was fast with only a few fallen trees to slow their progress. The fortified town Alex had seen on his first trip was still there, although its occupants seemed more agitated. Alex wasn't surprised; a constant stream of retreating Genesis soldiers limping past wouldn't have helped. They reached the turn-off to the M34 by late afternoon and headed south. Here, the road showed signs that it had been recently travelled with fresh tyre marks and tank treads. There were also multiple smoke spirals ahead that marked the approximate position of Newbury. When they reached the turn-off to Newbury along the A339, Alex decided to walk the rest of the way, calculating that he should reach the town centre by sunset. The darkness would offer ample cover against unwanted questions. Diego insisted that he should also take plenty of flares and a powerful spotlight. After going over their plans one last time and checking that their radios worked at the frequencies they had decided on, Alex set off in his Alpha uniform carrying a backpack with supplies and the radio.

The road into Newbury was a broad two-lane carriageway separated by a grass verge. Alex set a quick pace down the middle of the road keeping an eye out for packs of wild dogs. By the time he reached the outskirts of Newbury, the last rays of the sun had disappeared, and the cold chill of the night was beginning to bite. The place had definitely changed since the last time he had passed through, over two months earlier. The line of mangled cars that had previously obstructed their path had been pushed aside and heavy vehicle treads had flattened the undergrowth on either side of the road. As he moved through the more built-up areas, he saw the first signs of the Alpha army. Armoured cars and trucks were parked in rows along the side of the road and the inviting smell of wood fires permeated the air. There was also music and laughter coming from inside some of the houses. He walked on past many supply trucks, armoured cars and tanks – none were guarded. His earlier fears of being challenged by armed soldiers quickly evaporated as it was clear that this was an army in celebration mode. He got the impression of an army kicking back and relaxing as if they had already defeated their enemy.

Further into town, groups of soldiers passed him, laughing and chatting, often in French or some other European language, and sprinkled among them were the shaven-headed English recruits. Many also seemed happy; no doubt, he thought, fed on tales of a technologically advanced and defenceless city full of food and riches, just waiting to be plucked. Closer to the centre of town, the streets became narrower and more crowded. The smell of cooking fires wafted through the air and loud music blasted out of buildings, prompting some Alphas to let down their hair and start dancing. The whole place had a carnival-like atmosphere. He picked out a group of shaven-haired soldiers gathered around a fire, quietly chatting and drinking from a large wooden barrel with a tap valve at the bottom. In the centre of the group was an open fire with a crudely constructed spit. A soldier was drinking from a beer mug while he slowly turned what looked like the carcass of a large dog on the spit.

Alex picked out one of the soldiers who was busy draining a mug of whatever was in the barrel. 'What are you drinking?' he asked with a smile.

The soldier grinned back at him. 'Homemade whiskey. Tastes like piss but it's got a kick.'

'You mind if I have some?' Alex asked.

'Sure. Help yourself.'

Alex grabbed a cup from a box of utensils that was sitting beside the barrel and filled it with a pale-looking liquid. It smelt a bit like vinegar and had a cloudy appearance. He took a sip and realised the soldier was right about the taste. 'Where were you from?' Alex asked, feeling the liquid burn all the way down to his stomach.

The man leered at him in an unfocused, alcohol-induced haze. 'Originally or since the war?'

'Since the war.'

'A small place east of here, near Baughurst.'

Alex had no idea where that was. 'How long have you been with the Alpha army?' he asked.

'Hmm...maybe five...no, six weeks. To tell you the truth I've lost count, but it's been one hell of a ride.'

'In what way?'

The man frowned. 'You must be a new recruit.'

Alex realised it was a weird question to ask. 'Yeah...to tell you the truth I'm still recovering from the plague so I'm still trying to find my feet.'

'Huh...' The man grinned and pointed to Alex's shaved head. 'Thought so...freshly shaved.'

'Yeah.' Alex brushed a hand over his bald head. 'I was only shaved a few days ago.'

The soldier finished the last dregs of his drink then walked over for a refill. 'I guess you must be from around here then,' he said, returning with a full mug.

'Yeah. I live in Newbury.'

'Yeah, thought so.'

'So...tell me,' Alex persisted. 'Since this is so new. What's it like being an Alpha?'

'Great...yeah. These guys really know what they are doing. Fearsome fighters. They're teaching us to fight hand to hand. Bows and arrows...swords, long knives. And they got plans. Lots of plans.'

'What sort of plans?' Alex asked.

'Surely you've heard of Genesis?' the soldier replied.

'Oh yeah...they told me about this underground city when I was inducted,' Alex replied, trying to sound casual. 'But I haven't heard anything about when they plan to attack.'

'Well, they're not going to tell us that one. We are at the bottom of the food chain. All I know is that they are waiting for the armies to the south and north to join up in the next few days. Then we all head west to attack.'

'Hmm... And what do they know about the city?'

'Nothing official.' The soldier leaned closer as though he was about to divulge a ghastly secret. 'But I've heard that the government just before the war sent all their artworks, paintings and gold down there for safe keeping and they are a race of genetically modified people.'

'Really? That's amazing.' Alex tried his best to look amazed. 'Well, it should be a wild ride.'

'Yeah, cheers.' The soldier grinned stupidly and took another swig of his drink.

'So where is the command headquarters?' Alex asked. 'I thought I better see what I should be doing.'

'Nah... Don't worry about that. Stick with us. You're only going to be support staff anyway.'

'All the same, I might wander around and see what I can find. Which way is the headquarters?'

The soldier gestured over Alex shoulders. 'The Alpha command is over there in a church...St Nicolas's, I think. You should know it.'

'Oh yeah.' Alex gave him a knowing grin as he surreptitiously tipped out the remainder of his drink on the ground. 'Thanks for the drink. I'll probably be seeing you around.'

'Yeah, see you around,' he grinned, refocussing his attention back on his drink.

Walking on, Alex soon found himself in the main shopping district of Newbury. The place was alive with activity. Armoured cars, four-wheel drives and troop carriers lined both sides of the street, and large groups of Alphas

183

chatted and laughed against a backdrop of loud rock and punk music. Barrels of home-brewed whiskey and beer, balanced on stools, were scattered liberally along the street and formed the focal points of much of the activity. As he walked on, however, he noticed many more long-haired Alphas. There was a subtle change in atmosphere too. Many he passed conversed in a foreign language and brandished automatic weapons, along with bows and quivers of arrows, and long knives sheathed on utility belts. These were the Alphas from Europe and he felt a twist of fear rising in his gut as he passed them. They were not like the malnourished sickly looking English. In the flicker of the passing street fires, their stares felt cold and hostile. He had heard the descriptions of these Alphas from the retreating Genesis soldiers – their efficient brutality in combat and the methodical way they rounded up and executed those who wouldn't concede to their authority.

He reached a stone bridge over a fast-flowing river and found the way blocked by a line of armoured cars. Long-haired Alphas carrying assault rifles were patrolling the bridge and stopping anyone who wanted to pass. Only a short distance away the spire tower of St Nicolas's church rose above the skyline, dimly lit by the reflective glow from spotlights. Alex retreated into the shadows and watched. He noticed that anyone who approached was questioned, but most were let straight through without even a check done of their possessions. As he watched, several Alphas with obvious injuries were let through without questioning.

Guessing there was some type of medical station past the checkpoint he approached one of the guards. 'Excuse me,' he said mournfully, plastering a forlorn expression on his face. 'I'm not feeling well. I heard that there's a medical station here that can give me some help.'

The Alpha soldier shone a torchlight on his face. 'Yeah, you don't look so well.' He motioned with his head. 'On your left, 50 metres down the road.'

'Thanks,' Alex said, giving him a friendly smile.

On his right was the church, set back in a field of overgrown weeds that had been flattened by lines of armoured cars and tanks. Except for the shattered stained-glass windows, the church looked remarkably well preserved. Its solid sandstone blocks were an easy match for the hurricane force winds which must have battered the town when the bombs dropped. The delicate sandstone archway that led through to the church, however, lay in shattered pieces, crushed not by the holocaust but by the tanks that were parked at the front of the church.

Directly opposite the church was a craft beer and wine shop that had been converted into a field hospital. Inside were lines of makeshift beds – Alex estimated at least 100 – many filled with injured Alpha soldiers. The next-door barber shop was set up as a medicine dispensary. He decided this would be a good spot to watch for any activity from the church. And because he looked so sick, he may even be able to score a bed while he watched.

A man wearing a khaki shirt with a red cross embroidered on his right-hand pocket was behind a counter attending to a soldier who had just arrived. When he had finished, Alex approached the man and smiled. 'Hello, I was wondering if you could give me some help. I don't feel great; in fact, I feel really sick and exhausted. I don't think I have fully recovered from the Alpha plague.'

The man nodded his head sympathetically. 'Yes, we have seen a lot of persistent symptoms from plague patients. What specifically are your symptoms?' he replied in a strong French accent.

Alex decided to throw everything at him. 'Stomach cramps, vomiting, diarrhoea, fever, blurred vision, dizziness, aching joints...and tiredness.'

The man looked a bit surprised. 'No coughing or sore throat?'

'Ah...I had that earlier,' Alex replied cautiously, realising that he couldn't really fake a cough and a sore throat could be easily checked.

185

'Well, I better take a look.' He pointed to a vacant bed a short distance away. 'Sit over there and I will be back in a minute.'

Alex walked over and unclipped his pack, feeling pleased with his performance.

A few minutes later the man arrived back with a medical bag. He took Alex's temperature, examined his throat and checked his ears, then asked him to take off his shirt so he could listen to his chest.

Alex watched the display of emotions play out on his face as he struggled to diagnose a perfectly healthy person who had an alarming array of symptoms. Finally, he placed his stethoscope back in his bag and started examining the Alpha brand on Alex's arm. 'Your brand looks very fresh and inflamed,' he said after a moment of pondering a diagnosis. 'Maybe you have a bacterial infection, although you don't have any fever that I can detect.'

'I really don't feel well,' Alex pleaded. 'I haven't eaten in days because I can't keep anything down.'

This he seemed to believe. 'Where were you infected with the Alpha plague?' he asked. 'Here in Newbury?'

'Yes.' Alex nodded his head vigorously. 'A group of us were infected on the other side of town.'

'And who infected you?'

'What do you mean?' Alex asked, starting to feel uncomfortable at the change in topic.

'Do you know the name of the person who was in charge?'

'Hmm...' Alex scratched his head hoping to give the impression of someone deeply in thought. 'Look, I lost a lot of my friends and family. The whole thing is a bit of a blur. I didn't take any notice of who was doing this to us.'

The man took another look at the Alpha brand on Alex's arm. 'So, when were you branded?'

Alex shrugged. 'A few days ago.'

The man frowned, then peered even closer at the brand. 'This seems more recent than that. Are you sure it was a few days ago?'

Alex nodded. 'Afterwards I got lost and have been wandering around ever since, feeling sick.'

The man studied Alex for a moment and Alex saw suspicion and disbelief rising in his eyes. 'I will be back in a minute,' he announced, and before Alex could say anything further, he had walked off and disappeared through a door. Alex knew he was in trouble and thought about quickly walking away. But where would he go? No, he thought, he hadn't said anything that he couldn't bluff his way out of.

A few minutes later the man reappeared with a young woman with short-cropped blonde hair. Alex judged from the length of her hair that she had been shaven a couple of months ago. She was pretty with intense, searching eyes. She walked straight up to him and shook his hand. 'I'm Emma,' she said in an English accent, 'and this is Sebastian. He's asked me for a second opinion.' She gave him a warm smile.

She held his hand in a vice-like grip as she talked to him. Immediately, Alex could feel her energy and intelligence. It was like when he was being held down by Pierre. His memories were being searched. He pulled his hand away and for a moment they stared at each other. A look of surprise and shock appeared on both their faces as they recognised who the other really was.

'I didn't catch your name,' she said.

'Don't you already know my name?' Alex replied.

She blinked, then there was an almost imperceptible widening of her eyes and a furtive glance across at Sebastian. 'You are not what you seem.' She smiled.

There was a light in her eyes, but he didn't understand it and couldn't yet trust it. 'I don't know what you mean,' he said, acting dumb.

'Yes, you do. You are from Genesis and you've never been infected.'

187

Alex glanced at Sebastian, who was looking curiously across at him.

Her welcoming smile hadn't changed. If anything, it had crept further across her face. 'I will tell you what I saw. There were two scenes. The first was a man with long dark hair branding you with a hot iron bearing the Alpha symbol. And you were saying, "How does it look?" This man then replied, "Passable." The second scene was stronger, more emotional, and was the scene of two half-heads sitting around a table talking. One was Robison, who shot the other one twice in the chest. Then a woman was stabbed. I felt your reaction, your urge to kill the man who did it.' She leaned forward so her face was close to his. 'You want revenge and so do I. Robison shot my boyfriend. The only person I loved more than anything in this world.'

The accuracy of her words and her supreme confidence caught Alex by surprise. She was like Pierre, he realised. Any attempt to deny it seemed like a waste of time. 'I do want revenge,' he said. 'But not just for my girlfriend. The other half-head you saw was Pierre. You call him the Lion. The leader of the Alpha movement.'

'He was killed by a Genesis spy,' Sebastian said.

'That's not true,' Alex replied. 'The other woman you saw was my girlfriend, Elaine. We were there trying to convince Robison not to attack the Genesis army. Instead, Pierre wanted to collaborate with Genesis. Use the Genesis technology to understand what has happened to the Alphas and use this knowledge for the benefit of all. Instead, Robison killed Pierre and blamed it on Elaine.'

His words were clearly a revelation to Sebastian, but Emma was nodding.

'Is this true?' Sebastian asked Emma.

'Yes, all of it.'

Sebastian turned back to Alex. All scepticism had vanished from his eyes. Clearly, he had complete trust in Emma's abilities, Alex thought.

'Do you have a plan to stop him?' he asked.

188

Alex nodded. 'The man you saw branding me is a highly ranked Alpha called Diego. He was Pierre's personal assistant and knows the leaders of the army to the south. In the next few days, he will contact them and explain what really happened. If all goes well, when they arrive, Robison will be arrested and put on trial.'

'So, are you here just to watch?' Emma asked.

'Sort of... I have a radio in my backpack. The plan was to find a position where I could monitor Robison's movements and report anything unusual. If something went wrong and Diego couldn't convince them to act, or he was killed, then I would act.'

'To kill him?' Emma asked.

'Yes. To cut off the head of the snake.'

Emma and Sebastian looked at each other while Alex waited nervously to see what effect his words would have.

'Well, that sounds a lot better than my plan,' Emma said, cheerfully. 'We have a great spot to watch what is happening, but we were at a loss to know what to do next.'

'There is a bedroom upstairs that overlooks the church,' Sebastian added. 'From there you can watch everything that is happening. You're welcome to it.'

'Great,' Alex replied happily, breaking out in a smile.

'And there isn't really anything wrong with you is there?' Sebastian asked.

Alex couldn't help but laugh. 'I always look like this.'

Chapter 19

Diego judged it was late afternoon by the time they reached their destination. Half-an-hour earlier his car had been stopped at a roadblock and he had been interrogated by two rather aggressive and sceptical Alphas. He couldn't blame them; his story sounded like such complete fantasy they even broke out into laughter when he explained who he was. Only when he got angry and refused to back down did they concede to his demand to speak directly to Gerolf. It was somewhat gratifying to see the scowls of disbelief and mockery immediately dissipate when it became obvious that Gerolf knew him, and he was exactly who he said he was. One of the soldiers was then ordered to immediately drive Diego to Gerolf's headquarters.

The Alpha soldier parked his four-wheel drive in the shade of a twisted and broken oak tree by the side of the road. 'We're here,' he spoke into his two-way radio. 'What are your instructions?'

'Bring him in,' Diego could hear Gerolf say, 'and Diego, I hope you are ready for some serious drinking. Ursula has found a crate of French wine. I'm expecting you to help us demolish it.'

Diego laughed. 'I will give it my best shot.'

The soldier clipped the microphone back into the radio set and glanced nervously across at Diego. 'We were only doing our job,' he stammered. 'No hard feelings?'

'I would have expected nothing less. In fact, if you hadn't been very thorough, I would have reported you.'

The soldier gave him a relieved smile, then punched his chest in an Alpha salute. Diego tapped his chest lightly in reply then climbed out with his backpack. Gerolf and Ursula's temporary headquarters was an old English pub set in a grove of shattered oak and pine trees. At first glance the pub looked remarkably untouched, but on closer inspection, Diego noticed that part of the roof was missing, and a side wall had partially collapsed. This was typical of the buildings closer to the city of Southampton, which had received a direct hit from a nuclear blast. Few buildings had escaped the initial shockwave and the nuclear winter and harsh sun in the following years had only served to further reduce buildings into piles of rubble.

Looking around, Diego noted that the carpark was filled with vehicles, ranging from civilian cars and trucks to machine-gun-mounted armoured vehicles. There was even a row of tanks parked in a nearby field. He hadn't walked more than a few paces when a tall, fair-haired woman appeared at the front door of the pub, feverishly searching the carpark. When he waved, she gave a little squeal and rushed towards him.

When she reached him, she gave him a hug that almost squeezed the breath out of him. 'We were told you were dead. Killed by the Genesis spies,' she blurted out, pulling away from him and studying him at arm's length. 'I can't tell you how much Gerolf has missed you. We both have.'

After all that had happened, her welcoming smile felt like a beam of sunlight. 'And I you,' he replied, meaning every word. 'You look fantastic...like a Viking warrior.'

She laughed and hugged him again, then took is hand and led him back to the pub, talking non-stop all the way.

Gerolf was waiting for him at the front door of the pub and embraced him just as warmly. He looked much the same, although he did notice extra lines under his eyes and his beard was longer. Inside, a blazing fire was waiting, and a stew of meat and vegetables was simmering over the fire. The table was set for two, but Ursula quickly laid out an

191

extra plate and utensils and placed a bowl filled with freshly fried potato chips in front of Diego. 'Something to nibble on,' she chirped.

Gerolf pulled the cork from a bottle of red wine and liberally poured its contents into several large tumblers. 'Cheers.' They clinked glasses. 'Still alive.'

'Still alive,' Diego responded to the traditional Alpha greeting.

'Indeed, you look remarkably well for a dead man,' Gerolf commented. 'The rumour was that you were killed by the same Genesis spies that killed the Lion.'

'Huh...' Diego grunted. 'So that's what they have been saying. There were no spies. Pierre was trying to negotiate a deal with Genesis for their technology and was killed for his efforts.'

Gerolf's eyes widened. 'So, that's where you have been...Genesis?'

Diego nodded. 'Robison killed Pierre and pinned it on Genesis. That's why I'm here. He needs to be stopped before he attacks Genesis.'

His blunt revelations met with raised eyebrows and startled looks. Gerolf took a couple of gulps of his wine then placed his glass back on the table. 'You sure know how to ruin a party.' He sighed. 'Come on. You better tell us what's happened. I have a feeling we may need more than a few drinks.'

Over the next few minutes, Diego recounted everything that had happened since Pierre's meeting with the occupants of the Genesis medical bus. He spoke in detail about what Pierre had discovered when he searched Alex's memories, their discussion of cooperation with Genesis, Thomas's betrayal, the shooting of Pierre and the stabbing of Elaine. Gerolf and Ursula listened first with interest then with horror as Diego described the web of lies that Robison had perpetrated to push his own agenda.

When he had finished talking, Gerolf sat back on his chair and flicked the cork from the bottle of red wine into the coals of the fire. They all watched as it burst into bright orange flames.

'I always knew there was something not quite right about that guy,' Gerolf said finally. 'The way he insisted he was always right and wouldn't listen to anyone else's opinion.'

'I never liked the way he looked at me,' Ursula chipped in. 'It was creepy; it felt like he was planning something.'

'Pierre was also weary of him,' Diego added. 'But he never said anything specific.'

'Why doesn't he want to talk to Genesis?' Ursula said. 'If they are willing to collaborate, why doesn't he just talk to them?'

'It's all about control,' Diego replied. 'If Genesis offers their technology, they will want something in return. At the very least, a guarantee that they won't be attacked and infected with the Alpha plague. Robison would never accept that.'

'It's more than that,' Gerolf continued. 'Pierre was the symbol of Alpha. The leader who everyone identified with. He could not take control of Alpha while Pierre was still alive. Genesis was just a convenient way of removing him.'

'Alright,' Ursula said, massaging her forehead as though she suddenly had a headache. 'The question is...what can we do to stop him?'

'We should confront him with the evidence and arrest him,' Diego said. 'He needs to stand trial.'

'Hmm...' Gerolf took another sip of his wine. 'We could confront him, but I feel we would be the ones who would be arrested. He has a lot of support among the other commanders.'

'What about the army to the north?' Diego asked.

'The person in charge is Leon Martin – a good man, honest...but also loyal to Robison. It would take a lot to convince him.'

'Alex Carhill from Genesis witnessed firsthand what Robison did; he was even tortured by him afterwards. He will testify.'

'Where is he now?' Gerolf asked.

'The last communication I had with him he told me that he had contacted two people who were part of a medical facility that was directly opposite Robison's headquarters. A man and a woman, as I recall. Apparently, they hate Robison just as much as we do and are willing to help. I've told him only to watch and wait until I know what your response will be. He will only act on his own if something happens to me.'

'Good.' Gerolf nodded his approval. 'At least we have eyes on Robison's headquarters. The problem I see is that we can't just march up there and arrest him. It would start a war. We need to be much smarter than that. He's surrounded by a close-knit group of supporters who would quickly intervene if they felt he was in danger.'

'It sounds like we need a way of isolating Robison and luring him away,' Ursula commented, reaching across to grab a few potato chips. 'What about Diego? I mean, what if we tell Robison that Diego suddenly appeared with a crazy story about how Pierre was shot. We've arrested him and want to hand him over for interrogation.'

'Hmm...' Gerolf pulled at his beard in thought. 'That might work. At least it would guarantee a private meeting with Robison. Everyone knows Diego. He wouldn't want Diego flinging accusations at him in front of his commanders.'

'But Robison would never admit anything,' Diego said. 'It wouldn't help.'

'Not with all his command around him,' Gerolf conceded. 'But it does give us an opportunity to be alone with him. You mentioned that this Alex guy had befriended people at a medical station; they must also have access to drugs. We could drug Robison and say that he has collapsed. They would have to take him straight away to the medical station for treatment. From there we could easily kidnap him.'

'That might work,' Diego said, enthusiastically. 'I can contact Alex and see if these people would be willing to help.'

'And what will we do with Robison once we kidnap him?' Ursula asked.

'We will interrogate him here and see what the truth is,' Gerolf replied.

'And if what I say checks out?' Diego asked. 'Will you try to put him on trial?'

Gerolf shook his head ruefully. 'There will be no trial. If everything you have said is true, Robison is a psychopath who needs to be stopped. He also has Leon's support. If we tried to put him on trial there is every possibility that he would turn the tables on us and we would end up being shot. No... I would make sure he would disappear for good, without a trace.'

Diego nodded grimly and raised his glass. 'To the truth.'

Gerolf and Ursula also raised their glasses. 'To the truth and Alpha.'

Chapter 20

Events moved rapidly after Gerolf radioed Robison and told him about Diego. Robison's response was swift. He ordered Diego's transportation to headquarters for immediate interrogation. Gerolf requested that he and Ursula should also be present. At this request Robison hesitated, arguing that Gerolf should focus all his attention on the current campaign in the south. It was only when Gerolf insisted that his request was reluctantly granted. Two days later an armoured car and a four-wheel drive carrying Diego, Gerolf and Ursula set off to Newbury. Diego had radioed ahead to Alex and told him of the plan to drug then kidnap Robison. Alex, after a quick consultation with his contacts, had confirmed that they could supply the drugs that would knock out Robison and give the impression that he had had some type of heart attack. Everything was organised.

After a full day of driving, they reached the outskirts of Newbury just before dusk. It had been a long torturous drive and everyone was tired. The A339 arterial road north from Basingstoke was particularly degraded, consisting of little more than a series of potholes interspersed with fallen trees and clumps of creeper vines. About a kilometre from the church, they parked their vehicles in an open-air carpark. This was the predetermined meeting point, and Alex and his two companions were waiting. Diego climbed out of the vehicle and was immediately embraced by Alex. The two men had become close during their time at Genesis and their mutual respect was evident.

'This is Emma and Sebastian,' Alex said, stepping away. 'They have had their own horrible experiences with Robison, so they know what we are up against.'

A young woman with short-cropped blonde hair and intense grey eyes stepped forward and shook his hand. Her grip was surprisingly strong for one so small and she pulled him towards her when she shook hands. She was no shrinking violet, Diego thought, but he liked her energy and intensity. 'Nice to finally meet you,' she smiled warmly. 'Alex has spoken so much about you and told us all about how you saved his life.'

Diego was vaguely surprised by her comment, especially since she had not released his hand. 'I was just lucky.'

'Most people would have run away.'

It was a statement wrapped in a question that Diego felt compelled to answer. 'I couldn't leave without finding out what had happened. It was just luck that I came across Alex. I was just in the right place at the right time.'

'No, you stayed when many would have run away,' she added with a smile. 'Alex is lucky to have such a friend.' Releasing his hand, she turned her attention to Ursula, clasping her hand with both of hers. 'And it's great to meet you. I really like that scarf you are wearing.'

'Thanks,' Ursula replied, pleased at the compliment. 'I've had it for years. 'It is one of the only things I had from before the war.'

'Well, it matches your Alpha uniform perfectly.'

'Yes...I thought so too.'

'Well, I hope everything goes to plan and we can finally get rid of Robison and stop another bloody battle,' Emma continued.

'Yes, we must stop this madness. Robison has turned into a monster.'

Emma released her hand and nodded her agreement.

Alex smiled slightly and wondered how much extra information Emma had just gained from these handshakes.

Sebastian handed a syringe full of clear liquid to Gerolf. 'I thought about a powder you could add to a drink, but it would not have an immediate effect. Too many things could go wrong, so in the end I thought it would be easier to just inject the drug directly into his bloodstream. It will take effect within a minute. You just need to cover his mouth to stop him calling out.'

Gerolf nodded. 'I've requested a private meeting to discuss some of Diego's accusations when we arrive. Robison has agreed to this, so it shouldn't be a problem.'

'The drug will knock him out and give the impression he has had a heart attack,' Sebastian continued. 'It may also be useful to say that he complained of chest pains and clutched at his chest before he collapsed. They will immediately rush him to the nearest medical facility, which will be us across the street. We have a car loaded and waiting. Sometime during the night, we should be able to smuggle him out.'

'Good,' Gerolf said as he carefully placed the syringe in one of his pockets.

Meanwhile Ursula handcuffed Diego. 'Sorry,' she apologised. 'But we have to make it look like you are under arrest.'

'Showtime,' Diego said, shrugging his shoulders.

Ursula placed the key in one of Diego's pockets. 'You may as well hold onto the key yourself,' she said, 'in case something goes wrong.'

Diego was led to the accompanying armoured car and placed between two soldiers.

'Nice to meet you,' Gerolf called out to Emma and Sebastian as he and Ursula climbed into their car. 'Hopefully, we will see you shortly.'

With a wave, they sped off in the direction of the church.

They had barely rounded the corner of the road when Alex felt an urgent tug on his arm.

'Somethings wrong,' Emma said urgently. 'How well do Ursula and Robison know each other?'

Alex shrugged. 'I assume not very well, but I don't really know.' There was something in the way she framed these words that gave him pause. 'You saw something didn't you?'

She nodded. 'They had an affair.'

'What?' he gasped. 'Are you sure?'

'Yeah. It was intense. She was actually thinking about it when I shook her hand.'

'Do you think she will betray us?'

'Hmm... I think it was a while ago.' She paused, thinking. 'He told her something.' She frowned trying to pull her own thoughts together. 'He told her that he could see into a person's past.' She stopped walking and looked up at Alex. 'He's like me; he can see people's memories by touching them. He's a Witcher.'

It took a moment for Alex to grasp what this meant.

'No, that's not possible. He would have used his powers against me when he was interrogating me.'

'Was there anyone else in the room when he was interrogating you?'

'Yes, a couple of Alpha soldiers and Thomas.'

'That's why he didn't use his powers. He has ordered all Witcher's to be put to death. He would never expose himself. Much better to keep it a secret and use this power to discover who is telling the truth just by a handshake.'

'They're walking into a trap,' Alex breathed. 'If he shakes their hands, he will know what our plan is.'

Emma nodded. 'More than likely. The plan will be in the forefront of their minds. He can't fail to see it... You could try to radio Diego.'

The radio was in Alex's backpack. He quickly pulled it out and tuned into the correct frequency. Despite repeated attempts, however, there was no answer. It was switched off, he realised. There was nothing they could do but wait and be prepared for anything.

***

Before the holocaust St Nicolas's church must have been quite an impressive place, Diego thought, as he entered the west-facing steeple of the church. The structure remained largely intact despite the ravages of the holocaust, although the once beautiful stain glass windows were all blown out. As they moved through the church, they passed sandstone columns that formed towering archways spanning the length of the nave and culminating in a gothic archway that led into the chancel. All the wooden pews in the nave had been stripped away and were being used to feed a large fire that was burning in the centre of the church. Alpha soldiers milled around this fire eating and drinking from barrels of beer. The place had a relaxed party-like atmosphere with much laughter and loud music playing in the background. The group of strangers was given little attention, other than being pointed to a series of partitions at the front of the church when they asked for Robison.

Behind these partitions the chancel had been stripped bare except for a large table where Robison sat eating his dinner. Sitting next to him was a small man with a long, narrow nose and thinning hairline which he had attempted to conceal with a comb-over. This man immediately stopped eating and watched them suspiciously as they approached the table. Diego's heart sunk. From Alex's description it could only be Thomas.

Robison was bent over a large bone, digging the last bits of meat out with his fingers. When he saw them, he dipped his hands in a basin of water then wiped them on a towel. 'Excuse me, I haven't eaten anything all day. Can I offer you some food?' He gestured to a pile of ribs and neatly chopped up bones piled high on a large silver tray. Probably part of the church silverware, Diego guessed.

'Wild dog. There seems to be a huge number of them around this place. Vicious creatures, but they do taste delicious.'

Gerolf and Ursula looked at each other. 'We are fine. We won't take up much of your time. We just have a few questions.'

'Nonsense. I'm sure you haven't come all this way for just a few questions.' He walked around the table and grabbed Gerolf's hand and shook it vigorously. 'You've both done marvellous things down south. I hear you have added huge numbers of new recruits to our numbers and found new sources of supplies and food. Well done, both of you. You are a credit to the Alpha movement.'

He continued shaking Gerolf's hand, but his smile slowly slid into a grimace and a deep furrowed frown creased his forehead. He let go of Gerolf's hand and walked up to Ursula. 'And the beautiful Ursula. You look even fitter and stronger than when I last saw you.' He held her hand between his hands just as Emma had done and his eyes narrowed as if he was concentrating on something. 'You and Gerolf have achieved great things and soon we will have Genesis and all their technology to build our new world,' he continued, but there was a subtle change in his voice. The enthusiasm and conviction of his words of a moment ago had gone.

Diego was watching Robison closely now. With a shudder that shook his whole body he realised; Robison was a Witcher, like Pierre. He had just learned of all their kidnap plans from a simple handshake.

'We were hoping for a private audience,' Gerolf said.

'I have no secrets from Thomas,' Robison replied. 'He knows everything I do.'

Thomas, with a slight smile, wiped his hands on his Alpha uniform and stood up.

The alarm bells were ringing now. There was a hardness in Robison's voice that wasn't there before. Diego slipped his hand into his pocket and pulled out the key to his cuffs then stepped behind Gerolf to conceal himself while he unlocked them.

201

'So, what is so urgent that you had to come all the way up here to talk to me personally? Don't tell me that you believe the lies that I'm sure Diego has been telling you? Maybe you think you can kidnap me? Force me to confess into killing Pierre?'

At these words, Thomas reached under the table and swiftly pulled up an automatic weapon.

Gerolf indistinctively held his hands up in the air. 'We just wanted a friendly chat.'

'Friendly. Hmm... I'm not so sure about that,' Robison smirked, unclipping his handgun and pointing it at Gerolf. 'Empty out your pockets.'

'Why?'

'Just do it!' Robison ordered.

Gerolf, now visibly shaken, proceeded to empty the contents of his pockets onto the table. When he had finished, Robison used the barrel of his gun to poke through the contents. 'Now empty your right jacket pocket. The one that you deliberately missed.'

Gerolf reached into his pocket and pulled out the loaded syringe. 'It's just his medication,' Ursula explained. 'He's a diabetic. He has to take insulin shots.'

'I thought all the diabetics were already dead,' Robison replied sarcastically.

'He doesn't need it all the time – it's only a precaution.'

'Inject it! If he's a diabetic it shouldn't kill him. Go on!' Robison pointed his revolver directly at Gerolf's head. 'DO IT!'

Gerolf looked terrified and quickly glanced across at Ursula but there was nothing she could do. With little choice, he injected the contents of the syringe into his arm. For nearly a minute nothing happened, then his eyes began to flicker shut and he dropped to his knees before falling unconscious on to the floor.

'Insulin?' Robison sneered. 'Seems to have a strange effect, don't you think?'

Ursula rushed to his side and rolled him on his back. 'You could have killed him!' she cried. 'He hasn't eaten anything all day. He's probably having a hypo. He needs to eat something quickly.'

'The point is it wasn't insulin,' Robison replied, his voice as cold as steel. 'You were going to drug and kidnap me. Alex Carhill was waiting at the medical centre across the street to kidnap me.' He flicked off the safety on his handgun. 'I expected more from you, Gerolf. And you Ursula. We are so close to having everything and you let yourself be persuaded by trivial matters that mean nothing. 'You are both traitors to the cause. And traitors only deserve one thing.'

Robison stretched out his arm and his jaw tightened. At point blank range he shot Gerolf twice in the head. Blood and bone sprayed across the floor as the shots jolted his head backward.

'Nooo!' Ursula screamed. In an explosion of rage, she launched herself at him. Her body caught him in the chest, but Robison had already reacted. Two more shots tore through her body. She landed next to Robison, her body twitching with the last throws of life. Robison immediately pumped two more rounds into her.

The next moment, Diego was sprinting through the gap in the partition. He flew through the shadows of the church and past Alphas still drinking and eating their evening meals. Away from the fire, however, the church was in deep shadow and he tripped several times on makeshift beds. Each time he fell he immediately scrambled to his feet, but the falls had cost him valuable seconds and checked his forward momentum. Shouts of 'STOP HIM' arose all around him. Torch lights searched the darkness for him. Gaining speed again, he reached the front entrance, but pursuit was only a heartbeat behind.

He burst into the crisp night, his legs pumping. Ahead were more Alpha soldiers, who started turning towards him as more shouts of 'STOP HIM!' echoed from behind. To his right was a canal filled with the fast-flowing water of the river Kennet. He hesitated. The Alphas ahead of him were starting to collect their weapons and run towards him. He ran to the canal edge. In the darkness the water looked like liquid mud, twisting and foaming as it raged against the canal walls that contained it. The first shots rang out and he felt the thud of a bullet as it tore through his side. He leapt into the swirling torrent, letting the darkness and cold swallow him. The swirling current dragged him down, bumping his body along the bottom of the river. But he made no attempt to strike out for the surface, fearing the hail of bullets that awaited him. Finally, when he couldn't hold his breath any longer, he surfaced.

Upstream, searchlights were sweeping the water. Men were shouting. One voice above the others was claiming that he had shot him. Diego gulped in the air and let the current take him further downstream until the voices faded into silence. Even then he made no attempt to swim ashore. Only when there was complete darkness, and he could feel his strength seeping away, did he strike out for the shore. Here the river had widened and the roaring current gave way to a gentler flow. Exhausted and in pain, he latched onto a tree branch and pulled himself up onto the riverbank. The mud was thick and he sunk down to his elbows as he crawled his way up the bank. He crawled until the mud gave way to firmer ground covered in thick grass. Here he rested.

There was pain in his side where the bullet had struck him but the horror of what he had just witnessed was far worse. Gerolf and Ursula were dead, and he had barely survived. To gain so much information from a handshake meant that Robison was a powerful Witcher. Robison knew Alex was at the medical centre; his life was in the balance and he couldn't warn him. All he could do was hope that Alex and his companions had escaped.

***

From his vantage point on the first floor of the medical clinic, Alex trained his rifle sights on the church. Minutes earlier there had been shots. Not many, maybe six, but it only took one bullet to kill someone. Either way he reasoned something had gone seriously wrong. If Emma was right, then they could already be dead. As he contemplated these thoughts, he noticed soldiers spilling out of the church. These soldiers had their weapons drawn and were heading directly towards them. A small man dressed in Alpha uniform was barking out orders. Alex trained his sights on him. Thomas. He released the safety latch on is rifle and trained the sights on his chest. Only moments away from pressing the trigger he felt a hand on his shoulder.

'You can't,' Sebastian said urgently. 'It will alert them to where we are. There will be no chance of escape.'

He felt Sebastian's grip on his shoulder tighten. 'Another time. We have to leave now.'

Reluctantly Alex flicked the safety back on. More than ever, he regretted not killing Thomas when he'd had the chance.

Chapter 21

For a moment, Alex didn't know where he was. Above him was the nylon sheeting of his tent, weighed down with overnight dew. He was lying on top of his sleeping bag in nothing more than a thin sleeveless shirt and his underpants. He remembered being freezing cold during the night then stifling hot and continually zipping and unzipping his sleeping bag to suit. He had been sick from the Alpha plague for nearly two weeks, slipping in and out of consciousness for much of that time. If it wasn't for Emma and Sebastian's care, he was sure that he would have died.

They had nursed him, medicated him and cleaned up the filth of his body as he fought against the plague...and for that he would be forever grateful. His fever had begun to break a day ago. Before that, he only remembered fragments. The most vivid memories were of nightmares; a montage of his worst memories melded together into bizarre storylines. In one nightmare, Tina and Elaine, although they had never met, were having a conversation about him, bitterly complaining that his selfishness had killed them. He knew this wasn't true. But some part of him clearly remained unconvinced. He rubbed his forehead, trying to rid himself of these thoughts. His headache was still there but it no longer felt like someone was trying to prise his head open with an axe. His tent smelt strongly of a mixture of vomit and sweat so he unzipped it and climbed out. The cold rush of the morning air sent a shiver through him, but it felt good, like a splash of water on his face. The first rays of the morning sun were filtering through the trees and bathing the forest in shades of red and magenta. He always loved these early morning colours. The world felt unreal, like he was on another planet.

A short distance away, parked among some low-lying trees, was the station wagon they had used to escape from Newbury. He could just make out the shapes of Emma and Sebastian curled up in the front seats together. Looking around, he saw his Alpha uniform hanging from a line slung between two trees. The uniform looked freshly washed, but it was still damp. Still, he thought, it was better than walking around in the cold, half-naked. He pulled down his clothes and gingerly climbed into them, feeling like he was wrapping himself in a soggy blanket. Next to him was the remains of last night's fire. A small patch of ground had been cleared either side and several logs served as seating. To his delight, when he poked at the coals of the fire, some still glowed red. After collecting some twigs and sticks, combined with some rigorous fanning and blowing, he managed to coax a small flame. He hastily piled more twigs and sticks onto the flame until a healthy crackling fire emerged. He was just thinking about gathering some more wood when Sebastian emerged from the station wagon, stretching his limbs and blinking at the rising sun. 'You're up,' he said as he noticed Alex huddled by the fire. 'How are you feeling?'

'Hungry.'

'Huh. That's encouraging.'

'Don't suppose you have a steak, with chips and a pint of beer.'

'You must be feeling better.' Sebastian smiled. 'Your sense of humour has returned. I can offer you a tin of four-year-old potatoes and spam with mushy peas.'

'Sounds perfect.'

'Looking at the state of you, you need double portions. I also have some strips of dried pork and some packets of pasta. Something to build you up.'

Alex looked down at his twig-like arms and felt his protruding ribs beneath his shirt, suddenly conscious of just how much weight he had lost.

Sebastian opened the back of the station wagon and rummaged around before emerging with an armful of cans, some packets of food and a bottle of Irish Stout. 'I have been saving this for a special occasion,' he continued, holding the bottle up in the air like a trophy. 'This is what you English call stout. Can't stand the stuff myself, but it's definitely full of calories and nutrients.'

Alex didn't like to tell him that he wasn't really English, and he didn't like stout. He didn't want to wipe the look of delight from Sebastian's face. 'Great. Just what the doctor ordered,' he agreed.

Sebastian prised off the bottle cap with his penknife and handed the stout to Alex. It tasted surprisingly good and brought back memories of the last time he had been in an English pub. He had just turned 20, only weeks before the holocaust and Jason, his brother, was still alive. It seemed an eternity ago, yet it was less than four years. He remembered the excitement of being in England again. The smell of chips and beer. The pretty women with thick make-up, full of chatter and laughter. Thumping music...loud, frivolous conversations about nothing. He missed it all. Something deep inside of him wished that he had remained in London, directly in the path of the detonation. Then there would be nothing. No struggle...no death...no heartbreak.

A few minutes later Emma joined them and gave Alex a big hug when she saw he had recovered. He hadn't known them long, but already they felt like family. Together they shared a common enemy and had survived certain death. It was the formulae for close bonding between people – he knew that. He just hoped they would all live long enough to enjoy each other's company. The three of them prepared breakfast and chatted about anything: the lousy rations they were now forced to eat, what foods they missed most, even their favourite movies; anything but the true weight of circumstance that was now bearing down on them.

Finally, once they had settled into their positions around the fire and filled their bellies with food, Alex summoned up the courage to broach the subject. 'I fear that our chances of stopping Robison are now gone,' he stated, deciding to dive straight into what everyone must be thinking. 'Our chances died with Diego.'

'We don't know what happened,' Emma offered. 'They may have escaped.'

Alex studied her for a moment. There was a hint of hope in her eyes, but much doubt as well. 'I can't think of any scenario where Gerolf, Ursula or Diego end up shooting Robison. No, I think they were all executed within minutes of Robison shaking hands with them.'

Emma dipped her head slightly. A sign that she conceded the point that was never really in dispute anyway. 'So, what do we do?' she asked.

'Whatever we do, it has to be done quickly,' Sebastian said after taking a sip from a mug of herbal tea. 'I have been monitoring the chatter on the radio. All three armies have now merged at Newbury and will strike westwards in the next few days. It will only be a matter of weeks before they reach Genesis.'

'I will understand if you both don't want come with me,' Alex replied, 'but I have to go back to Genesis. I can't desert them.'

'Do you think Genesis can stop Robison?' Emma asked.

'They can't stand up to the Alpha army,' Alex admitted. 'But I have to try to help.'

For a moment, his words hung in the air with neither venturing a comment. Sebastian reached over and stirred the fire with a stick while Emma took another mouthful of canned peaches.

'I've seen...' Sebastian paused, as though trying to condense his thoughts into words, 'over the past few years the Alpha movement grow into a powerful military force capable of sweeping not only Europe but eventually the world. I'm sure that's what Robinson's ultimate goal is. He won't be satisfied with anything less.' He looked across at Alex. 'He won't be stopped. He reminds me of someone I used to know before the Alpha plague arrived when I was roaming the streets as part of a gang. We were what you English would call tough guys. We took what we wanted from those who couldn't defend themselves. I saw things...and I did things...that I can never forget.'

'We all have done monstrous things,' Alex said, 'but it doesn't mean we are monsters.'

'You haven't done what I have done,' Sebastian replied with an intensity in his voice Alex had not heard before. 'We had ultimate power. We roamed the streets heavily armed. We shot who we liked, raped who we liked and laughed about it afterwards. It was a competition of depravity. The crueller the act the more respect you got. The tougher you were. We ruled by fear and terror and killed anyone who dared to oppose us.'

The emotion welled up in Sebastian's eyes as he said this, and he quickly wiped away his tears. 'What I'm trying to say,' he went on more calmly, 'is that the leader of that gang was only interested in power. For him nothing else mattered. He didn't want to build a better world. He revelled in his own power. If the Alpha plague hadn't swept through and killed him, he would still be there roaming the streets with whoever followed him, killing, raping, destroying everything. I was part of that. I did terrible things to gain respect, I laughed at the cruellest acts and committed crimes that would have put me in jail for many lifetimes before the war. And I see the same things happening here. Robison is only interested in power. He pretends that he wants to build a new world, but he doesn't. If he's not stopped now, he will only become more powerful. He is also a Witcher, which makes him infinitely more dangerous.'

'What are you trying to say?' Emma asked.

'I'm going back to re-join the Alpha army. They don't know what I look like and I will change my name just in case Robison managed to prise that information from Gerolf, Ursula or Diego before they died.'

Alex looked across at Emma, who looked totally mortified. Clearly, he had not discussed this with her.

'I'm coming too,' she blurted.

Sebastian shook his head. 'Robison knows what you look like. It's too risky. You should go with Alex to Genesis.'

'You need me more than ever,' Emma countered. 'I can tell you who to trust.'

'It's too dangerous.'

'I agree with Emma,' Alex said, breaking the tension between them. 'I assume you are going to try to get as close to Robison as possible, then shoot him. To do that you will need to know who you can trust. You will have a much better chance if Emma is with you.'

He could see by the slight nod of his head that Sebastian was conceding his point. Alex knew the last thing Sebastian wanted was to be separated from Emma. Sebastian looked across at Emma and Alex could see the emotion rising in his eyes once again.

'We can do this together,' Emma said softly. 'I will vet everyone before you talk to them and you can work your way back into Robison's medical staff.'

'Are you sure?' Sebastian asked. 'We might not survive this.'

'I know,' Emma replied almost casually. 'I would rather die for something I believe in than die in some useless war that I have no control over.'

Sebastian nodded his relief obvious. 'OK, we will hunt down this monster together.'

'Good,' Alex said, 'then it's settled. All I ask is that you drive me to Genesis before you go back to the Alpha army. If we can arrive before they reach Genesis, I should be able to slip into the same tunnel Diego and I escaped from.'

211

'Are you sure that you're well enough to travel?' Emma asked.

Alex wasn't sure, but he knew there was no choice. 'I'll be fine. Especially if you have any more of that stout.'

Sebastian stood up and put his hand on Alex's shoulder. 'Thanks for your support.'

Anyone else may have been confused by the meaning of his words, but Alex knew exactly what he meant. When Emma hugged him, images had flooded into his mind of what Emma was thinking at the time. She was certainly not thinking about him. Her mind was fully occupied with reliving making love with Sebastian the night before – details he would rather have not seen. He was happy for them. Sebastian, until now, had simply not found the words to ask her to come with him. As he pondered this, it suddenly dawned on him that he was a Witcher, the same as Emma.

Chapter 22

'Stop. Hold your hands up in the air and drop your pack!'

Alex released the shoulder straps of his pack and let it drop to the ground then held his hands on his head. He was dressed in a pair of old jeans that Sebastian had given him and a long-sleeved flannel shirt. He had deliberately worn as little clothes as possible so that he would pose no threat when he was arrested.

While the first soldier kept his automatic weapon trained on him, a second soldier patted him down then took his pack.

Alex studied the walls of the tunnel and noticed a security camera trained on him. 'My name is Alex Carhill and I'm a member of the Genesis committee,' he announced loudly. 'I need to urgently speak to the chairman, Peter McCaffrey.'

'Just clothes, a radio and some food in his pack,' the second soldier announced.

The soldier who initially confronted Alex came closer, surveying him with deep suspicion. 'How did you find the tunnel entrance?'

'I know all the tunnel entrances,' Alex replied, returning the soldier's stare. 'I left here a few weeks ago to try to stop the Alpha advance. I have important information that I need to share with the committee.'

The walkie-talkie on the soldier's utility belt buzzed. 'Bring him in straight away,' Alex heard a voice say.

Alex was quickly escorted down the tunnel past several barriers that were reinforced with sandbags and machine guns. He also noticed what looked like explosives rigged along the sides of the tunnel. After a few minutes, the sides of the tunnel broadened and were reinforced with concrete walls, and he started passing rooms sealed with security doors. The soldiers escorting him stopped outside one of these rooms and input a code into a touchpad by the door. The door opened to an empty room except for a metal table and two metal chairs. It reminded him of the interrogation room that Elaine and himself were brutally interrogated in only six months earlier.

'Why have you taken me here?' Alex asked. 'I need to talk to Peter McCaffrey urgently.'

The soldier ignored his question, instead he punched a code into a second touchpad and left the room locking the door behind him. Alex had not expected this. He knew he would have some explaining to do, but he wasn't expecting to be locked up. He didn't need to wait long before the door opened again, and much to his disgust, Garrett entered the room.

'Still alive I see,' Garrett commented sarcastically, his bulldog face registering his disappointment.

'And I see they haven't locked you up yet,' Alex countered.

'Can't say the same for you.'

Alex noted the smirk on Garrett's face, and a bolt of anger surged through him. 'You know who I am. You have no right to keep me here.'

'I can do what I like,' Garrett said almost casually. 'After the stunt you pulled, do you think anyone wants to talk to you? I have every right to arrest a dangerous traitor.'

Alex could hardly believe what he was hearing. 'Traitor...? We were trying to start a revolt against Robison by his own commanders.'

Garrett's smirk only widened. 'Really? From where I sit you look like a traitor and most of the committee agree. In fact, you are no longer a member of the committee. You and your Alpha friend are considered criminals.'

Alex studied Garrett for a moment. There was a self-righteous confidence in his voice he had not heard before. This wasn't someone who feared being locked up for treason anymore. 'I need to talk to Peter,' he repeated.

'What makes you think that I would let you anywhere near Peter or the committee,' Garrett replied with a look of complete disdain. 'Look at you with your shaved head. You think we don't know what you and Diego are up to? I conducted a search of Diego's place and your apartment after you both vanished. We found all your hair that you had shaved off in a bin and tucked away at the back of a cupboard was your crude branding iron. Now...' he smiled. 'What do you suppose that was for?'

'I needed to pass as an Alpha to get close to Robison.'

'So you branded yourself. Sounds a bit excessive.'

'I was trying to kill the leader of the Alpha army. We wanted to leave nothing to chance.'

'Or alternatively you decided to switch sides...become an Alpha.'

'They killed Elaine. Why would I become an Alpha?'

'Well, we only have your word for that. Elaine could have died from any number of causes.'

Alex felt his anger boiling to the surface. 'Elaine died trying to stop the Alphas.'

Garrett just shrugged.

Alex stared at him. He wasn't just trying to wind him up...he was serious. He actually believed what he was saying. 'If I joined the Alpha army why would I come back here?' he asked.

'That is what I fully intend to find out.' Garrett pulled a pair of handcuffs from his trouser pocket. 'Put them on.'

'No.'

'I just have to tap on the door and two guards will come in and handcuff you to the table.'

Alex backed away into the corner of the room and crossed his arms.

'Okay.' Garrett tapped on the door and immediately the two soldiers who had arrested him entered.

'Cuff him to the table,' he ordered, throwing the handcuffs to one of the soldiers.

The soldiers dragged Alex across the room and forced him to sit on the chair, then handcuffed him to a short metal cable that was welded to the centre of the table. Alex pulled on the cable and tried to move the table but soon realised it was embedded in the concrete floor and wouldn't move. He was effectively pinned there.

'I need to know everything that you know,' Garrett said, taking the seat opposite him and opening a notepad. 'Now, where's Diego?'

'Dead. We tried to kidnap Robison to put him on trial, but he saw through our plot and killed Diego.'

'We?'

'Diego was close friends with the leader of the Alpha army that was south of Newbury. He convinced him to kidnap and arrest Robison. But something went wrong, and they were all killed.'

Garrett twirled his pen. 'I don't want fantasy...I want the truth.'

'You just got it.'

'Believe me, I will get it. Why did you come back here?'

'I told you, I have important information I need to tell Peter.'

'Well, that won't happen, you will have to tell me.'

'You have already proven that you can't be trusted.'

'Hmm...' Garrett leaned back in his chair and stared at Alex, a cold, calculating stare designed to intimidate. 'You don't seem to get it do you?' he said, his voice low and rumbling. 'You're not in a position to bargain...only beg.'

He nodded and a strong arm wrapped around Alex's throat, tightening into a chokehold. 'I want information on what Robison is planning and what he has told you to say,' Garrett said, leaning across the table so his perfectly square face completely filled Alex's vision, like a brick wall.

The more Alex struggled; the tighter the soldier's arm closed on his throat until he started having difficulty breathing. 'I told you the truth,' he croaked, feeling his face turn red.

Garrett leant across the table and struck him hard with the back of his hand. 'Do you know how often I've fantasised about this moment?' His thin lips parted in a smile. 'The man who found Genesis, escaped and brought the wrath of the survivors down on us. You're responsible for more death and destruction than I will ever be. To slowly and painfully crush you to no more than blood and bone then feed your body to the rats would give me the greatest pleasure,' he continued wistfully. 'You see, no-one is going to save you because no-one knows you are here.'

Alex couldn't breathe now, and he felt a trickle of blood run from his nose down into his mouth. He tried to prise the arm off his throat, but the soldier only tightened his grip. This would be the end of him, he thought. He wasn't terrified. The death that had eluded him for so long was upon him. It seemed particularly cruel that the last thing he would see was the ugly face of Garrett smiling back at him. Just when he felt consciousness slipping away, however, the pressure was released and he was left gasping for breath.

'It's only going to get worse from here,' Garrett growled.

Alex took a few more breaths then started to laugh.

Garrett frowned. 'Why are you laughing?'

'You haven't asked why I look so thin.'

'What? Garrett looked confused, then frowned deeply, realising there could be something he had missed. 'Why are you so thin?'

'I've been sick with the Alpha plague.'

Garrett frowned. 'You're lying.'

'No,' Alex shook his head. 'You can't be an Alpha without being infected by the plague. I'm an Alpha in every way. I have the plague, and you are probably now infected.'

Garrett immediately stood up and the two soldiers who had held Alex immediately backed away. 'That's why you came back...' Garrett gasped, 'to infect everyone.'

Alex just laughed as Garrett, accompanied by the two soldiers, fled the room.

Chapter 23

Alex wiped some of the dried blood off his chin onto his arm then lay his head back on the table and closed his eyes. He had been left alone for hours, although it was hard to judge time in a windowless room. He had been running through all the possible scenarios and nothing looked promising. The worst case would be if he was just left in the room to slowly starve to death. It was certainly a possibility. The brutal hatred he saw in Garrett's eyes frightened him the most. If he just ordered the soldiers to seal off the room and let him die, would they do it? This was Genesis he reminded himself. That sort of callousness only existed on the surface. Down here there were standards and ethics. Surely the soldiers wouldn't let that happen to him. Although, he reasoned, if they believed that he was responsible for the invasion of Genesis and all the deaths that followed, and now for bringing the plague, maybe they would leave him to rot. It would be a horrible death. He had long expected his death would be violent. But this? He did not deserve this.

The door clicked open and jolted him out of his morbid thoughts. Two people clothed from head to foot in biohazard suits appeared. Alex immediately felt a flood of relief, especially when he recognised who they were. Martin and Adriana stood before him. If he wasn't chained to the table, he would have hugged them both.

'Thank God,' he cried. 'I thought I'd been left here to die.'

Martin hurried around the table in his usual bustling manner and unlocked the shackles that held him. 'I'm very sorry about this,' he apologised, putting a consoling arm around Alex's shoulder. 'We only found out what happened to you about an hour ago. Garrett has been reprimanded.'

'Not arrested?'

'No, unfortunately since you left there have been a number of...let's say developments, which have made Garrett untouchable... For now anyway.'

Alex massaged his red-raw wrists where he had been pulling at his cuffs.

'Here, I have something for that,' Adriana said, placing her medical case on the table and pulling out a tube of cream. 'Before we can do anything, we have to establish if you are infectious.'

'I'm not,' Alex said bluntly, rubbing some of the cream on his wrists. 'I only said that to stop Garrett torturing me. I have had the Alpha plague, but my fever broke several days ago.'

'And what makes you sure that you aren't still infectious?' Adriana asked.

'I met a medic when I was with the Alphas. He has been treating this disease for over a year and knew everything there was to know about it. He treated me while I was sick and has assured me that within 24 hours of the fever breaking the patient is non-infectious.'

'Hmm...I'm sure you're right, but all the same we need to do some tests.' She took some blood collection tubes from her bag and a syringe. 'I need to swab your mouth and take some blood.'

'While you were away,' Martin explained, 'we developed a rapid test based on the Alpha bacteria samples you gave us. We should have the results within the hour.'

Alex held out his arm and Adriana applied a tourniquet then drew some blood. 'So how did you know I was here?' he asked.

'Well, I would like to say that it was Garrett who told us, but it wasn't,' Martin replied. 'In fact, initially he denied everything. It was the two guards who arrested you. They came to the hospital terrified that they had caught the Alpha plague from an Alpha soldier they had caught in one of our tunnels. When they were questioned further, they spilled the whole story, including your name. This information was immediately passed on and Garrett was placed in quarantine with the guards.'

'But you haven't arrested him?' Alex asked again.

'No,' Martin sighed, looking embarrassed. 'I'm afraid he has the loyalty of the Genesis military. We simply can't risk replacing him until this crisis is over.'

'After all that he has done?'

'He has more influence than any of us thought possible,' Martin replied. 'His roots go deep. If we remove him there is a real possibility there will be some type of military revolt. Something that we cannot afford.'

Adriana took his temperature, listened to his chest and checked his glands. 'Well, you seem healthy enough. Although you certainly have lost a lot of weight.'

'Oh yes, I almost forgot.' Martin placed the plastic bag he had been carrying on the table and pulled out a bottle full of orange juice. 'Freshly squeezed,' he announced. 'And I dropped into the bakery on the way down here.' He opened a cardboard box and proudly displayed its contents. There was an assortment of danish pastries, chocolate eclairs and cream tarts.

Alex laughed. He was home.

***

On the way to the hospital, Alex explained why he had left Genesis with Diego and how they had planned to kidnap Robison and hold him to account for his crimes. Martin listened, nodding and frowning deeply when he heard that the plan had failed, and that Diego was probably dead.

'I see,' he said thoughtfully when Alex had finished. 'I knew you hadn't switched sides. It made no sense. I'm sorry to hear about Diego. I truly liked him. I have had a lot of dealings with political and scientific leaders over the years and he always struck me as a straight shooter.'

221

'Yeah…he was. And he was probably the last person who could have stopped Robison.'

'Yes, the Alphas are at our doorstep now, but we have not been idle. When we sequenced the DNA of the plague bacteria you brought back, we found some very interesting sequences. This bacterium contained viral enzymes called integrases that enabled the bacteria DNA to insert itself into the host DNA.'

'By host you mean humans?'

'Yes, this bacterium has the ability to insert its DNA into human chromosomes, which is extremely unusual. We managed to capture a number of Alpha soldiers over the past few weeks and we have been examining their DNA and looking at what changes have occurred. Certain bacterium sequences had integrated into specific chromosomes. These sequences encoded new proteins that we think are responsible for the increased resistance to disease and radiation that the Alphas seem to possess.'

'So, it's true,' Alex said, somewhat surprised. 'It's not just propaganda. The Alphas are better at surviving on the surface.'

'Yes, we have grown some of the cells taken from Alphas in culture and they have increased tolerance to radiation. And tests on the Alphas indicate they have enhanced immune systems.'

'In what way?' Alex asked.

'Both their cellular and antibody responses are more rapid when exposed to invading pathogens. They are right... They are better adapted to the surface than we are.'

'Wow.' Alex realised that he hadn't really believed the claims that had so frequently been thrown at him by Pierre and Diego that the Alphas were a superior race, until now.

'Of course, our research is only at the preliminary stages, but the results are already obvious,' Martin went on. 'Our scientists are very excited by them. The Alphas could well be the key to survival on the surface.'

'Have you told Peter what you found?' Alex asked.

222

'He knows...which brings me to the latest development. A few hours ago, the main body of the Alpha army arrived at the entrance to Genesis. They have also occupied Box and are spreading out to look for any more tunnel entrances. Robison has contacted us and wants a face-to-face meeting. Peter feels it's important to meet with him in person to try to avoid any further bloodshed and he wants to use our latest results to try to persuade Robison not to attack.'

'How will these results help stop an attack?' Alex asked, frowning.

'He wants to offer Robison a partnership. Together we can investigate what the Alpha plague means. If they agree, we will open up the city to them. I know what you are going to say,' Martin said quickly, when Alex stopped walking and turned sharply towards him. 'Robison can't be trusted. The feeling was that we had to at least try. We will share our research and our city in exchange for their guarantee not to attack.'

'Has the committee agreed to this?' Alex asked.

Martin walked on. 'Yes, there is a feeling that anything is better than another attack.'

'Then you also agree?'

'Yes, we have contingency plans in place if they are not willing to negotiate.'

Alex scratched his head exasperated. He could hardly believe he had to repeat this mantra again. 'You can't trust anything Robison says. He has just killed Diego and his own commanders.'

'I'm sorry to hear that,' Martin replied after a thoughtful silence, 'but the situation is different. Many more lives are at stake. We feel that Robison may not want to risk destroying possibly the only technologically advanced city left on the planet.'

Alex sighed. 'And what contingency plans have you got in place?'

'The few tunnels that reach the surface from Genesis have been rigged with explosives which can be triggered remotely. If they try to invade, we will seal ourselves underground. We have also built more carbon dioxide scrubbers, which will mean that we can recycle the air more efficiently and our hydroponic gardens will supply enough oxygen to keep us underground indefinitely. Essentially, they will have to blast their way in, which considering we have a three-metre-thick concrete shell around the whole city, will be no easy task. And...' Martin hesitated, 'we released thousands of plague-infected rats onto the surface a few weeks ago. The disease is spreading fast among the dog population. The Alpha army won't be able to survive on the surface for long without taking large numbers of casualties.'

Alex felt the disgust swell up like bile in his throat. It was the same strategy that had been used against the survivors two years earlier by Genesis, but these were desperate times. 'We are too valuable,' Alex said, more to himself than anyone else. He knew the Alphas had powerful rockets and bombs that could damage the city. The mere attempt to crack open the concrete cocoon that encased the city could destroy it. The danger was real. 'I need to talk to Peter before he talks to Robison.'

'I'm sure that can be arranged,' Martin replied. 'As soon as your tests show you are negative.'

***

It took another hour before the tests came back and confirmed Alex was not infectious. Soon afterwards, he and Martin met with Peter in his office. Unlike his previous meetings in the committee, Peter was casually dressed in jeans and an open-necked shirt and had a series of maps laid across his desk. He greeted his friend with a warm handshake and a beaming smile and Alex realised Peter had probably assumed the worse and was not expecting to see him again.

'I'm sorry to hear about Diego,' Peter sighed after Alex explained what had happened. 'Do you know why the plan to kidnap Robison failed?'

'That's why I'm here,' Alex replied. 'Remember what we were saying before about Pierre's ability to read someone's thoughts and access their memories?'

Peter frowned, then the spark of understanding crossed his face. 'Robison's the same.'

'Yes. We didn't know it at the time otherwise we could have warned them to guard their thoughts if he shook their hands.'

'I see. So, you have come here to warn me.'

'I've come here with a plan to use this information against Robison,' Alex replied. 'He doesn't know that we know he has this ability. He uses this ability to uncover concealed information from his enemies, but he needs physical contact in the form of shaking your hand to do this. When you meet with him tomorrow, he will shake your hand and ask you questions that he hopes will evoke thoughts that will give him some insight into any possible vulnerabilities of Genesis. You must be very careful not to give away information.'

'Why not just refuse to shake his hand?'

'It wouldn't look good and besides I want you to shake his hand. We need to use this to our advantage. The one thing that Robison fears most is a treatment that will reverse what the Alphas have become.'

'You mean a cure?'

Alex nodded. 'I know we don't have one, but he doesn't know that. He knows we have advanced technology and that's all. When he shakes your hand, I want you to turn your thoughts to a treatment that will reverse the effects of the Alpha plague and that we are waiting to unleash it on the Alphas if they attempt to attack us. Such a treatment would destroy everything that he has been striving for. In short, it will terrify him. He wouldn't dare risk an attack with the possibility of the destruction of the Alphas.'

'It might work.' Martin nodded enthusiastically. 'It can't be very pleasant on the surface with all those packs of rabid dogs roaming around. And he must realise that we could stay underground for months or even years. Negotiation of some type of collaboration becomes the only option.'

'Huh...' Peter gave a faint smile as he worked though the possibilities. 'And you know for certain that he won't see through this deception?'

Alex thought about his own growing abilities and was fairly sure that he could not detect any such deception, but Robison may have had years to hone his skills. 'No,' he admitted, 'but he has no reason to suspect any deception. He doesn't know that I'm here and anyone who might have known about his abilities is dead.'

Peter looked across at Martin and the gentle smile of confidence softened his face. 'It's worth a try,' he mused.

'I will make a point of emphasising all our technological advances and how excited we will be to work hand-in-hand with the Alphas to build a new world based on them. That should clinch it.' Martin grinned.

'And if things go south, we still have the option of blowing up the tunnel entrances and we have the phage therapy which should neutralise the plague,' Alex added.

'Robison wants a face-to-face meeting tomorrow morning on the surface,' Peter said. 'I think we are as prepared as we can be.' He paused and brooded for a moment. 'And may God help us all.'

Chapter 24

Sebastian climbed to his feet and massaged his stiff neck. He was so tired. Fourteen straight hours without a break was numbing his brain; he desperately needed to eat something and snatch a few hours' sleep. They were located on the outskirts of Chippenham, about 16 kilometres north-east of Genesis, in a hastily set-up field hospital in a school hall. A short distance away, Emma was carefully applying antiseptic and a field dressing to a woman with bite marks on her left forearm. He could see the lines of concentration on her forehead as she carefully wrapped a field dressing around the woman's arm. Like him, she had worked without a break, bandaging up the wounded mostly, and ensuring the patients were hydrated. He had given her a crash course in field medicine before they re-joined the Alpha army a few days earlier. It turned out to be the right move.

Once he told them he was a medic and Emma was his assistant, and showed them their Alpha brands, they were welcomed with opened arms. Medics were in very short supply, especially since the attacks had started. As the Alpha army closed in on Genesis, they had come across probably their most deadly enemy yet: packs of wild dogs. These were not the types of dogs that he was used to seeing roaming the ruins after the holocaust in France. Those dogs were skittish and could be scared away with a shot into the air. But these dogs were different. Nothing scared them and they hunted in large packs.

Two days ago, he and Emma were caught in one of these attacks and witnessed firsthand what they could do. It was late afternoon and their medical unit had just found a suitable school hall where they could set up a field hospital. He and Emma were sent in search of extra bedding with a group of four other Alpha soldiers. They had the use of a transport truck to load up with any mattresses or bedding they found. It should have been a simple, straightforward task. The houses they were searching were on the edge of a woodland with fields beyond, thick with low-lying scrub and infused with thistles and brambles. In the distance he could also see the burnt-out hulks of tanks – remnants of a tank battle between the surface people and Genesis months earlier.

In hindsight they should have been more cautious. The warning signs were there. Barking, distant howls, large paw tracks in the muddy ground. Four of the party were armed with automatic weapons, but the instruction was not to use them unless absolutely necessary because there was a chronic shortage of ammunition. The first few houses yielded little more than a few blankets as their roofs had caved in and the mattresses were caked in mud. To cover more ground, the party had split into pairs to cover both sides of the street. He and Emma were searching the upstairs of a two-storey red-brick house when they heard barking coming from across the street. When they looked through an upstairs window, they were shocked to see a large pack of dogs gliding through the sparse undergrowth along the road. The lead dogs had picked up the scent and turned towards the house at the opposite side of the road. The pack followed, flowing through the open door like a fast-moving river. There were shouts, a short burst of gunfire, then horrible, terrified screams followed by the rabid sounds of the pack feeding. It was over in less than 30 seconds.

The remaining two Alpha soldiers in the house next door rushed out, opening fire on the few animals that lingered outside. It was a fatal mistake. As if they'd heard the sound of a dinner bell, dogs poured out of the doorway and flung themselves at the Alphas. They had no fear, no hesitation, just the lust for blood. Several animals were shot and fell but others poured over them. The Alphas were overrun and torn apart in seconds. Sebastian raised his rifle to shoot but Emma pushed the muzzle down. After what they had witnessed, it would have only given their position away. Somehow the dogs had learned that Alphas were a food source. And now they had the numbers and speed to tap it.

'Have you got something for my pain?'

The question snapped Sebastian back. A dark-skinned woman barely out of her teens was looking up at him with large pleading eyes. 'My arm really throbs.'

Sebastian knelt down and carefully unwrapped the dressing around her upper arm. A row of teeth bites stretched from her elbow to her shoulder. The animal that attacked her must have been huge and from the torn flesh around each tooth mark it was clear that the creature had tried to rip her arm from her shoulder. He gently squeezed some of the teeth marks and pus oozed from the wounds. 'Did that hurt?' he asked.

The women winced in pain and nodded. He felt the lymph nodes under her armpit and chin. All were swollen, indicating that the infection was probably systemic. Her forehead was also hot. 'Alright, I have some pills to help with the pain and my assistant will bathe and clean the wound.'

'Thanks,' the woman replied, 'but have you got any antibiotics?'

'Sorry, we ran out of them weeks ago.'

The woman said nothing, but her disappointment was evident. He could tell by the length of her hair that she was a recent Alpha convert. Maybe only a few weeks had passed since she had recovered from the disease. Her strength would not have fully returned. And now this.

'We used honey to put on wounds and mixed up herbs to stop infection,' she said. 'Don't you have anything like that?'

'Sorry we are down to the basics here. We have soap, detergent and alcohol to bathe your wounds, and medicine to lower your fever and help with pain. But that is about it.'

229

She stared at him a moment longer, her eyes filling with tears.

'I'm sorry. I will see that your wounds are cleaned,' he offered again. 'Other than that, you just need to rest.'

It was a lie. She needed antibiotics desperately and she knew it. Unlike before the war, bacterial infections going untreated could often result in death. But she was an Alpha now. That will help, he reasoned. He dispensed some pills for the pain then signalled Emma. When she came over, he explained the situation. Emma immediately set about cleaning the wound with alcohol. Sebastian took his medical kit and moved on to the next patient. This man had long hair and spoke Spanish. His English was limited but he could relay the basics of what was now a very familiar story – packs of wild dogs were running rampant. Attacks particularly at dawn and dusk were reaping havoc. He was just finishing up dressing his leg wound when someone called his name.

'You Sebastian?' an Alpha soldier with a ponytail and an assault rifle slung over his shoulder asked.

'Yes.'

'You are wanted at the front. You and your assistant are to leave immediately,' he ordered. 'We are planning a final push into Genesis and they want all the medical staff at the front.'

'What about here?' Sebastian asked.

The soldier shrugged. 'Genesis has all the medical supplies we need so we plan to take them. Pack up. There is a transport heading out in 15 minutes.' He turned to Emma. 'You both need to be on it.'

'Will Robison be there?' Emma asked.

The Alpha soldier frowned at the strange question. 'Of course.'

'Good.' Emma smiled. 'I like to be near our leader.'

Chapter 25

The meeting place was in an open sports field in the village of Box, surrounded by groves of ash trees. Only three representatives from Genesis were present: Peter, Martin and Garrett. The Alphas, however, were out in force. Most of the field was taken up with an array of light tanks, rocket launchers, armoured cars and troop carriers – a display of military punch to remind Genesis what they would be facing if they didn't capitulate. Music was playing in the background and some of the Alpha soldiers were dancing to it. When they saw their armoured car drive past, many of the soldiers punched their chests in an Alpha salute, then punched the air and began shouting, 'Alpha, Alpha!' Soon the chant was taken up by others until the whole encampment was chanting, 'ALPHA FOREVER!'

Peter watched the lines of long-haired soldiers with a growing sense of unease. Their burning conviction in their cause was as impressive as it was frightening. He realised that they weren't just facing an enthusiastic and confident enemy. They were facing a movement. A much more dangerous proposition.

They drove along a narrow track onto the grass in the centre of the field, which had been cut to ankle height. Overnight rain and wind had left the ground like a watery sponge underfoot. While Martin and Garrett were in waterproof military garb, Peter had opted for a casual shirt and jumper with matching trousers and shoes instead of boots in an attempt to project a less intimidating and more cordial persona. This was a decision he immediately regretted when he quickly sunk down to his ankles in the soft, muddy ground once he exited the vehicle.

In the centre of the field, Robison and three others were waiting, each dressed in the Alpha black uniform with a gold α insignia inscribed on their shirts. Positioned either side of Robison were two other soldiers with half-shaven heads and neatly trimmed beards. Peter assumed they were his generals from the armies to the north and south. Further back was a small-framed man with a long narrow nose and a thick ginger beard, who watched them approach with an eagerness in his eyes, like a dog about to be given a bone. From Alex's description, Peter realised it was probably Thomas. He instantly shared Alex's disgust for the man.

As Peter approached, Robison remained motionless with his hands clasped behind his back and his legs slightly apart in an at ease position. Peter was over six feet tall, but this guy was taller, with broad shoulders and heavily tattooed arms – he projected the essence of power. Peter stopped a few metres from Robison and studied him for a moment as Robison also watched him in silence. As the seconds passed the silence became increasingly uncomfortable. There was something very disturbing about this man, Peter decided. Apart from his intimidating size, there was an arrogance and hatred in those eyes Peter had not expected. If looks could kill, he thought. 'I'm Peter McCaffrey, the chairman of the committee that oversees operations at Genesis,' he stated formally. 'And this is Martin, our chief scientific officer, and Garrett, who commands my military.'

Robison acknowledged them with the slightest nod of his head. 'We are the Alpha,' he stated in a booming voice. 'The rightful inheritors of this earth. We have come to claim what is ours.'

Not much phased Peter. He had seen it all, experienced it all. But this guy was new. 'We haven't come here to surrender.'

'Then why did you come here?'

'To offer you collaboration and friendship, if you will accept it.'

A lopsided smile crossed Robison's face. 'Collaboration and friendship,' he repeated slowly, mocking the words. 'We have no need of your collaboration or friendship. You only offer this because you are outnumbered and facing an enemy you know you can't defeat. I know what you have done in the past and how you have treated the survivors.'

'I'm from Scotland. I'm one of those survivors and I now lead Genesis. I assure you we are no longer monsters.'

'Yet you sent an army against us only a few months ago.'

'That was a mistake,' Peter admitted, 'and it was not sanctioned by the committee.'

'You're saying it was a rebel army?' Robison's gaze settled on Garrett. 'Garrett, your soldiers speak very highly of you. I'm told it was you who ordered the army onto the surface and yet you are still in charge of Genesis's forces. How can this be?' He eyes turned back on Peter, full of laughter.

'The attack on your forces should never have happened,' Peter said firmly. 'Garrett has been punished for it; however, we also have confidence in his abilities to defend Genesis.'

Robison nodded his understanding, but Peter could only see mockery in his eyes.

'We are not looking for another war,' Peter continued. 'Not if there is any chance of avoiding it. That is why we are here, to offer you an alternative.'

Robison cocked his head slightly to show he was still listening.

'Over the last few months our scientists have been studying your Alpha plague and the effects it has had on your soldiers and they have made some amazing discoveries.'

'Yes, yes,' Martin stepped forward nervously. 'We have sequenced the DNA from this plague bacteria along with the DNA from Alpha soldiers that we have captured. The results have been remarkable. We found that this bacterium has managed to integrate certain DNA sequences in specific places in human chromosomes. When we looked closely at these sequences, we found they encoded previously unknown proteins. These proteins could protect human DNA from the effects of radiation.' Martin paused expecting some spark of excitement from Robison. When there was none, he cleared his throat and continued. 'What I'm trying to say is that you Alphas are more resistant to radiation than we are.'

There was only a slight nod of approval from Robison, but the two Alpha commanders behind him both smiled at each other.

'That's not all we found,' Martin went on, encouraged by the response of Robison's two commanders. 'We also found other bacteria genes that had inserted themselves into human chromosomes. These genes appeared to enhance the immune system. The Alpha soldiers that we studied had rapid cellular and antibody responses to infections.'

'You mean that they were immune from disease?'

'Ah...it's too early to say that, but they were definitely better at fighting off infection. We would love to study this more. There are clearly different insertion sites in different chromosomes depending on the individual. The picture is complicated,' Martin explained after a moment's thought. 'Each soldier was different. It may even explain why so many people die from this Alpha disease. If this bacterium inserted DNA into genes critical for survival, the human host could die. Either way, this needs a lot more research. We are just at the beginning.'

'The point is,' Peter interrupted. 'Together we can study what has happened to you. No-one has to die if we do this carefully and work out what is causing your new abilities. We are offering you a partnership. The chance to work with us to create a new race of humans. Even improve on what you are now.'

234

'And in exchange we would not attack you and infect you with the Alpha plague,' Robison added with a note of sarcasm.

'If you try to attack us, we will lock down and seal ourselves in,' Peter responded coldly. 'The city was built to withstand a nuclear holocaust and is surrounded by a concrete shell three metres thick.'

'We still have the firepower to break through,' Robison said forcibly, now keenly focused on Peter.

'Any attempt to smash through the concrete shell that protects us could cause massive damage. You could be destroying the only technologically advanced city left on this planet. You can still have your Alpha super race. You just need to give us enough time to understand and build it.'

Robison drew a sharp breath and looked up into the sky, just as the first drops of rain started to fall. When he looked back at Peter some of the intensity had faded from his eyes. 'So, if I agree to this, what will happen next?'

'Well...we don't have the capacity to take in all your people straight away, but we have extensive hydroponic gardens, and we can culture our own meat, so food supply is not a problem. We can accommodate a certain number of people underground, but they would have to surrender their weapons. That would be the only condition.'

Robison body visibly stiffened at the mention of surrendering weapons, but his face remained impassive, calculating.

'I will need time to consult with my commanders,' he replied, a reflective tone in his voice. 'You will have my answer in 24 hours.'

Peter watched his two commanders. They at least looked excited, even nodding agreement as he explained what Genesis could do.

'We will look forward to your answer,' Peter said, embedding some enthusiasm in his voice, even though he was unsure whether it was merited. 'If you agree, we can

235

take you for a tour and show you our facilities and have further discussions.'

'Yes, that sounds good.' Robison came forward and grasped Peter's hand with both of his. 'If Genesis is as impregnable as you say, it would be criminal to damage it.'

'Yes. Another war must be avoided at all costs,' Peter agreed.

Robison then moved onto Martin, again clasping his right hand firmly. 'I will look forward to hearing about your research.'

Finally, he moved to Garrett. 'And my commanders will be eager to talk to you.'

'And I them,' Garrett replied pleasantly.

With these words the meeting was over. They climbed back into the armoured car just as the rain started pouring down. Again, the crowds of chanting Alpha closed around them.

Little was said, each lost in their own thoughts as he decided if the meeting was a success or failure.

***

Robison watched the armoured car being swallowed up by the crowds of chanting Alpha soldiers. It had been a useful meeting. He had learned a lot.

'What do you think?' Leon Janssen, the commander of the northern army, asked.

Robison turned his attention to Leon. Like himself, Leon was tall, powerfully built and had a fearsome reputation both in battle and temperament, dealing harshly with anyone who displeased him.

'They offer peace, and they think that they are impregnable. I accept neither,' Robison said.

'You won't even consider their offer?' Leon asked.

'You do not let a wolf go once you have cornered it. We will attack tonight under the cover of dark. Ready your best men, small arms only. We don't want to damage their precious city.'

236

Leon looked surprised. 'Surely the offer is worth considering?'

'I have just considered it,' Robison replied coldly, 'and we attack tonight.'

The commander hesitated, then nodded. 'I will ready my frontline soldiers.'

'Likewise,' Commander Diaz, the newly promoted commander of the southern army, agreed.

When the commanders had gone, Thomas moved up beside Robison. He knew better than to say anything when Robison was in this mood. He also knew of his particular talent and guessed that he may have learnt something useful.

'I will put you in charge of rounding up all of these committee members once we have taken the city,' Robison ordered. 'I don't care whether they are dead all alive, but I want them all accounted for. Their leadership needs to be crushed as quickly as possible.'

'It will be a pleasure.' Thomas grinned.

Robison was in no doubt he was telling the truth. Thomas had proven time and time again that he was completely devoid of any morals or ethics. A useful tool to tackle dirty problems, and something to dispose of when the time came.

Chapter 26

Alex was enjoying his dessert at the Genesis canteen when the siren went off. At first, he didn't understand. Was there a fire? A power blackout? What did the siren mean? The staff at the canteen understood. They immediately began shutting down all the equipment, switching off the cookers, clearing away the trays of food and packing it away in cold rooms and freezers.

Alex drank his juice and walked up to one of the staff who was quickly wheeling away simmering pots of tea and coffee on a trolley. 'What does the siren mean?'

The man glanced at him. A look filled with a mixture of panic and confusion. 'Don't you know? It means that we are under attack from the surface.'

Alex listened; there was no sound of explosions or gunfire. Nothing. It crossed his mind that it was a false alarm, but equally Robison was capable of anything.

Outside the canteen, Alex stepped in front of a man in military uniform hurrying down the corridor. 'I'm a member of the committee,' he said, flashing his committee pass. 'What's happening?'

'The Alphas are coming through the escape tunnel we just dug to the surface,' he replied, trying to push past him.

The man had a strong Scottish accent and Alex realised he was from the surface. 'Why wasn't the tunnel blown up?'

'Nothing worked. The explosives didn't go off, then there was a power blackout and all the monitors went down. Before we knew it, they had cleared the tunnel and were spreading out through the sector.'

As if to reinforce his words, faint gunfire could now be heard echoing down the corridor. 'Can you stop them?' Alex called after him, but the soldier had already gone, weaving his way through the throng of running figures as everyone scrambled to reach the relative safety of their apartments. Alex could only think of one person who could be responsible. Garrett. Alex had been given a full briefing of the meeting with Robison earlier in the day by Martin. Robison had shaken all their hands. Peter had warned Garrett about Robison's abilities. All Garrett had to do is give him the position of the tunnel entrance on the surface, then when they attacked, shut down the monitors and power to that sector.

The more he thought about it the more certain he became. He could picture Garrett calmly switching off the power as the Alphas ran down the tunnel. The vision only fuelled his anger. He was annoyed that he had been taken in by the faint glimmer of hope that Martin had offered when he recounted their meeting with Robison. There was never any hope, he realised. In a moment of clarity, he knew what he had to do next. There had only ever been one solution. He would go hunting: Garrett first, then Robison, then Thomas. He didn't care that it would be suicide.

He took the lift up to his apartment and collected some items from his closet. Rope, torch, knives, his Alpha uniform and lastly his handgun that was standard issue for anyone on the committee. Before he packed his backpack, he checked his two-way radio at the frequency that Sebastian had selected for communication. There was only static. It was a longshot, but he kept the frequency open.

The nerve centre of the military was Sector 17, which was linked by light rail to the science sector where Alex's apartment was located. He set off at a trot towards the station platform, weaving through the rush of people scattering to their homes. The sounds of automatic weapon fire were now clearly audible along the corridors leading to the city centre. This made sense because the tunnel from the surface came

239

out close to the forest at the centre of the city centre. It was also bad news because it meant that the Alphas had reached the city.

The train pulled up at the station brimming with military reinforcements from the surrounding sectors. Many of these fresh recruits barely even knew how to hold a weapon. Their pale faces and wide eyes relayed the full horror of the situation. Within a minute of the train doors opening the surge of soldiers had cleared the platform and dissipated through the lifts and escalators. Alex boarded a now near-empty train. He checked his ammunition clip, then hid his handgun under his shirt.

At Sector 17, he swiped his committee pass to open the lift. The lift rose three floors and opened up directly into a large control room rimmed with flat screen panels displaying every corner of the city. As he suspected, many of the screens showed Alpha soldiers running through corridors and engaged in fire fights with the Genesis military. The battle-hardened Alphas were slicing through the resistance by methodically advancing in waves, each wave supporting the other with covering fire. He noted that nearly all of the dead lying in the corridors were Genesis soldiers. Streams of Alpha soldiers were running past the dead, collecting their weapons and ammunition before continuing the assault.

Garrett was standing in the middle of the control centre and barking instructions into a phone.

Alex clicked off the safety on his handgun. 'Garrett! I need to talk to you urgently!' he called.

At first Garrett didn't respond. He only turned when Alex raised his voice to a shout.

When he saw Alex, his eyes widened. 'What do you want?' he growled.

'I have a message from Peter.'

'What is it?'

'For your ears only. Is there somewhere we can talk?'

Garrett hesitated, disbelief and annoyance playing across his face. 'Alright, this way,' he grumbled reluctantly.

240

Garrett led him to a small conference room off to the side of the control room. Once inside, he quickly closed the door, but when he turned back to Alex, he found a handgun pointing at his head.

'What the fuck are you doing?' he demanded.

'Over here,' Alex motioned with his gun. 'Sit on the chair and tie your feet with this rope.' He threw the rope from his pack at Garrett. It bounced off his chest and landed on the floor.

'You can't be serious?' Garrett asked, now incredulous.

'Do I look like I'm joking?'

'We are about to be overrun by Alphas.'

'Did you switch off the power and let the Alphas in?'

'What? No. That's ridiculous.'

'Sit down and tie your legs.'

'No.'

Alex moved closer and stuck the barrel of the gun under Garrett's chin pushing his head up at an angle. When he thought of Garrett leaving him in a room to slowly die of thirst and hunger, he almost pulled the trigger. 'Don't you think I would shoot?' he whispered into his ear, his voice slow and venomous. 'You don't know how much I want to pull the trigger and blow your head apart.'

Garrett swallowed involuntarily and Alex saw the fear rise in his eyes. 'Alright, I will do what you say,' he muttered.

Alex pulled the gun away and Garrett tied his legs to the chair.

'Now put your arms on the arms of the chair,' Alex ordered.

Alex used another rope to bind his arms until he was satisfied that Garrett couldn't move. 'Now I'm going to ask you a series of questions and if I don't think you are telling the truth I will start shooting parts of you off, understand?'

Garrett nodded obediently and Alex had the pleasure of seeing his eyes water and the blood drain from his face.

Alex placed his hand firmly on Garrett's right arm and made eye contact with him. He immediately felt his fear. 'Did you switch off the power to the tunnel to let the Alpha soldiers in?'

Alex felt Garrett's fear escalate as he tried to avert his eyes. Images flooded Alex's thoughts. Peter was talking to Garrett, explaining what he had done, telling Garrett that he had shown Robison the position of the tunnel exit at Box when he shook his hand. 'I just couldn't risk it,' Peter had said miserably. 'We have the bacteriophage treatment. I couldn't risk the destruction of the city.'

'It was Peter,' Alex gaped.

'That's right,' Garrett breathed, relieved that Alex had guessed. 'He ordered me to cut the power. I didn't like it, but he is the commander-in-chief. I had to obey.' Garrett watched him with watery, hopeful eyes and visible relief when Alex released his arms. In the images that flooded Alex's mind, Peter had almost been in tears when he spoke to Garrett. He knew Peter. He would not have done this unless he felt Genesis was under serious threat. Peter thought Robison would attack and try to blast his way in with high-powered explosives. He thought he had no choice.

Garrett seemed to sense the change in Alex's mood and broke into a violent fit, straining against his bonds like a madman. 'Release me!' he ordered.

A disembodied voice suddenly broadcast from Alex's backpack. 'Alex? Are you there?'

Alex searched until he found the two-way radio. 'Sebastian?'

'You're alive. Great to hear your voice.'

'Where are you?' Alex asked.

'Emma and I are in Genesis. We have been following Robison. Can you meet us at the fountain at the centre of your underground forest? Robison is heading there now.'

'I will be there in about 15 minutes,' Alex replied.

'I knew it. You are a spy,' Garrett gasped, some of the old vitriol emerging in his voice.

242

Alex turned his attention back to Garrett. He still wanted to shoot him, but the sound of gunfire would certainly bring unwanted attention and he had more important things to do now. 'You still let the Alphas in. You didn't have to obey Peter. Now thousands of us are going to die from the Alpha plague.'

He stepped up to Garrett and in one swift movement struck him in the head with his handgun. The force of the blow sent the chair and Garrett sprawling onto the floor. With a loud thud Garrett's head hit the floor and a thin trickle of blood oozed down from his left ear. Alex packed up his backpack and left.

Outside one of the soldiers approached him. 'Sir, will the commander be coming out soon?'

'I have just given him some upsetting news that he has to think about,' Alex replied, sounding deadly serious. 'Give him five minutes then knock on the door.'

The soldier nodded, a concerned expression crossing his face. 'Yes, sir.'

Alex hurried past him. He was worried that the trains would stop running, but just as he reached the platform one pulled up. It was completely empty. These trains were driverless. Alex figured nothing would stop them short of a power failure or a major explosion. When the train reached the city centre, he jumped off and took the escalator up several flights, then ran through the main shopping arcades of the city. There were signs of fighting everywhere. The ground was littered with the bodies of Genesis soldiers strewn across walkways and piled behind makeshift blockades. They were all young, with the fresh, unblemished faces of the city. Only an hour earlier they were probably watching TV or eating their hydroponically grown dinners. He put these thoughts aside and tried to refocus. Sporadic gunfire could still be heard close by, and small groups of Alphas soldiers were going from shop to shop searching for any remaining military. Alex ducked into a shop and quickly changed into his Alpha uniform. Once changed, he looked at his reflection in a shop mirror. With his short, cropped hair and Alpha brand on his arm, he easily passed as a recent Alpha recruit.

***

Robison strolled down the beautifully manicured pathways of the Genesis botanical forest. He was impressed. Many of the plants and trees he passed he had not seen since the holocaust, yet here they were, thriving in an underground oasis in the centre of possibly the only advanced city left on the planet. And the city was all his. The Alpha soldiers were now spreading out quickly, mopping up what little resistance was left. This day would go down in Alpha history. He took a deep, contented breath. He looked around at the native animals running between the trees – shews scuttling along the ground, squirrels on the branches, and any number of different birds flying among the trees. 'Look.' He pointed at a red squirrel that poked his head out of the brough of a tree then quickly darted away.

'Not seen one of them for years,' Thomas commented, now in an equally merry mood.

As they walked on, the air became moist and the noise of cascading water began to dominate their senses. The path curved slightly before a magnificent water fountain came into view surrounded by thick sub-tropical rainforest. 'Beautiful,' Robison remarked, reaching the base of the fountain and gazing up at the many spouts of water shooting up nearly 10 metres in the air and cascading down in sheets of glistening spray. 'Truly spectacular. This city will be the base of operations,' he mused. 'From here we will spread across the UK then across to Ireland. Nothing will stand in our way.'

'Yes, nothing,' Thomas concurred, smiling happily.

Robison was so absorbed in his future plans he failed to see the ring of soldiers that was slowly closing in on him.

'You know that's recycled sewage water.'

Robison turned sharply to see Diego standing a short distance away with his automatic weapon trained on him.

244

'You...you're supposed to have drowned.'

'You do sound disappointed,' Diego mocked. 'But I assure you your disappointment will be short lived.'

The threat behind Diego's words was not lost on Robison. He turned around to see Leon, the commander of the northern army, surrounded by his lieutenants. Coming up behind them was Diaz and his commanders.

'I told them what you did to Pierre, and Gerolf and Ursula,' Diego said. 'How you have betrayed us and Genesis so you can cling to power. They know what you really are.'

'You see, the deal that Genesis offered was your last chance,' Leon added. 'If you had accepted their offer, none of this would be necessary.'

Robison's hand moved to unclip his handgun.

'I wouldn't,' Diego warned, taking aim at Robison.

A thin smile crossed Robison's face. 'I thought that you all understood. We are building a new world. I did what was necessary to keep us pure. There can be no compromise. The Lion wanted to dilute our bloodline.'

'No,' Leon shook his head. 'That's not why you killed the Lion. You killed him because he was a threat to your power. You represent everything that was wrong with the world before the war. You want to rule as a dictator. The Alpha movement was founded on the principles that we all consult and agree. You are not an Alpha.'

'You can't put me on trial. I'm the leader of the Alphas,' Robison said confidently, as though his words were law.

'You're right. We can't put you on trial. This is not an arrest,' Diego replied with equal confidence.

Robison backed closer to the fountain, frowning as the ring of soldiers closed in. Then he was gone. In one fluid movement, he leapt over the metal railing and vanished into a wall of cascading water.

Diego swore and shot several times into the water, but it was too late. 'Round the other side!' he yelled.

Emma was already on the move. The instant Robison disappeared into the water she took off around the fountain.

She reached the other side just as Robison burst through the water.

He had the look of a wild animal, swivelling left and right in search of his pursuit with his handgun ready to shoot. Emma was standing directly in front of him with her handgun pointed at his chest. 'Remember me?'

Robison stared at her. There was a flicker of recognition in his widening eyes before hatred flashed across his features and he swung his gun towards her. There was no doubt what would happen next. She shot him twice in the chest then once in the head. The bullets' impact flung his body backward into the fountain where he disappeared under a sheet of water. Moments later the Alpha soldiers arrived. Only the slow creep of red-coloured water spilling out from the centre of the fountain betrayed what had just happened.

***

Thomas was congratulating himself. When the soldiers closed in on Robison, he had managed to slip away unnoticed. He was now in the tunnel running towards the surface. As he had done many times before, he would reinvent himself. Cut his hair, shave his beard and fade into the mass of new recruits to wait and see where the dust would settle. He was confident something would turn up. What he didn't notice was the figure in Alpha uniform quietly shadowing every movement he made.

He reached the surface, entering a large warehouse full of transport vehicles and lines of four-wheel drive cars that would have been used to escape Genesis in case of an overwhelming Alpha attack. In the several hours since the attack, many of the supply vehicles had been pulled apart and their contents were being searched and catalogued by teams of Alpha soldiers. Thomas slipped through the groups of Alphas unnoticed and reached the lines of cars fuelled and packed with supplies at the far corner of the warehouse. He was just about to climb into one when he felt something cold poke him in the back.

246

'Hello, Thomas,' Alex whispered into his ear. 'I'm afraid this time you didn't quite make a clean getaway.'

Thomas turned to see Alex pointing a revolver at him. Alex took his gun and knives and threw them away, then ordered Thomas to climb into the driver's seat.

'Where are we going?' Thomas asked.

'We are going on a little sightseeing trip.' Alex pulled the keys out of the glove compartment of the vehicle and handed them to Thomas. 'Now drive.'

When they cleared the warehouse, Alex directed him onto the main road leading north-east to Corsham. Soon they were the only car on the road, driving through the darkness with only the silvery light of the moon for company.

'You know I never agreed with the decision to attack Genesis,' Thomas stammered. 'No, collaboration was always the best solution. And I said that to Robison. We should all work together. But he wouldn't listen...he didn't trust anyone. He thought it was all a trick. That somehow Genesis was plotting to use their technology against us. As soon as we let our guard down, they would do something terrible. He was totally paranoid.' He nodded to himself. 'This is the best outcome. Now we can all work together.'

'You and me?'

'I know we have had our differences,' Thomas conceded, 'but it's a new world now.'

'So, you think I should overlook the fact that you stabbed Elaine?'

'I was under orders and you know how ruthless Robison was. He would think nothing of killing me.'

Alex shook his head, disgusted at how Thomas was trying to twist the truth. 'You poisoned Robison against us. If it wasn't for you, we may have been able to stop all the slaughter that followed.'

'No, no, that's not true. Nothing could have stopped that. Robison was never going to do any sort of deal. He wanted to lead an army of superhumans, and nothing was going to get in his way.'

'Pull over to the side of the road,' Alex ordered, 'and put your hands on the dashboard. If you move them, I will shoot them off.'

Thomas quickly complied.

As soon as the engine died, the howls and barks of wild dogs could be heard. The sound sent an involuntary shiver through Alex. They were parked next to a playing field, complete with goal posts with the remains of the nettings flapping in the wind. The field itself was covered in a thick coat of ivy, but when Alex scanned the field with his torch, he could see dark shapes swiftly gliding across it. Directly across from the field was a row of houses that formed angular dark shapes against the backdrop of the rising moon.

'I know how you like playing games,' Alex began. 'Especially if they are stacked in your favour. I just thought of a new game. One that only you can play.' He looked across at Thomas, who still had both hands on the dashboard and a look of terror in his eyes. 'See those houses over there? I want you to run towards them. If you make it, you can lock the doors and keep out any dogs that might be sniffing around for a meal. I won't pursue you; if you survive, you are free.'

'You want me to run through a field full of bloodthirsty dogs? No way.'

'Do you think you have a choice?'

Alex watched the look of horror sweep across Thomas's face, then, when the answer became obvious, a calculating expression emerged. 'Can I at least have a knife?'

'Sure.' Alex pulled a small knife from his utility belt and handed it to him. 'Now I am going to count to five,' Alex continued in a low, menacing voice. 'If you are still in the car by the time I reach five, I will shoot you. If you run in any other direction other than those houses, I will also shoot you. Do you understand?'

Thomas nodded.

'One, two, three…'

Thomas gave Alex one last horrified look then flung himself out of the car and set off at a dead sprint towards the houses. The moment he left the car there was movement in the field. Dark shapes started racing towards him and the barking rose to a crescendo. About halfway across the field a large dog jumped up at his arm and another nipped at his heel. For a moment he stumbled and lashed out with his knife, then he was up sprinting again, his legs pumping like pistons. But by now the pack had coalesced behind him in a plethora of dark, swiftly moving shapes. Another dog grabbed his arm and he slowed to shake it off. The change in momentum proved fatal as more dogs latched onto his legs and arms, dragging him fighting to the ground. More dogs arrived and the barking and growling reached its peak amid the terrified screams of Thomas as the pack tore apart their prey.

Alex found he couldn't watch. He thought that he would feel good that he finally reaped his revenge on the man who had murdered Elaine. But he didn't. He knew that Elaine would be horrified at what he had just done, but Tina would have approved. Before the holocaust he would have also roundly condemned his actions and labelled himself as a monster. And maybe he was. He realised that it was Tina who taught him how to survive in this new world; he'd had to subjugate his humanity to survive. Elaine restored that. Made him see humanity again. He knew he wasn't Elaine or Tina; he was Alex and he still had to make his way in the world.

Thomas was right about one thing. It was a new world, an Alpha world, and he had an ability that he didn't understand. But its potential was undeniable. For the first time in a long time, he felt a vestige of hope for the future. He was an Alpha living in a technologically advanced city. They had the bacteriophage therapy to stop the Alpha plague from killing the Genesis population. The future was uncertain as always, but he felt strong; the strength of Alpha was now flowing through him. The new human race was emerging and just maybe, this time, we would learn from our mistakes of the past and a better, wiser human society would emerge. Only time would tell.

Thank you for reading my book. If you liked it, please take a moment to leave a review at your favourite retailer.

Rob Cole

Other Books by Robert Cole

Adult

Nuclear Midnight
(First book in Savage Dawn Series)

On a holiday in England, Alex Carhill is caught in the nightmare of a nuclear holocaust. In a matter of hours, a midsummer's day is turned into a nuclear winter. This is the story of his survival in a world that no longer has rules; where climatic extremes, murder, starvation and disease are commonplace.

As the land slowly heals, the survivors scratch together an existence in a contaminated wasteland ravaged by plagues of insects and disease. In this world, through hardship and pain, a new society is forged based on new rules and values moulded from the demands and necessities of life. After years of struggle, the survivors find themselves facing their greatest adversary. One they despised and thought had long disappeared in the first months of the holocaust. Now they must marshal all their resources and strength for one last battle against an enemy bent on their destruction.

The Ego Cluster

In a future world strafed with economic inequality, religious wars and climate extremes scientists discover a gene cluster that appears to govern the human ego. By suppressing these genes much of the ego-driven nature of the human decision process could be converted to a more empathetic, logical and considered approach, devoid of racial, religious and economic bigotry.

Visionary scientists Ethan Hendersen and Amelia Holt form both a romantic partnership and a working one in which their characters will be tested to the limit when they are employed by a mysterious cartel to develop a treatment to eliminate the human ego. Professional colleagues Dr Doug Ashton and Caleb Fuller are also swept up in the action as the real potential of the ego cluster treatment becomes evident. This is a story of an epic battle between scientific progress and its potential to change the human mind and the entrenched mind-set of the powerful elite.

Mytar series: suitable for older children and above

The Last Portal
(Book 1 of Mytar series)

Severe weather patterns - storms, floods and strong winds - are sweeping across planet Earth. Against this backdrop, three high school students, known and tormented for their strange abilities, fight their own battles against school bullies. The discovery of a strange key by their leader Chris Reynolds, plunges all three through a portal into a sister world, Cathora, in another dimension. In this world their behaviours, that labelled them as misfits on Earth, turn out to be the seeds of extraordinary powers.

They soon meet Batarr, the Guardian of the portal; he tells them they are not normal children, but are part of a group of six beings, called Mytar, who are periodically seeded throughout the dimensions to fight planetary invasions across these portals. Cathora has been invaded by an alien army, led by a creature known only as Zelnoff. After conquering Cathora, his next target is Earth. The Mytar alone have the power to stop him if the other Mytar on Earth can be found. There ensues many struggles and battles as Chris, Susie and Joe seek to evade Zelnoff's forces long enough for their powers to develop so they can detect the remaining Mytar back on Earth.

The Flight of the Mytar
(Book 2 of Mytar series)

Chris, Susie and Joe are transported back to Earth to find the remaining Mytar. To their horror, they find that two of the three Mytar were the bullies that had tormented them at school. With the agents of Zelnoff closing in, they are forced to transport them back to the underworld of Cathora against their will.

Once there, these new Mytar refuse to help and reignite old hatreds and conflicts. Hunted by the Nethral and the Taal, the Mytar children, guided by the Guardian Kaloc, are chased relentlessly through the underworld. When one of them is captured, it becomes a desperate struggle to rescue him and find the sixth Mytar before the forces of Zelnoff seize complete control of Cathora.

The Battle for Cathora
(Book 3 of Mytar series)

After many battles with a creature only known as Zelnoff, the children Mytar finally discover and transport the sixth Mytar from Earth to Cathora, completing the last member of their group. However, the Mytar powers are still underdeveloped and require intensive training to reach their true potential. In contrast, Zelnoff has gained more of the Mytar powers and his armies roam the planet unopposed. When a circling Zentor finds their hiding place, the Mytar children are forced to flee to the mistlands where they are ambushed and scattered.

With the situation seemingly hopeless, they discover critical information which points to a potential weakness in Zelnoff. With this information, one last desperate plan is devised. The Mytar must pool all their powers to fight an alien army and penetrate deep into Zelnoff's territory, if they have any chance of defeating him.

Printed in Great Britain
by Amazon